forget me always

Also by Sara Wolf

Love Me Never

forget me Always

A LOVELY VICIOUS NOVEL

SARA WOLF

Entangled Publishing, LLC
2614 South Timberline Road
Suite 109
Fort Collins, CO 80525

Entangled Teen is an imprint of Entangled Publishing, LLC.

Visit our website at www.entangledpublishing.com.

Edited by Stacy Abrams and Lydia Sharp
Cover design by Louisa Maggio
Interior design by Toni Kerr

ISBN 978-1-633753174
Ebook ISBN 978-1-633753280

Manufactured in the United States of America

First Edition November 2016

10 9 8 7 6 5 4 3 2 1

For A,
Death is really and truly only the beginning.

chapter one

"ARE YOU ALL RIGHT, SIR?"

I look up at the voice. A bellboy smiles cheerily at me. He has no idea who I am or what I've been through, yet he has the nerve to smile. It's been nineteen days since Isis Blake forgot about me, and he has the nerve to ask if I'm all right.

I light another cigarette.

"Get out of my face."

His expression falls, and he backs away. "S-Sure. Have a nice night."

I scoff and lean against a pillar of the grand marble roundabout of the Hilton. I watch ridiculously fancy black cars shuttle in and out, dropping off equally puffed-up old rich people. Bellboys and concierges scurry around, calling taxis and directing valets. Revolving glass doors with gold accents constantly whir and hiss over the mindless chatter. Women shriek with laughter, men guffaw; all of them are oblivious, happy idiots. I can see the truth in their clothes and posture—five of the men are cheating on their wives. Two of them with far younger women, one of them exclusively with prostitutes. He not-so-subtly taps the ass of a passing blonde in a peacoat. She hides her grimace with an actress's grace. When she sees me, she clips over in her heels with a mildly happier smile.

"Jaden! Oh my God! It's been forever!"

"Three months, Lily," I correct. Jaden is the name I use for my escorting work, and I've never let the other escorts I've met in passing know my real name.

"Three months, forever, same difference." She laughs. Perfume wafts off her, the expensive, strong kind. The kind you buy when you have to cover up the pervasive smell of sex.

"Finished with work?" I ask, and jerk my head at the man still watching her lecherously, his wife oblivious and clinging to his arm.

Lily sighs. "Yeah, for the night. I'm about to head back to my place. What about you?"

"Mayor's daughter." I motion to my tuxedo. "Winter ball."

"Bet you were the hottest guy there."

"It was a Catholic girls' school."

"And the hottest guy she'll ever have."

Lily is just a few years older than me, but she's been in the Rose Club far longer. Lily isn't her real name, just like Jaden isn't mine. I don't know her in real life, and she doesn't know me. But sometimes we work in the same hotels, and she's one of the few girls in the Rose Club who isn't annoyingly vapid. So we talk.

"Seriously." Lily elbows me. "I've seen her. She looks like an inbred Pomeranian on her best days."

"Now now." I blow smoke into the sky. "Let's not be nasty. She paid good money. And I respect and appreciate money."

Lily watches my face carefully as she waits for a taxi to cycle past. She knits her thin brows.

"What about your own prom?" she asks.

"What about it?"

"Are you going to that? Do you have a girlfriend? Or a date?"

I took Sophia to my junior prom. Sophia, the hospital-ridden girl I'd known since middle school—my first infatuation and first real friend. But it's not Sophia who pops into my head right now. An image grows strong of Isis, dressed up in some silk dress. Red? Or blue? Purple, probably, to match her hair. She'd dance and drink and start at least four fights. It would be awful. It would be hilarious. I smirk at the thought, but it quickly fades. She's in the hospital, too. And thanks to that scumbag called her mother's boyfriend, she doesn't remember me anymore. It's been almost three weeks since she asked who I was, with that blithe smile on, and only now have I really started to believe it.

"No. I'm not going to the senior one. It's pointless. I'm graduating in five months, anyway. High school barely matters anymore."

She plucks the cigarette from my lips and grinds it under her heel. "When did you start smoking?"

"When did you decide to start mothering me?" I ask.

"It's not good for you."

"Neither is sex work."

Lily glowers. "*Escorting.* And we both have our reasons for doing that. You don't have a reason to smoke. Unless you want to die early and painfully."

"And if I did, it would be none of your business."

Lily flinches, as if I'd slapped her. She hails a passing cab, then pauses in its open door to look back at me.

"You're one of us, Jaden," she murmurs. "Society looks down on us. Customers objectify us. All we have is each other. So it *is* my business." She pulls out her Rose Club card—white with pale gold stripes—and hands it to me. "If you ever need anything, or if you wanna talk, call me."

She's gone before I can throw it back at her, gone before the gaping chasm in my chest has the chance to bleed. I shake it off. I'm Jack Hunter. No one makes me bleed.

Except one girl, at a party, nearly five months ago.

I light another cigarette to cover the stench of weakness emanating from me. The women at the hotel's entrance are eyeing me. If I so much as blink in their direction, they'll accost me, flirting with tired tactics and worn eagerness. They are just as bad as the men. They covet things that look nice. And when they can't have what they covet, they squabble, quickly turning on each other in sickening displays of predatory possessiveness.

I consider throwing Lily's card in a nearby puddle. She has no idea what I'm going through. *I* have no idea what I'm going through. She can't help me. Besides, her help is offered solely because she has designs on me. Even an idiot can see that much.

Not everything with a vagina likes you, dipshit!

I whirl around at the sound of the voice. It's so clear, so perfectly loud and obnoxious, that it has to be her. But no purple streaks bob out of the crowd to greet me. No warm brown eyes crinkle with a smirk.

I fall against the pillar again and laugh, putting my head in my hands as reality slips through my fingers. Get it together, Jack Hunter. You're going to Harvard in seven months. Your mother is waiting for you to come home now. Sophia is counting on you. Her surgery is imminent. You can't go crazy. People are depending on you. You have a life to live, and no matter how much you wish on stars, no matter how much you bargain with God or with the doctors, that life does not include Isis Blake any longer. You're a stranger to her.

The hole she burned in the ice must be filled.

There is no warmth anymore. You barely tasted it, barely felt it on your skin. It brushed against you for a single second. Something so small should not retain this much weight. It is illogical. You are illogical for letting it affect you so much.

There is no warmth, Jack Hunter. Not for the likes of you.

You have blood on your hands. You have duty, and guilt, and you can't escape that. No one can help you escape.

Not even her.

"Jaden!" A shrill voice makes me look up. Cynthia, the mayor's daughter, waves me over to the limo. Her dark hair is over-curled and looks ridiculous. Her pink dress is too tight and too bright. Her circle of simpering friends have dropped off their purses and retouched their makeup, and now they're on their way to an after-party. *We're* on our way. I'm being paid to be one of them, after all.

I stub my cigarette out and put on my best smile.

My life has become a series of people asking me if I'm better.

Except I'm sitting in a hospital bed with a massive

bandage around my head like a turban. So no, I'm not better.

But people keep asking anyway because it's how you show concern for someone you care about, I guess, but frankly a giant box of chocolate truffles and reign over a small kingdom would be acceptable stand-ins.

No school. No home. All I do is sit in bed all day and watch crappy soap operas in which people faint dramatically all the time. Like, damn. That shit's an *epidemic*. I get so bored I try to mimic their faints, except the nurses catch me and say stuff like "you have a head injury" and "contrary to popular belief, the floor is hard" or some nonsense, so nobody can blame me when I steal the nearest wheelchair and bolt down the hall at top speed.

"Good evening, chaps!" I nod at two interns. They shoot each other looks, but before they can call security, I'm blazing around the corner.

"Bloody good weather we're having!" I smile at a man sitting in his bed as I pass his open room. He cheerily returns my greeting with a resounding, *"Go to hell!"*

I round the next corner and come face to face with Naomi, my nurse. Her hair's back in a strict bun, her face angry and worried and tired all at the same time. I don't know how she manages to look a million years' worth of tired and still keep up with me, but she does it well.

"'Ello, love. Fancy a cuppa?"

"You're not British, Isis," Naomi says flatly.

"I can be things," I insist.

"Yes, well, unless those things include a person who is lying in bed recuperating, I don't want to see them. And

I especially don't want to see them wheeling around the hospital like a madman."

"The madman is back that way." I jerk my thumb behind me. As if to prove it, a loud *"FUCK!"* reverberates. Naomi narrows her eyes and points at my room.

"Back in bed. Now."

"Why you gotta be like that?" I sigh. "We can work this out. There can be bribes. Of the monetary kind. Or maybe not monetary. Do you like adventures? I'm full of those. I can give you at least nine adventures."

"You've already given me one for the day. If you don't get back in bed, I won't let Sophia in after her checkup."

I gasp. "You wouldn't!"

"I would!"

I stand up and start to faint dramatically, but she catches me with her meaty arms and plops me in the wheelchair, pushing me back to my room. I grumble the entire way. In the doorway, I crawl out on my hands and knees and fake sob, collapsing into bed.

"Oh, quiet, you drama queen," Naomi chides and closes the door behind her.

"Drama *empress*!" I yell. "I prefer the title empress!"

My room's quiet. Too quiet. I huff and cross my arms and blow bangs out of my face. I need a haircut. And an escape plan. But looking fabulous while escaping is somewhat required, so I'm putting one before the other.

I grab my phone and text Sophia.

DEAD PROTEIN IS TRYING TO EAT MY EYES. BRING THE SHARP POINTY THING.

Her text comes seconds later.

You mean the thing you threatened that male nurse's balls with?

I sigh contentedly at the reminder of my own past brilliance. I'm so lucky to be me.

Yes. That.

She sends one smiley face: ☺

Sophia and I are the youngest people in this hospital, discounting the kids' ward, and they don't let you in there unless you're a doctor or a parent or you have permission, which is really hard to get. Which is why I use the windows. I hate Jell-O and it's all they give you at meals, so I hoard it and give it to the kids like a gelatin-laden Santa, and it's a big hit. Not so much with the nurses. And security officers. Regardless, Sophia and I make sense. Since the day we met at lunch a few weeks ago and I gave her my apple, I've felt like I've known her forever. Being with her is like a massive, run-on déjà vu. When she first told me her name, I blurted, "Oh! *You're* Sophia!" like it was a huge revelation. She asked me what I meant by that, and I searched long and hard in my own sizable brain and couldn't find a reason. I'd just said it, without thinking, and I didn't really know why. I still don't know why. I don't know a lot of things anymore, and it frustrates me, but it's not easy to maintain frustration when all people ask of you is to sit in bed and eat all day.

Besides that tiny bump in the road, she and I have been getting along famously. You can tell because A) she hasn't run away crying yet, and B) she always ends her texts to me with a smiley. Only people who like you do that. Or people who want to secretly murder you. But really, I don't think someone as delicate and beautiful as Sophia would want to murder someone, unless she wanted to be, like, beautiful and delicate *and* bloodthirsty, which, I'm not gonna lie, would add to her considerable mystique—

"Isis," Sophia says from the doorway. "You're thinking out loud again."

I whirl to face her. She's in a floral sundress, with a thick, cozy-looking sweater. Her platinum hair is kept thin and long, like strands of silver. Her milk-white skin practically glows. To offset all her paleness, her eyes are ocean-deep and navy-dark. In one hand she carries a book, and in the other—

"Scissors!" I crow. "Okay, okay, deep breaths everyone. Because I'm about to say something mildly life-changing."

Sophia inhales and holds it. I point at her.

"You're going to cut my bangs!"

She exhales and fist-pumps. "I'll chop them all off."

"Soph, soapy Soph soapbutt, we have only been together three weeks and I love you dearly, like a sister, like we are deer-sisters frolicking in the woods together, but this is extremely vital to my well-being and I am trusting you with my life."

"Ah, I see." Sophia sits on my bed, giving me an understanding nod. "You keep all your vital organs in your bangs."

"As well as all my future prospects with Tom Hiddleston. So you realize how important this is to me."

"Obviously."

"I am quite serious."

"Deadly."

"It's not like you can make me look any less hot, since that is impossible, but generally speaking—don't fuck up."

I'm not hot, definitely not compared to someone like Sophia, but it's the bravado that counts. She runs her fingers through my wild bangs.

"Straight across?"

"Uh, you're the fashion expert here. I just sort of throw on things that don't have holes in them and hope for the best. I read a *Cosmo* once on the toilet. Does that count?"

"Depends on how long you were on the toilet." Sophia experimentally brushes my bangs with her fingers.

"*Years*. They talked about face shapes. Like, do I have a square face? A heart-shaped face?"

"Definitely heart-shaped."

"Really? Because I was thinking more that-one-unfortunately-misshapen-Skittle-in-the-bottom-of-the-box shape."

Sophia laughs. "Just hold still and close your eyes. I promise I won't disfigure you for life."

There are the soft sounds of snipping and the feel of Sophia's gentle fingers, and then she tells me to open my eyes. I leap out of bed and dash into the bathroom. The age-stained hospital mirror reflects a short-banged girl, her slightly faded purple streaks gracing her forehead. A single bandage wraps around the base of her skull and up to the top of her head, like a headband, and leaves the rest of her head open. She looks tired, old. Her face contains two volcanic eruptions on her chin, one on her nose, and bags under her eyes that would make Coach jealous. And something's wrong. Something deep inside the girl is wrong.

Ugly.

"What's the matter? Don't like it?" Sophia comes up behind me. In the mirror, she practically radiates pale, waifish beauty, and I'm…

"No, I love it. You did great. Fab. Nothing's wrong!

Absolutely zero. Absolute zero. It's kind of chilly in here, isn't it?"

I run back to the bed and burrito myself in the blankets. Sophia follows, sighing.

"If you don't like it, you don't have to lie."

"No, I do! Shit, I really do. Sorry. It's not that, it's… other stuff. Stuff from before I came here."

"Ah." She settles on the foot of my bed. "The hard stuff. The stuff the hospitals can't heal."

I nod. Sophia's gaze isn't piercing, but something about it has weight, gravity, like she's decades older than she seems. I haven't told her about Nameless, mostly because she doesn't need to know when she already looks so sad all the time. Nameless was my first and last crush back in Florida, and he ruined me in ways that serrated my heart for good.

Sophia hasn't told me anything about her past, either, and it's better that way. I can tell she's had it worse than me. Sniffing out tragedy is sort of my entire deal.

"Was it a boy?" she asks finally. Was it a boy? Or was it a monster? I still don't have the answer to that, so I say the easy thing.

"Yeah."

She folds her hands over each other, like a dainty lady, and for the billionth time I'm reminded of how mature she is compared to me. The nurses gossip about her; the way she's been in the hospital for five years, the way she has no family—her mother and father died in a tragic "accident," and her grandmother raised her, but she passed a few years ago, leaving Sophia all alone in the world. Mostly they gossip about the boy who comes to visit her, Jack, the same guy who happened to see our house door open and saved Mom and me from Leo. He wasn't quick enough to stop Leo from flinging me into a wall and cracking my skull open, but he was quick enough to save Mom, and that's all that matters.

Infuriatingly good-looking, and an infuriatingly Good Samaritan, Jack apparently visits Sophia a lot. But since I got here, apparently he hasn't visited her at all. He's sent letters to Sophia (Letters! In this day and age!), but he hasn't come personally. The nurses love to gossip about that, too. I ~~scream politely from across the room~~ correct them whenever I can; I don't know him! He barely knows me! I'm indebted to him, sure, but there's nothing going on and there never will be because *duh*, all boys who aren't Hollywood actors with prestigious superhero careers are gross!

"I'm sorry," I blurt.

"For what?"

"For your boyfriend. He's…he's stopped coming around since I got here, and if it's because of me, I'm sorry, and I know that's arrogant to think, but the nurses blab and I can't help but think—"

She pats my hand and smiles. "Shhh. It's okay. They don't know anything. He's just busy. He works a lot, and he has school."

"I have school," I grumble.

She plops the book she brought down on my lap. "That's right! And you have two acts of *The Crucible* to read if you wanna catch up before you go back next week!"

I contemplate seppuku, but after remembering how big the medical bill for a cracked head is, I refrain. Mom's having a hard enough time paying without adding spilled organs and general death to the list. Besides, I can't die yet. I still gotta thank Jack properly.

Dying before you pay someone back for saving your mom is just plain *rude*.

“I don’t wanna go back to school,” I say.

“Yes you do.”

“I totally do. It’s a snoozefest in this place.”

“Then we’d better get reading.” Sophia smiles. I groan and roll over, and she starts reading aloud. She enjoys torturing me. Or she’s just happy to have someone here with her. I can’t decide which. We might get along great, but she’s still a huge mystery to me. Me! The ~~queen~~ empress of deducing what people are all about! I study her face, her hands, her dress as she reads. Everyone in the hospital knows Sophia, but no one knows what she has, exactly, except her doctor. The nurses don’t like to talk about it. I asked Naomi, and she glared and told me it was under doctor-patient confidentiality. Sometimes Sophia stays in her room for “treatments,” and those last for days. She doesn’t limp or cough or vomit, and no bandages or stitches are on her. Except for the fact that she’s so pale and thin and sometimes complains she has migraines, she’s perfectly healthy as far as I can see.

“Soph,” I interrupt. She looks up.

“Yeah?”

“I know this might be super invasive, and historically, invading has been pretty bad overall, but I don’t think I can physically contain my curiosity any longer. Or, I could. But I’d like, implode the star system from the stress.”

She laughs. “It’s okay, Isis. You can ask whatever you want.”

“Why are you in the hospital?”

Sophia slowly closes the book. “You really don’t remember, do you?”

"Remember what?"

Her eyes dampen with sorrow. She stares out the window for a long time before sighing.

"What?" I insist. "What is it?"

Sophia looks back at me. "Oh, nothing. It's just sad, is all. I'm sad for him. He was so happy, for a while. No—it was more than happiness. It was like he was alive again, with that fire in his eyes."

I wrinkle my nose, and before I can explode with the demand for answers, Sophia starts talking again.

"I have the same thing you have." She taps her head with one finger. My mouth makes a little *O*.

"You...split your head open like a melon, too?"

She laughs, the sound like bells made of crystal. "Something like that. Our heads are equally broken. Maybe not in the same ways, but broken all the same."

I look over at the bag she brought. A bunch of romance books crowd it, various clones of Fabio flashing their brooding frowns on every cover as a scantily dressed female is in the inevitable process of fainting on a rock somewhere nearby, preferably directly beneath his crotch.

"Why do you even like those? Aren't there just like, princesses and kissing and misogyny?" I wrinkle my nose.

Sophia shrugs. "I don't know. I like the princesses."

"They've got great dresses and fabulous hair and loads of money. Kind of hard not to like 'em."

"I suppose I like the way the stories always end happily. Since...since I know my story won't end as happily."

My heart twists around in my chest. She sounds so sure of herself.

"H-Hey! Don't talk like that. You...you're the closest thing I've ever met to a princess. Like, a real-life one.

Minus the tuberculosis and intermarrying. And, uh, beheadings."

Sophia laughs. "You're a princess, too, you know. Very brave. And noble."

"Me? Pft." I buzz my lips and a delightful spray of saliva mists the air. "I'm more like…more like…I guess if I was in one of those books I'd be like, a dragon."

"Why?"

"It just makes more sense!" I smooth my hair. "Fabulous glowing scales. Beautiful jewellike eyes."

"Wings for arms?" Sophia smirks.

"That's a wyvern! Dragons have wings independent of their limb system! But I forgive your transgressions. I've encountered a bit of heartburn today and am not in the mood to eat a maiden like you in the slightest."

"What would you do as a dragon?"

I shrug. "You know. Fly around. Collect treasure. Burp infernos on some townspeople."

Sophia is quiet for a moment.

"But I still don't get it," she finally says. "Why does a dragon make sense for you?"

"Think about it. I'd just make a badass dragon. I mean…nobody really likes the dragon. You get to be alone, in a cool, quiet place. No one likes you because you're too loud and full of fire. But if you're a princess, everybody likes you and you gotta be in the middle of hot sweaty balls all the time."

Sophia raises an eyebrow.

"Ballroom…balls. Dances. Ugh."

She laughs that chime-laugh, and I can't help the laugh that bubbles up, too.

"And I mean," I add, "you know. Dragons never have to worry about. Um. What I mean is, princes don't fall in love with dragons—"

Ugly.

"—they fall in love with princesses—"

Did you think that's what this was? Love? I don't date fat girls.

"—so it makes more sense, you know?"

Sophia nods, and for a moment we're both dead silent.

Finally, she smiles. "I think you underestimate princesses."

"Oh yeah?"

"Yeah! Everyone only pretends to like them because they have to. They don't have any real friends, because they're locked away in the castles all the time. Every princess wants to be free. Every princess wants freedom more than anything."

Her words ring with a deeper truth, like it's something she's been thinking about for ages, not minutes. But she smiles, and suddenly the tension is gone. She reaches into her bag, a little leather thing she keeps makeup and stuff in, and pulls out tiny airplane bottles of booze.

"Where did you get these?" I ask. Sophia shrugs innocently.

"Some rich college frat boy got checked into rehab in the next wing over. They made him empty his pockets, and then it was just a simple matter of sneaking them off the confiscation cart."

"You never told me you moonlight as a master thief."

"When you're trapped in a hospital most of your life, you learn how to YouTube everything. Including sleight-of-hand tricks." Her smile is so warm. "And, as a bonus"—she pulls out a can of spray paint—"the janitor left this in his closet."

"Oh my God, you're like a cat burglar. A *huge* cat burglar. A tiger burglar."

"I just know this hospital really well," she insists.

"And what debauchery have you planned for the evening with these supplies, madam?"

"I'm thinking we drink these." She motions to the bottles. "And tag that awful security guard's booth with a middle finger or two."

"Giant genitalia is much harder to clean off."

She points at me and winks. "Now you're thinking with evil."

"I prefer the term 'chaotic neutral.'" I unscrew a bottle's lid and down it, the familiar smell of rum searing my nose.

Rum. Rum and the fizz of Coke on my tongue. The warm heat of dancing bodies all around me. Music. Music so loud I can't hear myself think. A soft, smooth chest behind my shoulders, giving me stability, keeping me standing. A feeling of being safe.

"Are you all right?"

Sophia's soft voice breaks me out of the memory. I blink four, five, ten times, the hospital coming back into focus. What the hell was that? Who was the person behind me, making me feel that safe? Not even Mom makes me feel like that, not since I was little. She's been too fragile. But whoever that was gave me an inner peace I can still taste on my tongue.

"I'll be better when I'm drunk." I grab another bottle. If I keep drinking, maybe I'll remember more.

"Hey, slow down! Leave some for me," Sophia insists. She swallows a bottle eagerly. We trade sips, and when we start giggling at each other for no reason, I know we're drunk.

"I feel so warm and weird." Sophia laughs.

"Is this..." I hiccup. "Is this your first time drinking?"

"No!"

"It is!" I pat her shoulder. "I feel so honored to accompany you on your maiden voyage down the rabbit hole."

"Underage drinking is bad," Sophia whispers, then laughs. "Except I can't wait until I'm of age. Because by then I'll be dead!"

I flinch. Sophia stops laughing, her smile fading.

"Sorry," she says. "I don't mean to be a drag."

"The only thing that's dragging is your shot count." I pass her another bottle. "But it's okay for you to drink, right? You won't—"

"I'm not that fragile." She frowns.

"Sometimes medication makes people fragile! I was just checking."

"Why would you care?" Sophia snaps. "We barely know each other."

I freeze. Sophia goes still, too, her dark blue eyes widening.

"I'm sorry," she murmurs. "*I'm sorry*. Sometimes it happens like this, I say things without thinking. It just comes out and I can't stop it and then I feel so horrible."

"Hey, shhh." I pat her back. "It's okay."

"That's what they all say. They all say it's okay when it's not, and the resentment festers in them until they hate me."

"You...you don't know that. You can't read people's minds! It would be tight if you could, and you'd probably be some young adult novel protagonist with fairy powers, but you can't! Unless..." I look her over suspiciously. "You can?"

"I can't." She frowns. "But that doesn't change the fact everyone learns to hate me. Eventually. You'll be no different."

"No." I set my chin. "You were right. We barely know each other. That's the truth. But that doesn't mean I can't care. People like to say time is a big deal, but it's not. I care more than I should, faster than I should—"

The memory of someone's lips touching mine, someone I wanted to be happy. Someone I cared about, was starting to care about, more than I cared for anyone in a long time—

I shake my head.

"Time doesn't matter, okay? You're my friend. I don't hate you."

"You will." She stares sadly at another bottle. "Words hurt. And I say words without thinking."

"Why?"

She shrugs. "It's part of my condition. Irritability. Mood swings. Behavioral changes. I'm not who I used to be, and people are starting to leave me because of it."

There's a quiet, and then she laughs despairingly.

"You got off easy. Head injury, but nothing psychological. Except for—"

"The memories," I finish. She smiles.

"Sometimes forgetting can be a blessing. If I could forget him like you have, if I could forget it all, move somewhere new, start over fresh—"

She stops herself. I lean over and grab her shoulder.

"Wait, what? 'Him' who? What are you talking about?"

She chews her lip, then bolts off the bed and grabs the can of spray paint.

"Last one to the guard box is a pile of garbage!" she shouts, suddenly all joy and effervescence. Confusion ringing in my ears, I chase after her through the halls. The interns shout at us to slow down, but I can barely hear them over Sophia's chiming laughter. I follow it like a bloodhound, down the steps, around the hedges outside. The hospital is still and quiet on the east side—no parking lot, only an expanse of garden they grew for rehabilitating patients. The guard patrols the parking lot more than here, which makes it the perfect time to commit a crime and not do time for said crime.

"Sophia! Wait!" I shout after her, but she's so fast. She shouldn't be this fast—she's sick. Or is she only sick in the head? Is that what's wrong with her? I contemplate it as I catch up to her. She kneels by the guard box and shakes the spray can. She spritzes the air experimentally and wrinkles her nose.

"Oh, it smells gross."

"Here." I fish out a napkin from dinner and shove it at her. "Cover your mouth and nose so you don't breathe it in."

"It's nice of you to play mom." She laughs, takes it, and starts spraying a delightfully realistic middle finger on the white wall. "I never had a mom."

I'm quiet, half keeping lookout and half burning alive with curiosity.

"Well, I did." Sophia shakes the can and starts on the other half of the graffiti. "But she decided she didn't want me. Or Dad. No, Mrs. Welles decided she'd had enough of both."

"Soph—"

She finishes the middle finger and nods, satisfied. She offers the can to me.

"Anything you want to add?"

I shake the can once, admiring the vivid black obscenity staring back at me. I add a tiny, misshapen heart below the middle finger, like a signature. Sophia laughs and pulls me by the hand back into the hospital, the both of us high on adrenaline and paint fumes.

But it wears off, like all things do. Sophia goes back to her room for her medicine, and I spend some quality time with my laptop. Facebook is about as interesting as a sack of rotting tomatoes, except at least tomatoes don't post racist-slash-sexist rants.

Before I know it, I'm staring at an empty Google search bar. My fingers fly across the keys.

Sophia Welles Ohio.

I never knew Sophia's last name before now. And suddenly a world opens in front of me, a dark, twisted world. Article after article details exactly what happened to Sophia's family. Her mother, after struggling for years with schizophrenia and a heroin addiction, snapped one day and killed her father, then overdosed. Sophia came home from school and found the two of them when she was only seven years old. Her grandmother took her out of the big city of Columbus and came to Northplains to get away from it all.

Sophia's been through more shit than anyone.

I close my laptop and stare at the ceiling for a moment. How the hell do you keep moving on from something like that?

You don't.

You end up somewhere like here, covered in mental scars.

It takes me two days to work up the courage to go see Sophia again. She hasn't missed me, considering she's been going in and out of CAT scans and minor surgeries for twenty-two hours of it. When I open her door, she's lying in bed with deep purple circles under her eyes, a patch of shaved hair on the base of her neck split in half by an ugly threaded scar, and a faint smile.

"Hey," she croaks.

"What did they do to you?" I stroke her hand.

"Oh, rummage around in my head, pull out a few lumps, sew my cranium back up. The usual."

"You have lumps in there?"

She motions for her water bottle on the side table, and I give it to her. She unscrews the lid and takes a deep drink before sighing.

"I'm a drug baby. Lots of complications. I've been in and out of hospitals my whole life. And then one day, when I came with Gran, they found the tumor." She winces. "I didn't let it stop me, though. I convinced Gran to let me stay in school until at least the first year of high school. But then—"

Sophia looks at her hands. A bird outside her window chirps eagerly, its red breast bright against the bleak gray sleet of Ohio. We watch it fly off together.

"I should've died a long time ago." Her voice is small. "But they won't let me. They keep making me live."

"Because they care about you," I insist. "Who else in their lives is going to be as disastrously kind and beautiful as you? Who else will break the hearts of a thousand men and also ships because...your face launched them!"

Sophia sputters a laugh. "You mixed up those sayings a bit."

"Like a cake batter," I chime in. "Smooth and delicious."

Her laughter lightens her expression, the shadows gone from it for a moment. For a second I'd been scared.

For a second she sounded like Mom used to sound, at the beginning, when we were first reunited after her breakup with Leo. Hopeless.

"Isis?" Naomi knocks on the door and pokes her head into the room. "Ah! There you are. I knew you'd be here. Let's go. It's time for your session with Dr. Mernich. Hi, Sophia. How are you feeling?"

"Better," Sophia says, and smiles at me. "You should go."

"Ugh, no thank you. Mernich's going to ask about my feelings, and frankly I'd rather swallow a centipede than talk about those things. Or become a centipede and crawl away. Can I become a centipede? Do they allow that in America?"

"Isis," Naomi says sternly.

"You can become a certified light saber maintenance engineer in America, so I really think you should be allowed to become a bug—"

"Arthropod," Sophia corrects.

"—*arthropod.* And Naomi! My, what big hands you have. The better to grab me with, am I right? Ack, gently, woman! I'm damaged goods!"

Naomi steers me out of the room, Sophia cheerily waving as we leave.

Dr. Mernich is the kind of woman who forgets to brush her wild red hair but somehow makes the crazed lunatic look work for her, which is weird, because she works with crazies. Not that crazies are bad. I've met a few and am probably one of them. I just don't know it. Or I do.

But I refuse to let it get in the way of my fabulousness hard enough to require a shrink. Mernich is my way out of this place, in any case. She's the one who's keeping me here until she's satisfied I'm all right in the head. Which is dumb, because mentally I am a diamond fortress of impenetrable logic and sexiness.

Dr. Mernich clears her throat. "Isis, you're—"

"Someday I will not think aloud, and that will be a sad day for humanity. Also, quieter."

She heaves a sigh. "How are you feeling today?"

"Parts of me are feeling lots of things! For instance, my intestines are feeling lots of things. That means I need to visit a restroom. Sometime in the next hour. In addition to this riveting prospect, I'm slightly worried about Mom's meager finances and recent trauma, so if you could just write me a note so I can get out of here, that'd be great."

"What have we said about avoiding the subject with flippant jokes?"

I squirm. "Uh, it's vaguely negative. I think."

"And why is it vaguely negative?" she asks patiently and scribbles some more.

"Because I don't confront anything, I just run away from it," I recite.

"That's right."

"But to be clear, I run away from it like a *Baywatch* babe, not a roly-poly kid in gym class. I mean, I still *am* roly-poly, but it's an alluring sort of roly, you feel me?"

"Isis, do you really think you're large?"

There's a beat. The scale told me I'd lost eighty-five pounds years ago, but it never really sank in. I still catch myself thinking I won't fit into chairs, constantly worrying about how much space I'll take up, how much space people will see and laugh at me for, judge me for. I can't wear bathing suits without bursting into hives of stress. Even that pretty blouse my stepmother gave me was pushing it.

You're beautiful.

The words echo in my memories, but I can't put my finger on them. Who said that? And when? I shake them out of my head and refocus.

"Duh, I'm big," I reply. "And unlovable. But you already know that."

Her eyes spark. Of course she already knows that; she's spent two weeks with me, talking about my life. I'd stalled around her with jokes and lies for a good week, until I realized she was the one who gives the go-ahead to let me out. And then I had to start actually cooperating with an adult and Telling The Truth™. Ugh.

"You already know everything about me, right?" I tilt my head. "So c'mon. Why don't you just let me out of this—pardon my French—absolute shithole?"

She adjusts her glasses. "I'm afraid I can't do that. I'm certain there are still some things we need to work on. You're close but not quite there."

Even this shrink is full of herself. Her self-satisfied little smile as she says that gives it all away. The trophies and awards lining her stuffy walls give it away.

"You like it. Knowing things about people. It makes you feel powerful."

Dr. Mernich looks up from her scribbling, the faintest whiff of startled hanging around her. "Excuse me?"

"You. Like. The. Ego. Trip. Shrinking. Gives. You," I say slowly. "Aw, don't give me that look. I'm not judging you. I just understand. I see things about people, too, and I love knowing I know. It's weird. It's stupid.

Knowledge is a heady drug. But mostly it's fun and it makes me feel superior. Maybe I'll turn it into a way to make money someday, too. I gotta think about that kind of stuff, you know, with college and everything a few months away."

Mernich is completely frozen for point-four seconds, and then she starts scribbling madly. She does that when I say something super interesting that she can dissect. So she scribbles a lot. Because I am, objectively, an insanely interesting person. I'd better be! I work hard to be interesting, dammit!

"Anyway, what was I saying?" I scratch my chin. "Right, I feel really cooped up and sort of tired of hospitals. Also I feel bad for Sophia. Did you know she has no parents? And her grandma died? How sucky is all that death? Majorly sucktastic."

Mernich nods. "I'm her psychologist as well. She's quite the strong girl, if a little tragic."

"Wow. That's sort of condescending? I said I feel bad for her, but you went straight to giving her labels like 'tragic'? Wow. That's interesting. Wow."

I can see Mernich start a glare behind her glasses, but she quickly cuts it off and resumes her usual passive face. Oh, she's good. But not better than me. Not better than Jack.

I pause, my swinging legs stopping under the chair.

"Jack?" I mutter. "Where did that come from?"

How would I know Jack is any good? I haven't been around him for more than thirty seconds that first time when I woke up and he yelled at me.

"What about Jack, Isis?" Mernich presses.

"Uh, I don't know. It just…it just popped into my head. Which is weird. I mean, most things that pop into my head are really weird, like that one time when I thought about Shrek in Victoria's Secret underwear, but I think this actually beats Shrek's Secret."

Mernich leans back in her chair. "What do you remember before the incident, Isis?"

"I was applying to colleges. Boring."

"And before that?"

"I…I was at school. And I—I yelled. At someone. I don't remember who. Kayla, maybe. Maybe Wren? Yeah, I think Wren."

"What did you yell about?"

My palm suddenly stings, and I remember the harsh feeling of skin-on-skin.

"I slapped someone. I yelled and I slapped him. Wren must've done something stupid, I don't know."

"And before that? Do you remember any major events?"

"There was a party. A big one. Avery's house. Halloween—I dressed up as Batman. No—Batgirl?"

"Did Kayla go?"

"Yeah, she was a mermaid. She and her boyfriend—ugh, what's his name? I don't remember his name, but I know I slightly despised him."

"Despise is an awfully strong feeling."

"Yes, well, being alive is an awfully strong feeling."

"Isis—"

"I didn't like him. Or, something about him rubbed me the wrong way. I don't know."

"And can you recall what happened at the party?"

My head suddenly gives a massive throb, my spine tingling with pain. I squeeze my eyes shut and rub them.

"Isis? What can you remember?"

Leo's face comes back, leering at me from the

doorway. Panic wells up in my throat. I'm not going to be able to save Mom.

"I don't know! Stuff!"

"Try to remember specifics. Did you drink anything? Did you dance? Who was wearing what costume?"

"Wren was... He was a green guy. Link! Link from *Zelda*. And I drank...Coke. I think. With rum. Don't tell Mom that. We joke about me drinking, but she doesn't know I really drink, because I don't want to worry her, and I danced and there was someone—"

He's going to hurt her. He's hurt someone before. He hurt Sophia. Sophia? No, that's not right. Leo doesn't know her. Who, then, has hurt Sophia? A baseball bat. Avery came at me with a baseball bat, and someone grabbed it. I can see a broad, spidery hand wrapped around it, wrenching it from her, a low voice saying something with an amused tone to a startled, frozen Avery—

The pain ricochets through my head like a tennis ball on fire.

"Fuck!" I grab my forehead and put it between my knees.

"Take deep breaths, Isis," Mernich says softly. "You're doing well, but don't give up now. What else happened there?"

A bed. A soft bed, someone's soft lips, someone whispering my name.

The pain splinters, blossoming in my brain like a demented flower. I can't see anything. The world goes black and my ears ring.

That's what you get for trusting someone.

Ugly.

Maybe I'll love you. If you hold still.

Mernich says something, but I can't hear her. It hurts.

It hurts and I want it all to stop.

You got guts. I like that.

Have fucking fun trusting nobody for the rest of your life!

I don't go out with ugly girls.

Ugly.

Ugly.

"Isis! Look at me!"

I look up. Mernich's face is pale.

"It's okay. You don't have to push yourself anymore. I'm sorry. Just breathe. In and out. There you go. Slowly. Sit up."

When I lean back into the chair, I realize my hands are shaking. My whole body is trembling, like a thread in the breeze.

"Why?" I murmur. "Why can't I remember what happened?"

She pulls her clipboard out again and clicks her pen. "Well, to find that out, we need to go to the beginning."

"You mean like, biblical Genesis? Because I have three rules for a happy, fulfilling life, and 'Never Time Travel Ever' is one of them. Because, you know. Dinosaurs killed things. And the bubonic plague killed things. And let's face it—with my supreme amounts of unnatural charm, I'd be burned as a witch."

She chuckles. "No. Not that far. I just want you to tell me your story. The real one. The one about Will."

I flinch, my skin crawling at the sound of his name.

"Pulling my own tongue out and setting it on fire would be preferable to talking about that guy."

"I know. But I think it's time to stop running. I think you know that, too."

I hate her. I hate her so much. She's the reason I

can't leave. I'm racking up more and more pricey bills the longer I stay here. She's the reason Mom worries. But I can tell she really wants to know about Nameless. If I tell her the story, maybe she'll let me go. Nothing else has worked so far. It's worth a shot, even if that shot will pierce through my guts and leave me to bleed all over the floor.

"From the beginning?" I ask softly.

"From the beginning." She nods.

I inhale and then let it out as a long sigh. Somewhere outside, a bird chirps. I want its freedom more than anything.

"When I was in fifth grade, I developed a crush on a boy. This was my first mistake. He wasn't a particularly attractive boy, he was sort of quiet and spit sometimes, but he had pretty, dark, silky hair. The female teachers complimented him on it. I wrote him a love note that said, 'I like your hair,' and he wiped his nose on it and gave it back to me at recess. I should've seen the warning signs in the mucus. But I was smitten. He'd paid attention to me! Me, the fat roly-poly girl with frizzy hair and a constant cloud of BO surrounding her. He actually didn't snub me, or push me in the mud, or call me a fat whale, he just wiped his nose on my declaration of love and gave it back to me. It was the most promising social signal I'd received in my short ten years of life on the planet earth."

Thus began my descent into utter madness.

"I did anything short of committing crimes to get his attention. Also, I committed actual crimes. Like riding my bike on the freeway shoulder lane to get to his house and stare at him through his window while he played video games. But then I found out it was illegal! You can't ride your bike on the freeway at all! So I started taking the bus to look at him through his window while he played video games.

"Anyway, so there I was, in the prime of my life, and by prime I mean not prime at all. Mom and Dad were going through the divorce, which involved a lot of shouting and money and guilt, so Aunt Beth offered her home for a few months so I wouldn't have to switch schools, which turned into nearly five years, but Aunt Beth was totally cool about it. We had grilled cheese almost every night and she let me watch R-rated movies. So basically I'd died and gone to heaven, and neither of my parents gave a diddly-damn except Mom who sometimes got guilty and sent me lots of exceptional socks. I love her, but really, *socks*?

"So while my lovable gene donors were off debating who owned what vase for sixty months, I grew up in the loudest ways possible. Well, I wasn't exactly loud back then, I was more an indoor-mouse-whisper kind of gal, but you get my drift. There were fights. One time, a girl tried to run me over with her scooter! Do you remember scooters? I remember scooters. My shinbone remembers scooters. One time that girl even gave me a frog! Because she was so nice! I found it in my locker! Actually I had tons of friends and by tons I mean everyone in the library who squeezed around my bulk to reach their books."

"And what were you doing in the library?"

"Hiding. I read a lot of Jane Austen and cried. It was a formative experience."

Mernich nods, motioning for me to continue. She's doing it. She's making me bring out the big guns. I sigh.

"All right. No more pussyfooting around it. I talked

to…Nameless…I can still call him that, right?"

"If that's most comfortable for you, yes."

I take a deep breath.

"After stalking him for most of middle school, the first time I exchanged words with Nameless was at Jenna Monroe's beach party in seventh grade. The girls were wearing pastel tankinis and swimming. I was wearing two sweatshirts and yoga pants and sitting with her mom. I was still at a loss as to why Jenna Monroe invited me at all—Jenna was all legs and brown ponytails and glitter pens, the total opposite of my pudge and pencils. We'd been friends once, when we were still pooping ourselves and learning not to eat said poop, but judging by the way Jenna's mom waved to me when I first came, I got the impression Jenna had no hand in inviting me at all.

"Anyway, there I was, waist-deep in an element that sure as hell wasn't mine. Girls were giggling, splashing water on each other's boobs, and boys were around! Staring at the girls! Well, all the girls except Jenna's mom and me. Nameless was there, so I hid behind the soda cans on the picnic table and tried to look like I wasn't there. Being almost two hundred pounds is sort of counterproductive to invisibility, though. Everyone saw me. Even Nameless. It was like, two seconds of eye contact, and then he looked away. And I thought I was done for! Because, you know, when people look at you and you're fat, you think you're done for."

I look up, and I can see the faintest glaze coming over Mernich's eyes. She's skinnier than a beanpole. Probably has been her whole life. She has no idea what I'm talking about. No amount of college can teach her that. I laugh.

"You know what? Screw it. Just…I'll just talk about

the part you really wanna know. It's what everyone wants to know. They don't care about the how or the whys, just when and where and how quickly they can say, 'awww, I'm sorry' or try to fix it."

"That's...that's not what I meant by this, Isis—"

"No, you know what? It's fine. It's probably better this way. This way I don't have to drag out my entire sordid history for you to pore over. Saves you time! I'm sure you're a busy lady with a lot of crazy people to talk to and I'm, frankly, a total purveyor of common sense and not—time wasting. So you know what? Yeah. The day it happened it was raining. I was at his house. The frogs were outside and croaking because he lived near a marsh. That's what Florida is. Marshes. Marshes and assholes. His mom made us popcorn. My hands were oily. His hands were oily. We'd been secretly going out for two months, but he wouldn't let me tell anyone and when I tried to talk to him at school, he ignored me, laughed at me, and told me to buzz off. But then he'd apologize. When we were alone he was nice. Nicer. Marginally. I was fourteen. Fourteen, okay? I was fourteen and I thought I was in love and I would have done anything to keep him from leaving me—"

Bile rises in my throat, but I swallow it back and clench my fists on the armrests.

"Do you know what it's like? Never wanting to lose another someone? Everyone else leaves. Mom and Dad left. I didn't want him to leave. If he left, I would've lost it. He was the only normal thing in my life. He made me feel... When he smiled at me, he made me feel pretty. Do you know what that's like, either? Feeling huge and gross and then finding someone who makes you feel pretty? Do you know what you'd do to keep that person? You'd do anything. Anything in this world short of killing yourself. Maybe even that, if he asked for it."

Mernich's eyes are softer now. But I don't trust them anymore. This is what she wanted. She's getting it. Her pen is scrabbling madly across the paper even as she opens her mouth to speak.

"I'm sorry, Isis. I didn't mean to seem callous. But this is good. You, saying these things aloud, even if you hate me for bringing them out…it's good. It's helping."

"Sure. Whatever."

I'm shaking. My body trembles with a rage I can't express. It's not all anger at Mernich's voracious curiosity, though. I'm not all mad at her. The anger is directed at someone else, too. Nameless for hurting me. Mom and Dad for leaving me. Myself, for letting them do these things to me.

Mernich pushes back in the chair. "We'll stop here."

She gets up and doubles around her desk, pulling out a familiar yellow slip.

"What are you doing?" I demand.

"Writing you a discharge."

"Not gonna grill me more? Not gonna ask me to come right out and say it? You were the one who said I needed to confront it, not run away."

"This isn't running away," she says calmly, and rips the paper off and hands it to me. "I've been doing this for fifteen years, Isis. Some people need me—a total stranger—to listen. However, some people are only further injured when a total stranger listens. As a doctor, and with you as my patient, I can't suggest you continue speaking to me on this matter with a good conscience. I'm not the one who should hear it. Someone else—your mother, your father, maybe Kayla, or Sophia, or perhaps someone you haven't met yet—one of them will make you feel safe enough to say it. One of them will be the one you decide to tell. It's up to you."

I stand and grab the paper warily, like it's a trap. But Mernich just smiles.

"Would you like your diagnosis?"

"I'm crazy."

"Not at all. Do you know what disassociation is?"

"Something crazy people have."

Mernich's smile turns patient. "It's what occurs when a person goes through a traumatic experience. It's a… Think of it like a coping mechanism for the brain. Say someone throws a snowball, and it's going to hit your eye. Your eyelids react much faster than the snowball flies to protect the cornea. Disassociation is like an eyelid for the brain. A traumatic event can cause the brain to disassociate the event. Sometimes this manifests as a simple case of shock that quickly wears off. Other times, we see intense reactions, such as withdrawal, PTSD, and in your case—"

She looks up, and I dread the next words to fall from her mouth.

"—memory gaps."

"What?" I scowl. "I don't—"

"You have periods of painful blackouts when you try to recall a certain person in your life. Your brain has identified this person as the source of overstimulation, and perhaps pain. You have what's called lacunar amnesia. It's a very centralized and rare thing."

"So I've lost my brain? Part of my memories? I've totally forgotten them?"

"You haven't really forgotten—the brain never truly forgets. I believe in your case, the memories are still there but buried beneath layers. It might take months to get them back. But you may also never get them back at all."

"Who…which person was it? The one I forgot?"

"Think back. What have your friends told you? Have they been acting strangely toward you, concerning a certain person?"

It filters in slowly—weeks of Kayla's weird looks, of Wren's concerned sighs, and Sophia, shaking her head and saying it's sad. And then Jack's fractured expression when I first woke up and said I didn't know him. I stare, wide-eyed, at Mernich's passive face.

"Jack. That Jack guy. Everything they say about him doesn't make sense. But why do I have this lactose amnesia thing? I mean, my head was bad, but…"

"You suffered significant head trauma. I believe the lacunar amnesia is a combination of that and your own disassociation of the traumatic event of fighting off your mother's attacker."

"Did Jack— How do I know him?"

"You'd be better off asking Sophia that question, perhaps. But you're leaving the hospital with that discharge slip right away, aren't you? You were quite eager to go."

I look at the crumpled yellow note in my hand and close my fist around it.

"It can wait."

Mernich smiles at me.

"Yes. Yes it can."

chapter two

3 YEARS, 25 WEEKS, 5 DAYS

MY MIND IS A WHITE BLANK of confusion. I knew Jack. I know Jack. The underwear model-esque dude with the rude mouth *knows* me.

Before this extremely vexing realization, he'd just been a guy I was grateful to. But now he's a guy I know! I know *guys*! Guys who aren't harmless Wren! Why hadn't anyone told me? It's not like I'd hate them for telling the truth. In fact, I kind of actually encourage truth-telling for everyone on this planet! It fosters clear communication and ensures things mildly don't fucking suck!

I find Sophia in the common room, reading a romance novel. The heaving bosom on the cover distracts me for point-two seconds before I realize I have better boobs than that and slam my hands on the table.

"Sophie! Soapy! Soapbutt!"

She looks up calmly and puts a bookmark between the pages. "Yes, ma'am?"

"Not to be rude or overly confrontational, but why the *fucking hell* didn't you tell me I had amnesia?"

She gasps. "You have amnesia?"

"Soapy!" I lament. She stands, putting her book

under one arm and offering her other to me.

"Oh, stop. I'm kidding. Come on. Let's take a walk."

I debate how effective screaming until I get my way will be and decide not very and then lace my arm with hers. She leads me down the too-sterile whitewashed halls. We weave around interns and gurneys. An old woman waves hello from her wheelchair, and Sophia waves back.

"Hello, Mrs. Anderson. How are you feeling?"

"I'm well, dear. What about yourself? I heard you have that surgery coming up. Dr. Fenwall is very excited about it."

"Oh, you know him." Sophia smiles wider. "He's excited about everything. I'm not getting my hopes up."

"Don't talk like that, sweetie! I'm sure it'll be a success and you'll be out of here and on dates with that dashing young man of yours in no time."

Sophia laughs, but once we've turned the corner, her smile fades rapidly, like a flower caught in a first frost.

"She seems, uh, nice," I try. "Also, dying. But nice."

"We're all dying, Isis," Sophia says. "Some of us just a little faster than others."

Feeling somehow chastised, I try to look around instead of at her.

"They really need to redecorate," I say. "Maybe paint some hearts on the walls. And puppies. Just strew puppies everywhere. Puppy bonanza. Pupanza."

She doesn't say anything, leading me to a stairwell. Maybe this is it. Maybe she's going to stop being my friend forever. Maybe she hates puppies. Maybe she hates painted hearts on walls! Maybe my big mouth has finally landed me in trouble I can't get out of, except I could totally get out of this stairwell by jumping over the railing and straight down—

"Isis, you're being silly."

I look up. "Was I thinking out loud again? Mea culpa."

Sophia holds open a door at the top of the stairs, and sunlight streams into my eyes. She ushers me through it. I burst onto the roof, fresh, crisp winter air lapping at my face. From here, you can see most of Northplains, Ohio, nestled in the rocky valley below. Thrushes swoop around the treetops, a massive flock of them sitting on the roof, pecking at nothing. They look so calm. So small. So peaceful.

"AHHHH!" I scream, charging at them. They scatter with angry squawks, the noise deafening for a split second.

"That's what you get for being so damn cute!" I shout. Sophia walks up beside me, the wind toying with her beautiful platinum hair.

"This is where I come when I'm sad or feel alone."

"It's great!" I shout too close to her ear. "It's great," I whisper.

"I'm glad you like it. I've never shown anybody. Well, except Jack. I've shown him. And Naomi knows I come up here."

"Because she's nosy as balls."

"Because she's nosy as balls," Sophia agrees. She perches on the edge of the roof. Warily, I lower my hands and inch toward her. I look over the edge—it's a long way down. As in, an extremely dead way down. But Sophia doesn't seem worried at all. She just gently kicks her heels against the building.

Not wanting her to feel left out, I sit next to her and gingerly ease my feet over. She hums. The sun is thinking about going down—still bright and full but drooping tiredly. The world is at peace. Or it's ignoring us. It doesn't know we exist. Sick and recovering people live in separate worlds. The regular world is focused on living, and ours is focused on not dying. And sitting up here, inches away from death? That's another third world entirely. It's the edge, the in-between. Everything is fragile and could change at the slightest breeze, a single, soft push.

"What are you thinking?" Sophia asks.

"Deep, intense thoughts. So deep. At least two indie songs' worth of deep."

She laughs and hums higher. A thrush starts chirping with her, or maybe at her.

"What's that on your arm?" she asks. I pull my sleeve down over it instantly, out of habit.

"Nothing."

"If it was nothing you wouldn't wear long sleeves all the time."

"It's nothing, honestly."

"Did you try to kill yourself?"

There's a beat. The thrush stops chirping.

"No," I say finally. "I'm crazy. Not stupid."

The silence returns with a vengeance. The weight of every world ever is on this roof, bearing down on the two girls sitting on the lip of it.

"Have you ever had sex?" she asks. I abruptly start wobbling for no discernible reason. She grabs my arm and I gasp for air.

"You really *are* trying to kill me!"

"It's just a question."

"But this isn't answering *my* sort of direly important question about my amnesia and Jack!"

"I had sex." Sophia picks at her dress. "With Jack."

"That's great!" I feel my throat tighten, and deep in the pit of my stomach something burbles. Perplexed at my sudden bodily reactions to her words, I do the smart thing and brush them off entirely. "I mean, good for you, really! I mean. Good! I hope it was good! You two are good! Together!"

"Jealousy doesn't suit you." She laughs.

"Jealous? Uh, did you miss the part where Jack is a giant black hole in my brain instead of an actual person?"

It hits me with the force of a dozen Godzillas break-dancing over the ruins of Tokyo.

"Did I…did I—"

"No! Oh no!" Sophia says. "Sorry, I didn't mean to wind you up like that. I don't think. Um. I don't know what happened between you two for certain, but last I heard, you and Jack were engaged in a brutal, egotistic battle. Not sex."

"Sounds rad."

"He said you called it a war. Occasionally, 'crusade.'"

"He must've done something really shitty if I pulled out the medieval terminology."

"I don't doubt you and he had some misunderstandings." She nods. "He can be cold. Cruel, even. And you're the opposite. But he's really not trying to be. He just ignores people's feelings in favor of logic and rationality."

"Ugh." I stick out my tongue. "One of those."

"He blackmailed you."

"That's standard issue in a war."

"You planted fake weed in his locker and nearly got him suspended."

"Jolly good."

"He kissed you."

I feel the blood drain out of my face and down to my feet.

"Uh, yeah, no—"

"Uh, yeah yes," she corrects. "Avery told me. I forgot to thank you, by the way. Even if Jack doesn't visit as much with you around, Wren and Avery do. And it's so nice to see them again. It's been years. They're feeling very guilty, you see."

"Wait, wait, hold on one flaming-ass second!" I get off the edge. "You're telling me your boyfriend *kissed* me?"

"I don't know, did he?" She cocks her head to the side. "I trust Avery's word, even if she is unforgivable, but I trust your memory more. You should try to get it back. Then we'd both know the truth."

"If he kissed me, you should…you should just break up with him! He's a scumbag! And don't even talk to me again. I'm even more of a scumbag."

Sophia laughs and gets off the edge, putting a hand on my shoulder. "It's okay. How could you know he had me? You were new, and he doesn't talk about me a lot."

My skull suddenly throbs, the pain imploding along my forehead. I gasp and massage my temples as a jumble of memories come flooding back—Jack's face going soft when he talked about Sophia. A cigar box. A letter with her signature. His anger at me for snooping and trying to get to know Sophia, so palpable and cold I felt frozen down to my lungs. Something that happened in middle school. A baseball bat. A kiss. Someone kissing me (Jack?), and the knowledge he had Sophia ringing through my head the entire time.

"Are you okay, Isis?" Sophia asks gently. I grip her

hand and clasp its slender frailness between one of my own.

"He talked about you," I say. "I remember now. *Jesus*, he didn't talk a lot about you, but when he did...he was so overprotective. So thorny. He wanted to make sure no one hurt you. He wanted to—he wanted to keep you safe. Once, I tried to read a letter by you; I mean, I broke into his house to do it, but it was with good intentions, I promise. He keeps them all in his dad's cigar box in the dresser. They're all neat and you can tell he— He cares for those letters more than his life. And he found me reading one, and he was so mad, I thought he was going to literally ax me. Ax me a question. And that question was, 'Do you want to die quickly or slowly?'"

Sophia's face flares pink, and she looks at the ground.

"He loves you, Sophia," I say slowly. "Don't ever doubt that. I mean, I can't remember most of him, but there's a sliver of him I remember now, and my gut tells me he loves you, without a single fricking doubt. My gut isn't wrong. Except when it has food poisoning. Then it is very, *very* wrong."

Sophia looks up, her deep blue eyes welling with the softest of tears. She chokes back a laugh. "I'm sorry. I didn't mean to accuse you—or anyone. I just... I've been with him for so long it feels like I can't tell anymore. And ever since you transferred to his school, his letters—"

She looks my face over, like she's searching for something in my expression. Then she shakes her head. "I'm sorry. Never mind. Thank you."

Before I can say anything more stupid, she walks through the door and takes the steps two at a time, leaving me to the wind and the birds.

I look down at my hands. The memories were so vivid. The smell of stir-fry Jack made. His mother's face, his mother's painting. Their dog, Darth Vader. Jack's room—the smell of sleep and boy and honey and mint, a smell so familiar it comforts me.

Comforts?

I make a face and throw that trash thought in the brain-trash. The dude is clearly an asshole. He kissed me when he had a girlfriend! Me! I'm not even kiss-worthy! Not compared to someone like Sophia. He had Sophia and he kissed me, so he clearly must be a blind idiot as well as an asshole. He's two for two, and the third strike's the last. If there's one thing I can't stand, it's guys who take advantage of a girl's trust to do sleazy things like mack on another girl.

I take the stairs two at a time. I don't see Sophia anywhere in the lobby, so I go back to my room, turning over the semi-what-the-fuckery I'd just encountered. The memory of that Jack smell hits me again for no reason when I turn a corner. I furiously shake my head. Nuh-uh. Whatever I had with him is over. As soon as I find out the details, the past is going in a vault and never coming out again. Sophia is too nice. And she's my friend.

And Jack is the only thing she has left.

"Besides, I don't even like him. I don't even know him. How can you like a carbon-based cootie machine?"

"Who's a carbon-based what?"

I look up to see Wren standing by my bedside, holding a stack of papers. His green eyes shine behind his horn-rimmed glasses, his floppy hair even floppier. The second I register it's him, I open my arms and run toward him, but when I realize the papers are math worksheets, I back up to the wall.

"What are *those*?" I whisper accusingly.

He blinks. "Your makeup work for Algebra II?"

I hiss and arch my back. Wren sighs and puts the papers on my bedside table next to a vase of wilted sunflowers Mom got me.

"You have to do them sometime if you wanna graduate with the rest of us."

"Yes, well, in case you haven't been paying attention, I'm not one to follow the *conventional traditions of the masses*. Also, there are roughly four hundred people in our graduating class and I like maybe three. You being one. Kayla being the other."

Wren looks expectantly at me.

"And Knife Guy."

He exhales. "Still not fully recovered, I see."

"Actually! I am. So now I can ask you! Why didn't you tell me about Jack?"

Shock paralyzes his face for a second.

"You seemed sort of traumatized, Isis. How could I tell you when you were lying in bed with that huge bloodstained bandage around your head? I was just happy you were alive. We all were."

"Yes, I appreciate being alive and well and all, except you forgot the *I-love-my-brain-and-would-like-to-know-what's-going-on-with-it-at-all-times-jerkwad* part!"

"Look, I'm sorry, all right?" Wren takes off his glasses and rubs his eyes. "It's my fault. I'm...wary of girls in fragile states. I don't know how to help them. I've never known how to help them. All I do is hurt them. And with Sophia here in this hospital, too, I've just been on eggshells. I'm sorry. I was wrapped up in my own head, and I forgot about you."

I feel the anger drain out of my body when Wren grins sheepishly.

"You've really…I haven't told you how much you've helped me," he says. "But you have. You really have. Before you came, I just stayed friends with people on the surface. I didn't feel comfortable getting to know people for who they really were. I was fine with them just liking me superficially. But then you— I'm sorry. I didn't want to hurt you. So I didn't tell you. I should've. I'm sorry."

There's a terse quiet. Finally, I lightly punch him. In the ear.

"C'mere, you piece of shit!" I yank his head under my arm and noogie him. "You think you're so cool, worrying about everyone else like a dumb worry warty ass. I'll show you—"

"Ahem."

I look up. Sophia stands there. Wren goes white down to his roots and pulls out of my headlock all in a split second.

"S-Sophia," he stammers.

"Wren." She smiles. "It's good to see you. Tallie misses you. So do I. But Tallie misses you the most."

Wren's white face gets green-tinged as he struggles to speak.

"I've been…busy."

"Too busy for Tallie and me?" Sophia cocks her head. "Busy for four whole years? Jack and Avery visit her, but you don't anymore."

The tension in here is hells thick and no attention is on me, so obviously I have to rectify this situation by asking annoying questions.

"Who's Tallie?"

Wren won't look at me or Sophia, his eyes riveted on the floor instead. Sophia just keeps smiling.

"A good friend of ours. Don't worry about it. I'm sorry I barged in. I'll come back later."

When she's gone, Wren releases the breath he'd been holding.

"I thought you two were talking while you were here?" I ask. "Why are you so shaken up?"

"If you can call it 'talking,'" Wren whispers. "She just stares at me from across the room, or the hall, and smiles. We don't actually talk. That was the first time in… years."

"Is Tallie someone important?"

Wren knits his lips shut, and I know I won't be able to wheedle it out of him.

"Ah, look, never mind. It's cool. You got some secrets, I got some secrets. Our secrets should get married and have babies."

Wren looks shocked.

"Platonically," I add. "Entirely platonic baby-making."

"Is that…a thing?"

"Everything is technically a thing!"

I turn and hop into my bed, smoothing the covers to feign a modicum of decency like a proper lady would. Wren looks like he's having some internal battle. His mouth's all screwed up and his shoulders are shaking.

"Hey? Are you okay?"

"I told you before. I had the camera," he blurts.

"Camera?"

"Avery gave me the camera that night in middle school. She wanted the whole thing on tape."

The thing. I remember it vaguely, but the second he says it in his own words it comes flooding back—Jack, with a baseball bat. Middle school. Avery, Wren, and Sophia were all there. Two? Three men? Avery said she hired those men to get back at Sophia, because she was jealous.

"Avery bullied me. No. Back then I let myself be bullied." Wren spits the sentence. "We hid in the bushes. It was up by the lake—Lake Galonagah. The nature preserve. Avery's parents had a cabin up there. She invited us all to a party and then lured Jack and Sophia to the woods, where the men were waiting."

My heart beats in my ears. Wren clenches his fist.

"I got it all on the tape, Isis. It was horrible. I should've stopped—I should've put it down and saved Sophia. But I didn't. I was a coward. I was frozen. All I could do was stare at that screen, and as long as I stared at it, I could pretend it wasn't happening, that it was a movie instead of real life."

He gives a shuddering gasp. I leap out of bed and put my arms around him.

"Hey, hey, shhhh. It's all right."

"It's not." Wren chokes. "It's not all right. Jack saved her. I couldn't do anything, but he saved her."

I pet circles on his back. "What about the men? What happened to them?"

Wren looks up, eyes red on the edges. The fear takes over again. Reality seeps in—I can see it in the way his expression fixes itself. He rearranges his face, his body, so that he's standing straight and tall.

"I'm sorry," he says, his voice much firmer. "It's been a rough day. I need to get home. Try to do some of that math work, okay? Text me if you have questions."

"Wren, I—"

"Don't, Isis. I'm still… You're recovering. And I'm

recovering. Just—just don't. Not right now."

I take a step back. "All right. Get home before it's dark, okay? And don't forget to eat something."

He smiles. "I won't."

I watch him pull out of the hospital parking lot from my window. After a half hour, I text him: **EAT SOMETHING YOU MASSIVE DOOF.** He responds with an emoji of a grilled cheese sandwich. It's not nearly enough, but it'll do for now.

Mom comes to visit after dinner. I'm picking at rehydrated saltwater crocodile slash Frankenstein's butt jerky slash chicken, so when she holds up a bag of fast food, I run into her arms, imagining roses all around us.

"I love you," I say. "Truly, my love for you has never been larger than in this moment. Except that moment you pushed me out into the world screaming and covered in goo."

She laughs. Her trench coat is still chilly from the air outside, and her hands are cold. I rub them with mine to make them warm. She sits at my bedside, and we quietly eat french fries and burgers, enjoying each other's silence. The hard stuff doesn't get talked about until we've had a good laugh or two. Some normalcy has to be put between the darkness and us. That's how you get enough strength to face it. And by now we're experts at scrounging around for the strength to move forward together.

I wave the yellow slip Mernich gave me. Mom's eyes go wide, and she dabs the corner of her mouth with a napkin.

"How did you get that?"

"Blackmailed a few congressmen. Bribed some drug lords. The usual."

"Isis!"

"I got it from Mernich, how else?" I laugh. "You need to sign off on it and give it to the front desk. And like, I guess they'll do one last CAT scan of my head or whatever, and take the bandages off."

"I wouldn't let you come home unless they did," Mom says sternly. "I'll give it to them when I leave tonight. I'm surprised—Mernich said you wouldn't be ready for another week."

"I managed to win her over with my svelte charm and palaces full of money and boys. Mostly boys."

Mom barely hears me, her focus all on the slip. She looks up and grins. "Are you ready to go home?"

I can practically see the relief on her face. The bills always stick out of her purse when she comes to visit. I'd taken a peek at some when she went to the bathroom—the amount of money is ridiculous. Now she won't have to worry about it as much, though. Praise the J-man.

"Are you kidding? I'm ready to belly-flop into the driveway of home! I'm ready to smear my soulful existence all over the roof of home. I'm ready to corporeally merge into the walls of home. I'm ready to graft the windows of home *onto the skin of my butt*."

Mom tactfully ignores my superlative theatrics and nibbles a pickle. But I know the look in her eyes. She's nervous.

"Something wrong?" I ask.

"The trial." She swallows. "Leo's trial is this Friday."

"You told me." I nod. "I'll be there with you, okay? If I could just testify, if your lawyer would just let me testify—"

"You remember what she said." Mom shakes her head. "Even if you did, the defense would argue your head injury and rule it as inadmissible."

I snort and down soda. "What about Jack?"

Mom looks startled. "Jack? What about him?"

"Is he testifying?"

"I'm not sure. You've never mentioned him before. Why now?"

"I remember him. My session with Mernich made me remember him."

"Oh, that's fantastic!" Mom smiles.

"Why didn't you tell me I'd forgotten him?"

"Honey, I'd been meaning to. But Mernich advised me not to. She wanted you to come to the realization on your own. She said it'd be healthier."

"It's not healthier, it's just more fricking confusing!"

"I wanted to tell you so badly," Mom says. "Believe me. But I was so scared for you. I did everything the doctors told me to, so nothing would go wrong. I didn't want to take the chance I'd mess up your healing process."

When I don't say anything, Mom sighs.

"He's a nice boy, you know—"

"I don't know what he is, Mom."

My voice is sharper than I meant it. Mom flinches. I eat a fry and exhale.

"Sorry. Today has been so weird."

She gets up and kisses my head. "I know, sweetie. Try to get some rest. That bag on the table has your clothes in it—"

"Real clothes!" I crow, eyeing the lumpy bag. One of my Converse shoelaces sticks out over the bag, and I've never been happier to see a shoelace before in my life.

"So don't forget. You'll be out by tomorrow, and at home, where I can take care of you. Oh God, Isis. I'm so glad you're coming home."

"Me too, Mom."

Mom leaves, and Naomi comes in for her final night check a few hours later. I pick at the last stubby french fry and let the mindless cartoons on the TV start to lull me to sleepland.

"I heard you're leaving," Naomi says.

"Yeah."

She quirks an eyebrow. "No cartwheels? No screaming?" She crosses the room and feels my forehead. "Are you feeling all right?"

I lean back. "Everyone lied to me."

"Yeah? Why'd they do that?"

"You did, too."

"I most certainly did not!" Naomi looks offended.

"You could've told me I had amnesia."

"That psychology stuff is up to Dr. Fenwall and Dr. Mernich. They told me about it, but I wasn't allowed to tell you. They are my bosses, after all. I could get fired if I did."

"Oh." I frown. "Sorry."

Naomi sits on the bed and crumples my hamburger trash into her palm.

"Why do you think everyone else kept it from you?" she asks quietly.

"Because they wanna see me squirm."

"Nonsense. They wanted to protect you. They wanted to see you get better."

"Even Sophia knew."

"I wouldn't be surprised; that girl knows everything. Sometimes it's like she can see right through people." Naomi shivers slightly, but the room isn't cold. "Now, promise me you won't sneak into the kids' ward tonight, all right?"

"But…I gotta say good-bye to them."

"I'll take you in the morning to say good-bye. Promise me."

"I promise."

"Be specific."

I huff. "I promise I won't scale the wall and pull myself up over a precarious windowsill ledge into the kids' ward."

"That's what I like to hear."

She readjusts my IV and taps the monitor. After a quick check of my chart, she closes my blinds and turns the light off.

"Good night, Isis."

"'Night."

The hospital bed is comfortable enough, but too much comfort nags at you after a while. Makes you feel useless and lumpy. But I'm leaving. Tomorrow is the last day I'm here. The real world is out there waiting for me. My real memories are out there, waiting for me.

chapter three

ISIS'S FRONT PORCH is as rundown as ever.

The wind chime clinks pathetically in the night air. The lights are on, warm squares of golden light fighting off the darkness. I pull my keys from the ignition and grab the still-warm lasagna from the backseat. Mrs. Blake's decorated the front door with a Christmas wreath and a string of white lights. I smooth my hair and knock twice. The mottled glass on either side of the door has been repaired since that bastard broke it, but seeing it still makes my throat twist.

Mrs. Blake answers in a sweater and yoga pants. She looks happier and more clear-eyed than my previous visits.

"Jack!" She opens the door. "Come in, quick! You must be freezing."

I step into the warmth of the hall, and she takes my coat and fusses over the lasagna.

"Did you make this yourself? It smells lovely. It must've been time-consuming!"

"Not extremely difficult. Just some meat and sauce."

"Nonsense. I can't make a good lasagna to save my

life. Thank you so much."

"Eat it while it's still warm."

She laughs. "I will. Let's sit in the kitchen. Do you want a piece?"

I ignore the gnawing in my stomach. "I already ate."

"Well, have some juice at least. Or do you want soda? I could make you some hot eggnog!"

"Water would be fine."

She makes a *tsk* noise that sounds so familiar. Isis does the same thing, in the same tone, when she's disappointed in something. Mrs. Blake fills a glass, slides it to me, and dishes herself a portion of the lasagna. We sit at the table and I watch her eat. Her wrists are thinner than I remember last time.

"Have you been eating?" I ask softly. Mrs. Blake shrugs.

"Oh, you know. Things at the museum are so hectic lately. I don't cook as much as I should."

"You forget."

She smiles sheepishly. "Yes. Isis is so good about that—she always packs me lunches and puts them in the car so I won't forget them in the morning."

Her eyes light up as she takes another bite.

"You really are a wonderful cook, Jack. This is amazing. Thank you."

"It's the least I could do."

"No, no. You didn't have to do this at all. The visits, the food, all of it. I'm...I'm very grateful. You've helped us so much."

I clench my fist under the table. "I haven't helped at all."

"Without you—" Mrs. Blake inhales, like what she's about to say requires more air, more life force. "Without you, Leo would have—"

"I didn't do anything. I couldn't save Isis in time," I snap. "She got hurt because I wasn't fast enough. I failed."

The last two words ring in the near-empty, dim kitchen.

"I failed," I say, stronger this time. "And she forgot me because of my failure."

"She didn't— Jack, no. That's not it at all."

Yes. It is. It's my punishment. And I'll take it. It has been a long time coming, after all.

I stand and go into the hall, pulling on my coat. Mrs. Blake nervously follows.

"I didn't mean— I'm sorry. You don't have to leave," she says.

"I have work."

She doesn't know what work. She just knows I have to leave. And she knows it's an excuse as much as I do.

"All right then. Drive safely."

Before I get a foot out the door, Mrs. Blake grabs my coat sleeve. I turn my head over my shoulder, and she murmurs softly, sympathy glowing from her eyes with near-uncomfortable warmth.

"You're always welcome in this house, Jack."

I'm quiet. Mrs. Blake reaches up and hugs me. I quell the urge to push her away. Her arms are gentle. For a moment, she feels like my own mother. I'm the first to step away. I always am.

"I should go," I say. She nods.

"Will you be there? At the trial?"

"I'll try. I don't know if they'll let me in the courthouse. I'll ask my mother's lawyer."

Mrs. Blake watches me go from her doorway. There's

no fear in her eyes—not anymore. Not like the fear I saw that day. She didn't try to stop me or the bat. She let it happen. Maybe she feels guilty she let me beat Leo nearly to death. It's useless to tell her she couldn't have stopped me anyway. The thing in me—the thing that's lusted for blood and anguish and justice since that night in middle school—could not have been stopped. It had been starved for too long, and the bars of its ice cage melted too thin by an idiotic, annoying girl.

It will not happen again.

I get in the car, start it, and pull away from the curb.

The beast will not come out again. I will restrain it next time. That's what I've told myself since that night in middle school. I promised it would never happen. But it did. And I couldn't control it. I'd nearly beaten a man to death because of it.

~~He deserved it.~~

~~I was as terrified as he was.~~

I shake my head and merge onto the highway. The beast will have to wait. The fear will have to wait.

Blanche Morailles, on the other hand, cannot be kept waiting.

Few women on this earth are as intimidating as Blanche Morailles. She's a frightening combination of chilly poise, svelte cheekbones, and a wickedly sharp smile. It gives her a disarming presence, always cloaked in dramatic, floor-sweeping velvet coats. No one knows her real age—countless beauticians she no doubt pays by the bucket keep her looking younger than she really is. Blanche is the daughter of a French ambassador. She isn't cheap enough to resort to Botox, so the fine lines around her eyes tell the story of a woman in her late forties. Perhaps fifty-two. But that's pushing it.

I spot her perfect dark-haired coif over a dozen typical heads of Ohio dishwater blond, and weave around the tables. De l'Ange is a prestigious restaurant, and the one I used to work in before it was bought out and taken over by a new staff and crew.

I slide into the seat opposite Blanche. She sips ice water and twists her amethyst ring around her finger, raising one eyebrow to indicate she acknowledges my presence.

"Feels familiar, doesn't it?" she asks, her voice rich and strong, with the barest French accent.

"The opposite," I correct. "I'm an alien in this place now."

"You've only been away a year. Less than that."

"A year and one month."

She sips her water again, pauses as if thinking, calculating, and then she nods. "So it has. I should've known better than to test your memory."

"What's that supposed to mean?"

Blanche smiles. For all her upkeep on her face, she's rarely touched her teeth—they remain slightly crooked.

"It means I know you're far smarter than the average man, Jack. And the above-average man. In fact, you are smarter than most men. This is a compliment, I assure you. Almost every man I've met is an idiot in some way. But not you."

"Does my intelligence concern you?" I ask. The waiter offers me bread, but I refuse it.

"Aren't you going to eat?" Blanche tries to change the subject.

"No. Does my intelligence concern you?"

She sighs. "Yes. It concerns me. Every personality of a working member of the Rose Club concerns me. I have not gotten this far—I have not become the best simply by ignoring the strengths and weaknesses of those I hire. I use them appropriately."

There's a long pause. The waiters bustle about and bring Blanche a lobster pasta. She thanks them in French and begins picking at it delicately.

"I'm sure you already know what I'm going to say, Jack. In fact, we both know what I'm about to say. And you also know I'm going to say this thing only because I know what you're going to ask. That's why you set up a meeting with me, is it not? To ask me something."

I nod. She smiles and folds her hands.

"Then ask."

"But I already know the answer."

"Ask anyway."

It's a command, not a request. My eyes dart around the room. Blanche doesn't have bodyguards, but her manservant Frasier is constantly at her side, and in his own quiet way he is every bit as protective as a bodyguard. I spot him eating at a table to our left by himself. His dark tailored suit hides his slight yet powerful frame. I've seen Frasier deal with the more unsavory clients of the Rose Club when Blanche feels the need to send a message to the escort community at large. It isn't pretty. I don't know Blanche and Frasier's story. No one does. All we know is Frasier handles the business Blanche is too ladylike to touch.

I turn back to Blanche. I'm not afraid of Frasier, but now that I know his eyes are on me, I feel less brave.

"I only need two more weeks of payment. Then I want out."

Blanche looks down into her dish and smiles. "This is what I was afraid of. The smart ones always know when to leave. Usually they are not as handsome as you, my dear, and thus earn less. So I feel more inclined to let them go."

"You aren't 'letting' me go. I am leaving of my own volition in two weeks."

Blanche's expression turns steely, a frown carving her face. I see Frasier straighten in his seat out of the corner of my eye.

"You seem to have forgotten our agreement, Jack," she says.

"Our agreement was you get me the clients to earn myself sixty thousand dollars. And I did. I earned more than double that, considering you take sixty percent."

"And you'd earn a lot more, if you stayed. You turned eighteen recently, right? You could start making enough for yourself. Real money."

"I don't need the money." I can barely contain my sneer.

"Oh, I know. Full scholarship to Harvard. Read all about it in the local newspaper. You certainly are going places. With or without me."

I'm quiet. Blanche flicks some hair away from her face, expectant.

"Thank you," I say finally. "For working with me. I learned a lot."

"I'm sure you did."

"On the fourteenth, our agreement is over. I'm hoping you'll be amicable about this."

"Of course I will, Jack. I'm a businesswoman. I'm simply lamenting the fact that you and I won't be able to build more together."

She looks down at her phone as it buzzes. A shadow

crosses her face for a moment, but a faint smile replaces it as she looks back up at me.

"You know, you're right. It *is* time you left. You're much too good to be stuck in little old Ohio forever. You'll do well at Harvard, I'm sure."

She extends a hand to me. Everything in me screams not to trust it. It's too sudden. The shift in her mood was instantaneous—that text message must have said something about me. Or maybe I'm paranoid. Maybe it wasn't about me at all. Maybe it was another Rose Club business deal going smoothly and netting her a lot of money. That's much more likely.

"Why the sudden pleasantries?" I ask.

Blanche laughs. "Oh, Jack. Always so suspicious. Don't worry. Honestly, don't. I knew you wouldn't be an escort for much longer with me. That's bittersweet, assuredly. But I did mention, didn't I? When we first met? What did I say again? You have that stellar memory, surely you can tell me my exact words."

The moment comes flooding back. I'd just turned seventeen. We were sitting in Blanche's car, a silver Rolls-Royce or something else stupidly showy. I'd just gotten off shift at De l'Ange when Blanche stopped me in the alley as I was throwing away the day's trash and asked to give me a ride home. I don't know why I went with her, but she reeked of money, and money was all that was on my mind since I'd found out just a few days before how much Sophia's surgery would cost. I went hoping some of her wealth would rub off on me, maybe. I was desperate. And she could smell that like a fox downwind of a rabbit's den.

We talked. She proposed I join her Rose Club. She told me what it meant and what I'd have to do. There was no trickery or secrets. She was very honest and up-front, and I was prepared to do whatever it took to get the money for Sophia. And when we were done, when I'd agreed to it and signed the contract, she'd snapped her Louis Vuitton handbag closed and smiled at me.

"This club isn't just a way to provide people with luxury experiences, Jack. You benefit from it with more than just money. You meet politicians. Their daughters. Their wives. You meet stockbrokers and dot-com billionaires who have daughters. You meet the movers and the shakers of the world. You become connected. It's a web that spreads far and wide, and you've just become a single string of it."

Coming back to the present, I recite the words to Blanche. She claps her hands softly.

"Very good. A single string. That's what you are. Even if you leave the web, the web will never truly leave you."

I narrow my eyes. "What does that mean?"

"You're smart enough to know what it means."

She makes a motion for Frasier, and he gets up and pulls out her chair. She stands, and he smoothly puts her coat over her shoulders. Blanche pulls her gloves on one finger at a time.

"In two weeks, our contract is over," she says. "The payments will proceed as usual until that time."

"I suppose this is good-bye, then?" I ask. Blanche flashes one last smile at me.

"No, Jack. I'm certain you and I will meet again."

I watch her go. My phone buzzing tears my attention away from her figure. It's a call from a blocked number. I answer.

"Jack? It's Naomi—"

She doesn't have to say anything more.

"I'll be there in ten," I say and then hang up.

chapter four

3 YEARS, 25 WEEKS, 6 DAYS

ONE TIME I HAD this really sweet dream where I had wings made of crystal feathers and I was slender and beautiful like an elf queen made of light and purity and also maybe I barfed rainbows but that isn't the point—the point is it was a wonderful dream, probably the best of my life. Most importantly I am not having it right now, because right now I'm having a dream about a giant spider.

It's chasing me through a forest of some kind, and I'm sort of peeing myself while hoping I'm not actually peeing myself in real life. It's a weird mix of lucid dreaming and lucid terror, so I can't get scared enough to wake myself up, but I'm awake enough to be scared.

And then all of a sudden, the dream changes.

The spider disappears, the forest disappears, and I'm suddenly in the shower of my old house at Aunt Beth's in Florida. The tiny one, with green tiles and mold in the cracks and the wind chime hung over the bathroom window. I'm three years younger and naked and my fat is obvious to the world, hanging in great chunks off my belly, my thighs, my chin. I'm crouched in the shower, curled up in a not-so-little ball, my flesh pressing against the enamel and the water trickling down from the showerhead. It's cold water. I don't know how I remember that, but I do. Aunt Beth had a solar heater. I stayed in the shower that day until the water got cold.

And I'm crying.

That isn't anything new, really. But seeing myself like this, in a third-person bizarro out-of-body experience, is a first. I know this moment. I'd know it anywhere.

The girl in the shower clutches herself—her stomach, her face. But her hand keeps wandering back to one place: her right wrist. I know what she's feeling. That wrist burns. No amount of cold water can douse the pain coming from it. She'll put a bandage on it later. But it takes her four hours to sit up. Five hours to stop crying with no sound. Six hours to dry off and get dressed. Seven hours to stop staring at herself in the mirror as she makes a decision.

It takes eight hours for the girl to decide to change herself.

It takes three years for his voice to stop ringing in her ears every time she walks out the door. And even then, it doesn't fade. It still hasn't.

Two weeks from the day in the shower, she stops eating so much. The girl loses five pounds. Then three more. A month later she's ten pounds lighter. She puts on layers of sweatpants and sweatshirts and runs in the eighty-degree Florida summer for hours. Aunt Beth thinks she's at Gina's house sleeping over when in reality she's on the side of the road behind a hibiscus bush, passed out from heat exhaustion. When the sun sets and it cools down, she wakes up and starts running again. She runs because she can't stand the thought of who she was a step behind. One step. A new Isis. Another step. A newer Isis. She leaves herselves behind over and over because she can't stand any of them—because she can't stand the girl who thought the boy who destroyed her could be her everything. He was the only one in the world who looked at her like she was human, treated her like she was more than a sack of too-much skin.

She rarely eats, and if she does it's only in front of Aunt Beth, to convince her she's all right. But Aunt Beth is smarter than she lets on. One day, she and Isis talk, and it's the sort of talk aunts are supposed to give—boy talk. I remember her every word as clear as day, and that reflects straight into the dream.

"You haven't been eating much, Isis." Aunt Beth, with her gentle smile and bright red hair held back by a head scarf, treats me every bit like her daughter. I was the kid she could never have.

"I'm not hungry," I say lamely. And then my stomach gurgles and my charade is thrown headfirst over a cliff.

Aunt Beth sighs. "It's about that Will kid, isn't it?"

My stomach goes from gurgly to vomity. I flinch. But that flinch is important. It's the first flinch I made when I heard his name. The first of hundreds.

"Did you two break up?" she asks softly. I shrug like it doesn't matter but it does, it does, it's the only thing that matters.

"I didn't break up with him. He broke up with me. I sort of just broke down. You know how it goes."

"Oh." She puts her arm around my shoulder. "I do know how it goes."

There's a massive silence. The ocean laps just a half mile away from our tiny, kitschy beach shack. The sun slants through the window, throwing turquoise and emerald shadows around the kitchen as it passes through a collection of sea glass on the sill.

"Whenever someone would break up with me," she starts, "I'd sit myself down and make a list."

"Of what? Ways to blast yourself to another planet?"

"No. I'd make a list of traits my dream man would have. And by the end of it, I'd always feel better."

"That sounds stupid."

"Of course it's stupid. That's the point. It's supposed to make you laugh with all its stupidity!"

I knit my lips together. Aunt Beth nudges me.

"Well? Go on. Describe your dream man."

I mull it over for an agonizing few seconds.

"I want him to know the alphabet backward, and fast. He'll make perfect cinnamon sugar doughnuts. He can jump rope a million times in a row. He'll have bright green eyes and be left-handed and be a master of the obscure lost art of ocarina playing."

"He sounds impossible."

"That's the point!" I insist. "He's my dream man, right? So, if my dream man is someone who can never really exist, then he can't hurt me. He can't come up and make me fall in love and smash my heart."

"Oh, Isis." Aunt Beth pats my knee. "You don't have to think like that. Not everyone is out to hurt you."

"He'll be really kind." I smile down at my hands. "He'll call me the prettiest girl he's ever seen. Those things are even more impossible. So. So there. That's him. And he doesn't exist and he never will. So I'm safe."

The dream shifts. The kitchen table disappears. Aunt Beth disappears. And then it's suddenly four months later. Four months of passing out and stumbling through classes on nothing more than a piece of bread and celery. I didn't need food. The word "ugly" reverberating through my head sustained me better than any calorie could.

I was punishing myself.

I know that now, far too late for it to help.

By the time Aunt Beth notices, everyone else is noticing.

Jealous, Gina disappears to Costa Rica for one weekend and comes back fifteen pounds lighter. But no one notices. Not when Isis Blake goes from two hundred pounds to one-twenty in the span of six months. Nameless notices. And now, instead of ignoring me, he laughs with his friends whenever I walk by. Smirks. Scoffs. He thinks I did it for him.

I did~~n't.~~

I never get the chance to work up the courage to get angry at him. I feel it brewing in my stomach, like still-warm embers of resentment. But then my mother arrives. I walk in the house one day to see Aunt Beth and Mom drinking tea and discussing my future. I get a say, of course. And I say I want to leave. Ohio is the perfect place to start over. Anywhere no one knows me is the perfect place to start over. Anywhere that isn't where Nameless is.

It's my dream, but it's more like my life. It's not quite *true* to life—the colors are too bright and the faces wobble. But it's exactly what happened.

I wake up to the whitewashed hospital room. I wake up realizing I ran away like a little coward.

I haven't changed at all.

I'm safe. My counter is safe. Three years, twenty-five weeks, six days. I am still safe.

But I haven't changed *at all.*

Isis Blake of Northplains, Ohio, is the same cowardly fourteen-year-old girl curled up in the shower. Just a little older, a little lighter, and a little stupider.

It's dark—probably the middle of the night. I get out of the hospital bed and pull some clothes out of the bag Mom brought. Stepping outside in Ohio in the winter is like suicide without all the flashy brain bits, but I'm doing it anyway. I can't stand this tiny room. It's trying to suffocate me with all the beeps and smiling posters of kids getting shot up with flu vaccines. Who smiles when they see a five-inch needle? Sociopaths, that's who.

I promised Naomi I wouldn't use the window to sneak into the kids' ward. But last time I checked, a hall is not a window and there is a hall that goes right by the kids' ward. I just never use it because it's near Sophia's room, and that's the one place Naomi would think to look for me if she found me missing from my bed. I pile pillows under the blankets of my cot, reach under it and grab four leftover Jell-O cups I'd been hoarding, and ease out the door. The hallways are quiet. I readjust the Jell-O cups by stuffing them into my bra. I take a moment to admire my considerable multicolored breasts and feel a single tear spring to my eye. Beautiful.

But back to business. I've got some gelatin to deliver to several grubs. I just need to make it around the corner, and I'll—

I hiss and flatten myself against the wall. A group of interns passes, all carrying coffees. I quell the urge to become fleetingly radical. I want to slide across the floor behind them on my shoes like James Bond, silent and suave, but I also want to see the kids no matter what. Too much is riding on this. So like a lame normal spy I tiptoe behind them. And pirouette.

And that's when I hear it. It sounds like a dying cat far off, but as I get closer and closer to the kids' ward, I realize it's a person. Someone is screaming like they're being ripped apart. In the empty hallway it's eerie, and I start to consider maybe my life has turned into a horror movie and a girl with long black hair will be hiking up my phone bill as she calls to tell me I'll die in seven days, but then there's the shuffling of feet behind me, and I duck behind a gurney. Naomi, with a few other nurses, charge toward the scream with winded urgency.

"Who forgot to up Sophia's cc's?" one of the nurses asks.

"No one forgot. Fenwall said to ignore the change entirely," Naomi pants. "But someone was supposed to give her Paxtal. Trisha?"

"It wasn't me!" Trisha insists.

The first nurse sighs. "Jesus, Trisha, not again—"

"Do you know how hard it is to get her to take them? When she's like that?" Trisha hisses.

"Did you call him at least?"

"Of course! He's the only one who can calm her down—"

They run past, out of my earshot. They must be talking about another Sophia. The Soapy I know always listens to nurses. She'd definitely never refuse to take her pills.

I inch closer to the door the screaming is coming from. The nurses closed it, but I can hear it through the walls.

"Why does she get to go?" the scream reverberates. "Why does she get to go and I don't? I want to leave! Let me go! Let me go! Get your hands off me, you filthy bitch!"

I recognize that voice. Sophia. But that can't be right. Sophia wouldn't sound so harsh, so feral.

"I hate her, I hate you all! I fucking hate you! Get away from me! Leave me alone!"

The words are all wrong. I slowly peer around the corner and into a tiny slit of window unprotected by the curtain. I can't see much, but I see Sophia's legs flailing on the bed as the nurses try to restrain her. I see Naomi walk by with a syringe in her hand. Sophia fights, the bed shuddering as she beats her legs harder. And then her feet move slower. Her screaming becomes softer, hoarse shouts I can barely hear anymore through the glass.

"Please," Sophia sobs. "Please. I want Tallie back. Please, just give me Tallie back. Just let me out of here. I want to see her. *I want to see her!*"

One of the nurses starts toward the door. I pull back around the corner. As much as the curiosity is burning me up inside, I can't hang around much longer, or I'll be in deeper shit than an elephant keeper at a circus. I take the stairs to the kids' ward without looking back.

Sophia has tumors. I know that much. She'd never been like that with me—not that harsh or angry. I feel like I've seen something I wasn't supposed to—something private and embarrassing. She'd definitely feel awful if she knew I saw it, so I can't bring it up with her. Sophia's endured a lot from me—from my nonstop talking to my terrible jokes and thorny defensiveness. I've made mistakes in front of her, and she's never mentioned them again. The least I can do is forget what I saw, too.

The commotion Sophia made was the perfect cover—the guard isn't even at the door. The sleeping room is lined with beds, stickers, and colorful sponge art pressed onto each headboard. Toys and books are stacked on the ground, and the gently beeping monitors glow in the darkness.

James is the first to notice I've come in. He sits up and whispers groggily, "Isis? Is that you?"

"Yeah," I whisper. "Hey."

He points at my chest, his bald head shining in the faint lights of the monitor. "Why are you jiggling?"

"I've always been this stacked."

James rolls his eyes. I laugh and shove a Jell-O cup at him. He rips the top off and then slurps it down in one gulp. I inch over to Mira's bed and carefully place her Jell-O cup on her bald forehead. She sleepily opens her eyes and groans.

"Isisssss. It's cold."

"Hurry up and eat it, then."

They eagerly stuff sugar down their throats, and I clear mine, trying to find the words to say good-bye.

"Listen," I say. "I'm getting out of here tomorrow."

"You're leaving?" Mira sniffs.

"Yeah. I got better." I smile. "Just like you will."

"I won't."

"You will. You will, and don't you dare let me catch you saying you won't."

"Will you come back to see us?"

"Is the sky mildly blue? Duh, I will!" I give her a noogie. "Also, toys. I'm gonna bring some cool new ones for your birthday, and James's birthday, and Martin Luther King's birthday, and my own birthday, because frankly these dinky little hand-me-downs do not suit Your Highness."

Mira grins. A light flashes out in the hall and I duck behind her bed.

"The guard!" I exclaim. "Shit. Take mushrooms. Shiitake mushrooms."

"Shiitake," James echoes. I bop his head.

"Hey! That's a bad word."

"But it's a mushroom! Nothing's wrong with mushrooms!"

"Haven't you played *Mario*? *Everything* is wrong with mushrooms."

"He's coming this way to check," Mira hisses at me. The guard's so close I can hear the jangling of his keys.

"Okay, everyone calm down. Don't panic. OhmygodwhatamIdoingwithmylife. Don't panic!"

"We're not!" they insist together.

"Right! Okay!" I breathe out my nose and charge toward the window. I always have a harder time climbing down than up, but it's the only place in the room to hide; every piece of furniture in here is kid-sized and too small. I open the window and leap over, clinging by my fingertips on the sill. My Converse scrabble on the cement of the wall, the cold winter air nipping at my butt, which hangs fourteen feet above certain death, or at the very least a broken kneecap. The door to the ward creaks open into utter silence. The grubs are good at pretending to be asleep.

"Who left the window open?" I hear the guard murmur. My heart rockets into my throat. He strides over and I pray to whatever god is listening that he won't see my fingers. I must be praying right for once! He doesn't see my fingers at all! He just kindly closes the window and shoves them off the sill instead. My hands jump to the ledge on the outside, but it's so tiny and slippery, and I fight, my hands aching—

All I can think about is how to fall elegantly so

my dead body doesn't look stupid, because I've seen a million crime shows and honestly existentialist panic is no reason to not try, in your last moments, to contort your body as you fall so you strike a dramatic pose. It's your last pose ever! You have a moral obligation to make it fabulous! Or at the very least not-disgusting.

I could pose like Beyoncé, but one thing is still for certain.

I'm going to die.

Which is a whole lot of very not good.

My last fingers slip off the ledge. And then there's weight all at once on my wrist as someone grabs it. Whiplash rocks my body and hard cement collides with my belly, scrapes my elbows. I look up into icy blue eyes shaded by wild tawny hair.

"Y-You!" I sputter.

Jack pulls me back up through the window, Mira and James on either side of him, wide-eyed and ecstatic.

"You almost died," Mira whispers shakily.

"You were all like 'WHOA' and the guard was all like 'BYE' and Jack came in and was like 'GRAB'!" James shrieks.

Jack straightens. I stand up on shaky legs and contemplate life and the refreshing fact that I still have a life to contemplate at all. Jack freezes when our eyes meet and then turns on his heel abruptly. I run and put myself between him and the door. He stares at me and I stare at him, some unsaid pressure bearing down on my lungs. Adrenaline sears my veins, and a twisted pain tears through my chest. I can't look away. He's not even that good-looking. He just looks so…*sad*? And that sadness is condensed in an arrow that he's shot right into me with his dumb antarctic eyes.

"How—"

"I was walking behind you in the hall. I followed you. I have a knack for knowing when you're about to do something stupid," Jack answers in clipped tones.

"Why—"

"Sophia. I came to the hospital for her. Now move."

Jack tries to maneuver around me, but I stop him at each turn.

"I've had years of practice being fat. We are good at blocking things. Also, floating in salt water."

"Let me through."

The smell of mint and honey floats toward me, that same disconcerting smell of him I found in my memories earlier today.

"See, I think I should *not* let you through, since you are a really bad boyfriend, and logic dictates a bad thing should not be near a good thing, so essentially, Sophia doesn't need you around."

He scoffs. "You have no idea what you're talking abo—"

"You kissed me," I say. "Sophia told me you kissed me. And I remembered it. A bit. And even if you saved me, and Mom, and pulled me up from the ledge or whatever, I can't forgive you for hurting Sophia like that. I can't forgive you for kissing someone you didn't like. That probably hurt me, too. You've hurt a lot of people, haven't you?"

Mira and James watch us, our words like ping-pong balls their heads inevitably follow. Jack is expressionless, wordless, like a recently wiped chalkboard. I can't read him. But tiny wisps of incredulousness give way to shock, and then his face sets in an icy mask of irritation.

"Get out of my way," he repeats, a deadly quality in his voice.

"No. See, I'm a good dragon. Does your small-yet-somehow-still-functioning brain know what a dragon is?"

"Scaly!" James chirps.

"Breathes fire!" Mira adds.

"I'm the dragon," I say. "And Sophia is the princess. And it's my job to guard her from the likes of you."

Jack raises a brow. "Likes of me?"

"A bad prince. The kind that ruins princesses forever."

The ice-blue splinters of his eyes darken, shading over. His eyes are easier to read than his face, but not by much. Is it anger? Guilt? Frustration? No. It's none of those. It's helplessness.

"You're too late. I've already ruined her forever," he says, and he pushes past me with such force I don't have time to brace. He's long gone when Mira decides to speak up.

"They call him sometimes. Naomi does. When Sophia gets really mad."

"What do you mean?"

James shuffles, staring at his feet. "Sometimes… sometimes she gets weird. And mad. And when we ask about it, Naomi says it's someone else yelling, not Sophia. But it's her voice. And then they call Jack, and he always comes no matter what time it is and she calms down and gets quiet again."

"How long has this been going on for?"

"A couple years, I think," Mira says. "Since James came here. She used to be so nice to us all the time. I mean, she still is. But sometimes…sometimes she gets weird. So she stopped visiting us. And Jack started visiting her more. I think she feels guilty."

"I think they both feel guilty." James scoffs. "They both got the same faces my dad does when he visits me."

I watch Jack's figure grow smaller down the hall.

She remembers.

Isis Blake remembers me.

The world doesn't move for me. It stopped that night in middle school. It trembled when Isis first punched me and grew to a quake with every day I fought the war against her. And then it went still for weeks. For weeks that felt longer than years.

Today the world shakes, and it shakes with her name and her set, determined face as she looked me in the eyes and told me I was a bad prince. Today it shakes because she might think I'm terrible (You are terrible. Your hands are bloody and *you are terrible.*), but she remembers me. A small fragment of the old Isis—the one who recognized me and despised me months ago—shone through in her eyes. She hates me. But she remembers me.

She remembers a kiss ~~(which kiss which kiss which kiss the fake one from the beginning or the true one in Avery's house?)~~.

Today my world shakes. Not hard. But it moves under my feet and reminds me that yes—*yes*. The world can still move. I'm really still alive. I am not ice. I am not a freak or a monster. I am not something people are afraid of or avoid. I am human and I have done bad things, but the world shakes and I am human. I am not untouchable. I can be shaken.

By Isis Blake.

As I walk into the hospital room more familiar to me

than home, Naomi walks out of it, her hair frazzled and her nurse scrubs wrinkled. A scratch mark mars her arm from elbow to wrist. It isn't deep, but it's red and angry and very noticeable.

"That bad?" I ask.

Naomi shakes her head. "I have no idea why she… She hasn't done this for an entire month, and now—"

"Something must have triggered her," I say, and try to push past her into the room. "Let me talk to her."

"She's sleeping. Trisha administered a tranq."

The elation from knowing Isis remembers me drains away. A dark fury starts to broil over me, but Naomi backtracks.

"Jack, listen. Listen to me. It was the only thing we could do. She was threatening to hurt herself with a pair of scissors."

"How did she get—" My own anger chokes me off. "Why did you let her have those?"

"I didn't! You know me better than that, for Christ's sake! I don't know where she got them or how, but she had them and all we could do was stop her before she could do any real harm to herself."

Dread replaces the anger, layering over it like a sickening cake. I can barely open my mouth to speak, but the words somehow escape.

"She must have been triggered. She's gotten so much better. You know she wouldn't do this unless someone said something that upset her."

Naomi waves a tired hand toward the sleeping Sophia tucked under the white covers too perfectly. Too peacefully.

"You're welcome to talk to her when she wakes up."

I instantly spot the fine wrinkles under her eyes, the

weary bags that all nurses get sometime in their long and stress-ridden careers. She's so tired. She's been Sophia's best nurse, the only one she really likes and trusts.

"I'm sorry," I mutter. "For being so caustic."

Naomi's eyebrows shoot up into her hairline. "Excuse me? What was that strange word I just heard?"

"Don't make me say it twice."

I push into the room and close the door behind me. I watch Naomi leave through the frosted glass of the room's divider, her smirk evident even through the translucence.

The room is dim and quiet, save for the beeping of the monitors that staccato out her vital signs in too-cheery chirps. Every bouquet I've given her this year is still in the room—wilted and browning and not enticing in the slightest. But she keeps them all. She keeps each vase full of water and all the vases in chronological order. The room smells like molding flowers and antiseptic.

It's then the guilt hits me like a steel maul to my chest. I haven't visited for two weeks. There's a two-week gap she's carefully left in the line of flowers, two empty vases waiting for me to bring them the blooms they need to serve their purpose.

I let my guilt at not being able to save Isis override my duty to Sophia. And that's unforgivable.

How can I be so excited about a girl remembering a kiss when the girl who needs me is suffering?

Selfish bastard.

I sit on the end of her bed gingerly. The white blankets fold like snow under my weight, and contour gently around her outline. She's so much thinner than I remember. Her every bone sticks out like a bird's—frail and hollow-looking. Her cheekbones are sharp and evident. There's no trace of the rosy bloom I'd gotten so used to seeing growing up. That went away after that night long ago.

"I really am a bad prince," I mutter.

I smooth hair away from her forehead. She mumbles softly and rolls over.

"Tallie..."

My fists clench in the sheets, and the molten spike of feverish regret bakes my insides, starting in my heart, working its way to my lungs and stomach and everything in between.

Tallie.

Our Tallie.

You've hurt a lot of people, haven't you?

chapter five

3 YEARS, 26 WEEKS, 0 DAYS

DR. FENWALL IS SANTA. If Santa went on a SlimFast diet and wore corduroy pants every day of his life and used terms like "endometrial tissue."

"Now, Isis, if you could just lie back…"

I slump on the CAT scan bed and huff. "I've done this before, doc! I've done lie-backs every freaking day since I've been here! At least seventy billion lie-backs!"

Fenwall's eyes crinkle and his white mustache curls with his smile. "You should be a little used to it."

"You never get used to being slotted into a giant doughnut's vagina." I motion at the CAT machine. It beeps excitedly. I plot its demise.

"Well, this is your last time doing it. Come on now, lie back."

I shout "UGH" and flop back and bang my head.

"And be careful, will you? We spent a lot of hours sewing that cranium back together," Fenwall chides. He presses a button and the CAT bed slides in, a tunnel engulfing me in dimness.

"You okay in there?" he asks.

"Everything's cramped and smells like cotton balls."

"Perfectly fine, then. Start it up, Cleo!"

A woman at the control panel in the next room waves through the window and the machine starts to whir. I hear Fenwall leave, and then it's just me and Big Bertha. And her vagina.

"How's...how's the weather up there in...robot land?" I try.

The machine gurgles.

"Good. That's good. And the kids?"

Big Bertha bleeps enthusiastically and a blue light blinds me.

"Ahh!" I shield my eyes. "Th-They must be going through teenage rebellion!"

The machine blips sadly and the light goes out.

"It's okay," I assure her. "When they're in their twenties they'll think you're smart and worth listening to again."

"Tilt your head to the left, Isis," Fenwall's intercom blasts in my ear.

"Rude! I'm having a discussion here!"

"Are you talking to inanimate objects again? Mernich would love to hear about that." I can hear his grin.

"No! No, I'm not talking to anything! Nothing at all! Just...myself! Which is basically nothing. Nothing special. Except my butt. My butt is definitely something hells special—"

"Left, Isis." Fenwall doesn't take my shit. In a friendly grandpa-y way. I tilt my head and Bertha beeps once, twice, and there's a pause. The regular white lights come back on and the bed slides out slowly.

"Phew!" I leap up and shake off the claustrophobia. I hate small spaces.

Fenwall comes in. "Feeling all right?" he asks.

"Well, I need to spend five therapeutic years on the open plains of Mongolia, but other than that I'm good."

"Fantastic. Your results will be done in just a second. Let's go get your mother."

I follow him out to the hall. It feels so good to walk around in my real clothes, not a hospital gown anymore. And the absence of a stinky bandage turban clinging to my head is a mild plus. I practice shaking my hair out like a majestic lion but almost hit an intern and stop. They have enough problems without strands of fabulous hair in their eyes. Mom's waiting in the lobby. She smiles and gets up and hugs me.

"So? What are the results?"

Fenwall looks at the papers in his hands. "Everything looks fine. The hemorrhaged tissue has cleared up remarkably well."

"What about this?" I point at the scar just to the side of my hairline and above my forehead. "The hair isn't growing back. I'll never get married!"

"The scar will shrink and fade, but that will take time. Years," Fenwall says.

Mom pats my head. "It's not too big, sweetie. Unless someone is seven feet tall and can look straight down on your head, no one will ever see it."

She's right. What's one more scar on a girl full of them already, inside and out?

"Do I get any meds?" I ask. Fenwall smiles.

"Nope. You're free to go. We'd like to set up a checkup appointment in a few weeks."

He motions to Mom, and the two of them go to the counter and speak to the nurse. There isn't a big crowd, but there are more people than normal on a Saturday. That doesn't stop me from noticing the bright red hair walking through the lobby.

"Avery-boh-bavery!"

The flame-haired girl turns, perfect porcelain skin freckled as ever. But her eyes are all wrong—tired, bloodshot. Her clothes are perilously unfashionable. And the way her expression stays the same instead of a grimace or sneer forming when she recognizes me? Something is really off.

"You." Her voice is tinny.

"Yes, me! I am alive! But that can be easily remedied."

"Get out of my way."

"How've you been? Busy? Beautiful bitch duties as usual?"

Avery's mouth remains straight, not even the faintest of frowns appearing. "If you don't move, I'll make you move."

"You can try! Push me a little, maybe? Throw me around? Don't get too enthusiastic, though. If you cut me in half, nothing but rainbow sparkles and Bacardi would spill out. Also you would be a murderer."

"I *should* cut you in half," Avery finally snarls, her emotionless mask breaking. "You fucked her over."

"What?"

"You." Avery jabs her finger at my chest. "Sophia finally started talking to me, and then you ruined everything."

"How did I ruin it?"

Avery's expression is a cruel, twisted thing. "How fucking fair is it? I've been trying to make up for my mistakes with her for years. She's shunned me for years. And then you come, for three weeks, and she likes you already? Now you're leaving her. She won't talk to anyone. Not the nurses. Not me."

"I'm—I'm not leaving forever."

"It doesn't matter. She thinks you are. She thinks everyone leaves her."

There's a long pause. I know that feeling, more than I'd like. I nervously pick at my sweatshirt. Avery scoffs.

"But I can't be all mad at you. When you came, she told me I could visit for once. So I did. And I got to tell her I was sorry."

She looks off into the distance wistfully.

"I got to apologize, to at least try to make things right. So. Thanks. I guess."

"You're welcome? But also I'm going to see her before I leave? And I'll come visit her? So I'm not actually, uh, leaving."

"She's having her surgery soon." Avery doesn't seem to hear me. "And now I can't even say good-bye to her."

"You can. I mean, you can say it. She might not be talking to you, but she's listening. I'm sure of it."

Avery shrugs, her face becoming blank and despondent again as she shoves past me.

That's not Avery. That's a hell-bent shell of the glorious bitch she used to be.

Mom and Fenwall come back, talking amicably. Mom says something about my checkup in February, but I barely hear her.

"When is Sophia's operation, doc?" I ask. Fenwall looks alarmed.

"She told you about that?"

"Yeah, duh! Can I come see her before it?"

"Of course. You're always welcome to visit. Sophia needs more visitors, in my opinion."

She needs more friends. Not visitors. But I don't say that. People always complain about me saying things. I say too much. Too fast. Too loud. Maybe I should hold things back. Maybe that will make me smarter, or more mature.

I squeeze my eyes shut, thinking about Mom, Dad. About Leo. About how maturing seemed to be less about accumulating dignity and more about accumulating pain on top of pain.

Maybe I don't want to mature.

Sophia's room and the hall leading to it look different in the day. Naomi came and said good-bye earlier and took me to say good-bye to Mira and James for the last time. But somehow, this good-bye is the hardest. Standing outside this door and trying to knock is the hardest thing I've done in a while. What I saw last night, her screaming—the way Jack looked when I mentioned her—all of it's confusing and stops my throat up like a cork. How am I supposed to look her in the eyes and say good-bye when I heard her screaming that she hates me just a few hours ago?

How do I say good-bye to Sophia when maybe she isn't the Sophia I thought I knew? It's hard.

But I'm Isis Blake. I've done harder things. Like live.

I knock twice, and Sophia's voice emanates faintly.

"Come in."

She's sitting up in bed. Her platinum hair fans all around her on the pillow, her skin milk-white and glowing. She looks like a princess of starlight and snow. None of the thrashing anger I saw last night is in her. She smiles.

"Hey. You're leaving, huh?"

Her voice is so soft, so Soapy-like. Normal.

"Yeah. I ran into Avery downstairs and she said—"

Sophia shudders, and I recognize it. It's the same

shudder I give when someone says Nameless's name out loud.

"Sorry," I cover up instantly. "I didn't mean to—"

"It's fine," Sophia manages. "She's just the worst person alive, is all."

"But she said...she said you've started talking to her again. After I came here."

She's quiet, staring out the window, but then she nods.

"I felt sorry for her." Her voice is bitter. "The same way you feel sorry for a lost dog. She tried to apologize, but nothing she can say now will undo the pain she's caused me. Nothing. And yet she still tries. It's pathetic."

It's my turn to flinch.

"Maybe she's really and truly sorry," I try. Sophia laughs.

"Maybe. But that doesn't mean I have to forgive her for what she did."

"What...what exactly *did* she do?"

It's a dangerous question, one that Sophia doesn't answer. Finally, she opens her mouth to speak.

"Come here. I have something I wanna show you before you go."

I inch over and sit on the chair by her bed. She pulls open a drawer and brings out a stack of letters bound with pink ribbon. She unties it slowly and riffles through them before settling on a single letter and handing it to me.

"Read that, will you?"

"Out— Out loud?"

"If you want."

I glance down at it and clear my throat.

"'Dear Sophia—'"

It suddenly hits me—these are the letters she and

Jack send each other. This is Jack's wide, impeccably even handwriting. I glance up at her nervously, but she just smiles and waves me on. Is this some kind of sick trick? Why does she want me to read her boyfriend's letters to her? I search for any resentment in her eyes, but there is none, just a cool, sweet passivity.

Does she really hate me?

I only knew her for three weeks. And we were only "friends" because we were the only teenagers in the hospital. We hung out—texted each other and showed each other stupid cat pictures from the internet and talked about music, but do I really know her? I don't. I don't know who Tallie is. I don't know why she screamed like that last night. I don't know what her disease is. I don't know anything about her.

I look back down at the letter.

"'I'm sorry I haven't written to you in a week. There is no excuse, and I don't expect you to forgive me, but I hope this longer letter gives you more comfort than two shorter ones would've.

"'I'm doing well. Mom has been painting again—horses, mostly. She loves them. She said she was painting one for you, for your birthday. July is so far. But she says a masterpiece will take time. I can only hope she doesn't paint you an entire hospital wall worth of ponies.'"

I snort and instantly regret it. Sophia's eyes are locked on me, and the pressure they exert is crushing. Gently crushing. Crushing like a quaint spring breeze. From a typhoon. I read again. "'By then, you'll be done with your surgery. You can choose—I'll take you anywhere you want to go. The sea? My grandfather's beach house in California is empty for most of the year. We could go there for the summer. Just you and me. The warmth would be good for you, I think.'"

It's so bizarre—this isn't the Jack I know. I mean, I barely know him, but a cold, sneering douche bag with a savior complex and a penchant for cheating on his girlfriend shouldn't sound this…gentle. This kind. It doesn't make any sense. It does, though, because he loves Sophia, but if he loved her this much, why would he kiss me?

"'There's a new student in my class—an annoying gnat that constantly buzzes around my skull. Can't keep her mouth shut. She annoys the teachers, the principal—practically all the people with functioning eardrums find themselves instantly repelled by her idiocy. I'd tell you her name, but it's a plant—Ivy or Iris or some nonsense like that. I can't be bothered to remember. She spread some stupid rumor because I politely let her friend know I wasn't interested at a party last week. She punched me. It didn't hurt. Much. Anyway, she spread the rumor we kissed in juvenile retaliation.'"

My voice wavers. I did? I don't even remember—

The party. The smell of spilled Pepsi and the sound of drunken laughter. Avery's house. A grand chandelier with cocktail wieners stuck in it. Kayla. Kayla and me talking for the first time, Jack walking in for the first time and the crowd parting around him and Kayla working up all her meager courage to talk to him, his jaded, bored words as he ripped into her, and my punch—straight, true, blood coming from his nose—

The memories dart up like sprouts after a long winter. I read frantically. This is my past. These are the things I can't remember, here, in this letter.

"'It was so annoying, Sophia. God, I wanted to strangle every idiot who kept asking me about it. Finally

I got so sick of it, and I lashed out. I debunked it by kissing her. I'm sorry. You understand, I hope. It was disgusting and sloppy and she's—'"

My voice catches as I process what the next words are. They don't sting. They just ache. Ache like everything does when I see people who are better than me at love, who know more, who've had more real, soft, true experiences.

"'—inexperienced to the extreme.'"

I look up. Sophia frowns.

"I'm sorry he's so mean about this, Isis. I just wanted you to know the truth."

"Like I care what he thinks," I scoff. "This is the truth. I gotta know it. Let me keep reading."

Sophia nods. "If you're sure."

"'I nearly threw up in my mouth. No more rumors about kissing, though. I'm telling you this for honesty's sake—I apologize. It won't happen again. Some idiots just need to be silenced before they become worse.'"

I snort. He's the idiot. The king of 'em, actually. Someone should inform him he's won the crown. I read the next few lines to myself and feel my cheeks start to warm.

"'I miss you, Sophia. Every day.

"'I'll come visit soon.

"'Yours,

"'Jack.'"

"Uh, never mind. I think I got the gist. That last part is, uh, private."

Sophia giggles and takes the letter back. "He is quite the silly romantic."

"Yeah. So. Thanks. Now I know."

"Now you know," she agrees.

"He kissed me to get me to shut up." I nod. "Not bad.

It's the one thing that would probably shock me into silence."

"Why is that?"

"Well, you know. Guy like that kissing a girl like me. Unnatural. Not right. Unequal, really. Hell, any guy enduring my close-up face long enough to kiss me just plain goes against the laws of nature. I mean, there are lots of other girls out there. Like you! And Kayla! And like, everyone! Choosing *me* to mack on? That's like choosing plain yogurt over a bunch of awesome cakes for dessert!"

I laugh. Sophia is quiet, her hair shading half her face. I can't see the other half. She doesn't speak for a good minute, and I nervously shuffle. Me? Nervous? I shake it off and put my hand on her shoulder.

"Hey, Soapy, are you—"

"You're disgusting."

The contempt in her voice freezes my insides. It's the voice I heard last night. The other Sophia. She tilts her head, the hair sliding off her face and her eyes heavy-lidded.

"Do you really think anyone is falling for that?" she asks.

"What do you—"

"Those depressive little comparisons you make. The way you pan off any worth of yours. You're a sick, masochistic bitch who likes playing 'modest' to make people like her. To make people feel sorry for her."

The words hit hard. Harder than the impact when Leo threw me against the wall.

"Is that what you really think of me?" I ask. "You think I— You think I say these things so people will *like* me?"

Sophia laughs, full and rich and downright dark.

"Don't play innocent. I've done the same thing countless times. You and I are exactly alike, Isis. That's why I understand you. Neither of us is our real self around other people. Because that would scare them. So we pretend. We don't say what we mean. We don't say what we really think, and everyone else believes we're normal. Harmless. But that's far from the truth."

She seems so different—her posture is totally relaxed in a luxurious, satisfied way. Her eyes are slits and her lips form a subtle smile.

"I get it now. That's why Jack is so fascinated with you. *That's* why he kissed you. That's why he even bothered getting to know you. Because you're exactly like me. Hopeless like me."

"Sophia, this is crazy."

"Is it? Am I crazy? Am I just an insane girl cooped up in a hospital, taking my frustrations out on you? Am I seeing things that aren't really there? How can I know what's going on, when I'm trapped in here?"

She throws her head back and laughs that intimidating laugh again. Her head snaps down all of a sudden and her eyes blaze, two stony sapphires exerting their full pressure on me.

"You and I are alike, Isis. But you and I are also different. You get to leave. You're healthy. You get to be normal, to run and jump and have sleepovers and have dreams and go to school, and go to college, and all the things normal girls get to do, you do. Because you're normal. Or are you special? Do only special girls get to do those things, and I'm the normal one? No. Don't answer that. I'm not normal at all. I'm defective. You pretend to be defective, but I really am. So go ahead. Give me your fake-modest bullshit one more time. Do it."

For once, I'm silent. No comebacks run through my head. No quips. All I can do is ball my fists and tremble. Sophia smiles.

"That's what I thought. Now leave."

I get to the door before I turn. Sophia's watching my every step, her sickening smile never fading. But I can't just leave it like this. I liked her. Like her. Genuinely.

"When the surgery is over, you'll be normal, too. And we should… If you don't hate me still, we should go… shopping. Drinking. Or something. Something normal girls do. Because I think…I think we could be friends."

"I don't," Sophia says lightly. "Now get out, and never come back here."

"You're pushing me away," I say, my voice getting stronger. "You push people away first before they can leave you. You did it to Avery, and with good reason, probably. But you still did it. And now you're doing it to me. And that's fine, but I know what it's like. I know what it's like to be lonely and scared. I know what it's like to not want someone to leave you."

Sophia's smile just hangs there, but it's like a painting now, instead of something with real feelings behind it. A facade.

"Thirty-eight percent," she says.

"What?"

"That's the likelihood I will survive the surgery. Thirty-eight percent. And if I don't go through with the surgery, I only have two months left."

I'm quiet. Sophia folds her hands and leans back, her smile fading.

"No, Isis. You don't know what it's like. You have no idea what it's like to wait to die. Now get out. And leave me alone."

I shake my head. "No. I'm not going to. Even if you ask me. Even if you won't talk to me. I'm coming back here. A lot. And there's nothing you can do about it."

"I could sic security on you," she snarls.

"Clearly you are underestimating how many times I've evaded plump Taser goblins with badges before."

"Screw you," Sophia lashes out.

I take a deep breath. Is this what Naomi's been dealing with? Is this what Jack's encountered? It must be so hard for them, but it's harder for Sophia. It's harder to watch yourself from inside your physical shell as your emotions and hidden pain take over. I know that most of all. Being consumed by emotion made me starve myself when I was fourteen; it made me torture myself. I was my own worst enemy for so long, and there was nothing I could've done about it. I could only watch myself taking a ride headfirst down to shittersville. Why? Why couldn't I stop myself back then? Why didn't I just wrest control back from myself?

The answer hits me instantly, like the punch line of a bad joke: because I didn't want to be in control.

Back then, I was hurting so badly I didn't want to be in control anymore. The Isis who'd been in control fucked up and allowed herself to be hurt. I didn't trust myself, I realize. That's why I went off the deep end, why I didn't want to be responsible for my actions. I didn't want to face them, or face the fact I'd messed up really, really badly by trusting Nameless. So I handed over the reins to my darker side and sat back for the ride, wanting to punish myself.

Sophia's eyes are the same. I recognize them as the same look that Isis in the mirror had so many years ago. I still have that look in my eyes sometimes—a look like a saw blade is tearing you in half inside. Sophia doesn't trust herself, either. And so she definitely can't trust anyone else.

So I smile.

"I know it's hard. Leaving is always hard. But coming back won't be hard. I think you're wonderful, Sophia," I say. "I promise—I'll be back."

She glares daggers at my chest, straight into my heart. But I can't feel pain. All I feel is compassion, understanding. All I feel is a kinship—and no amount of awful words can change that.

I've never been happier to see home in my life.

Except that one time Kayla let me have her burrito and then Wren let me have his burrito, so I ate three cafeteria burritos and then sat through algebra thinking intensely about toilets and I've never driven home faster in my life.

My cat, Hellspawn, is the first to greet me when I get home. He comes bounding around the corner, and I run toward him, ready to smother him in a hug of pure love and friendship. He thoughtfully gnaws my ankles.

"Ow! Ow, that hurts, you little shit!" I hiss. Hellspawn hisses back.

"Aw, look at that. He missed you so much," Mom says as she comes in behind me.

"He missed me or the ability to eat my shoelaces?"

Mom chuckles. I drop off my backpack upstairs—my room feels so foreign. It smells so weird compared to the faint scent of antiseptic and bleach I'd gotten used to. I flop onto my bed and stare up at the ceiling. Who knew I could miss a hunk of plaster so much?

Ms. Muffin the stuffed panda droops sleepily. I put her on my chest and hug the Chinese stuffing out of her.

"I'm back."

I laugh at my own words, still a little sore from the hospital and the mental toll it took on me. Still sore from reading Jack's words. But I'm too grateful to be home to dwell on it much. For now.

"I'm really back," I exhale.

The smell of something delicious wafts up and yanks me out of bed. It's saucy? And cheesy? Downstairs, Mom pulls a lasagna out of the oven.

"You made that? For me?"

Mom smiles sheepishly. "I bought a cake. But no, I didn't make this. Someone…someone very nice did. They brought it around."

She serves me a plate and urges me to eat. I take a bite, and the flavors explode in my mouth. It's the best thing I've tasted in a while—hospital food doesn't have shit on this. Hell, an actual Italian restaurant would be hard-pressed to beat this.

"This is… Who made this?"

"Do you like it?" Mom takes a bite. "I think it's very good."

"Uhm, I'm kind of the master of avoidance, Mom, and you smell like five whole avoidings! Who brought you this?"

Mom frowns. "Jack."

I look down at the lasagna, then back up at her, then down at the lasagna before I run to the bathroom and attempt to stick my fingers down my throat.

"Honey!" Mom bangs on the bathroom door. "What

are you doing?"

"He poisoned it!" I yell around my fingers. "Eat some bread and Pepto-Bismol to slow the spread of it in your blood!"

"Don't be ridiculous, Isis!"

"Uh?" I throw open the door. "Have I not updated you on how evil he is? He cheated on his girlfriend, he practically abandoned her these last three weeks, he hates me—"

Mom's frown turns absolutely deadly. She grabs my ear like she used to do when I was little and twists, pulling me back to the table.

"Ow ow ow ow I NEED THOSE TO DIFFERENTIATE SOUND."

"You will sit down, and you will eat this meal, and you will finish every last bite of it, so help me."

"He's poisoned—"

"He has not poisoned anything!" Mom exclaims, banging her fork. "He's been nothing but kind and considerate since you went to the hospital. He's been bringing food nearly every night and checking in on me, and may I remind you he was the one who saved you, Isis. So you will be respectful and you will eat it and I will not hear you complain about it again."

I wince. After a long staring contest with a bit of cheese, I take a slow bite. Only then does Mom relax, marginally, and start eating her own. Something like resentment takes root in my heart, but I quickly prune that shit. She has no idea who Jack really is. *I* barely know who he really is. So it's understandable that she'd defend him.

Halfway between our slices of slightly stale store cake, Mom breaks her stony silence with a single tear that plops onto the tablecloth. She buries her face in her hands.

"I'm sorry, Isis. I didn't mean to hurt you. God, I'm so sorry."

The sorry is a little deeper than the usual apology.

I get up and go behind her and lace my arms around her neck, resting my cheek on her shoulder blades. I can see the court papers and police statements piled on the coffee table in the living room, my medical bills among them.

"I'm s-so sorry," she sobs. "It's my fault. It's all my fault. And when I saw you in the hospital, your head all bloody—oh my baby." She turns and grasps me in a hug. "It's my fault you got hurt. I let Leo into my life and he hurt both of us. It was fine, I thought. It was fine if he only hurt me. I could take it. But I never thought—I never wanted—"

Her sobs turn to chokes, and she's shaking so hard I can hear her teeth chattering.

"It's okay," I whisper. "It'll be okay. I promise."

That night, she asks me to sleep in her room with her, and I do. The old air mattress is a comfort, the familiarity of the floor beside Mom's bed welcoming. I've been here many times. This exact spot is where I do the most good—comforting Mom, making her feel safe. It's the most I can do for her.

This is where I belong.

chapter six

3 YEARS, 26 WEEKS, 3 DAYS

EAST SUMMIT HIGH could take a nuke and nothing about it would change. Except the PE field. And maybe a bit of architecture. But the food would survive the blast because I'm 99 percent sure it's cockroach flesh, and Mrs. Borsche would remain standing because let's get serious, everyone knows she's an undercover Cold War agent genetically engineered to survive minor things like rapid atomic decompression.

When I pull into the parking lot, Kayla is standing there on the curb, waiting for me. She dashes over while someone almost runs her over and we ~~smash into each other~~ hug.

"You're alive!"

"Marginally." I laugh. She smells like coconut and the tears of every boy who will never have a chance with her. It's like coming home. Hugging her is the best feeling next to the feeling I got sleeping in my own bed—er, air mattress—last night. And then I see Wren walking toward us. And Kayla sees him, too. She darts to his side and drags him over, his glasses nearly falling off but a small half smile on his face.

"Isis!" he exclaims.

"Yes, it is I. Alive in the flesh. Temporarily. In roughly seventy years I gotta die again."

Wren laughs and one-arm hugs me in that awkward way boys sometimes do. "It's good to have you back."

"Things have been totally boring around here," Kayla laments. "Avery's been quiet and weird and Jack's been quiet and weird, like even more quiet than his iceberg days. It's so *weird*!"

"Global warming," I offer.

"And no one's tried to escape out the science lab window—"

"Cowards!"

"—and Principal Evans won't shut up about Jack—"

"A crime worthy of execution!"

"—and someone wrote 'Isis Blake is a crazy fat bitch' on the bathroom stall in F building."

"Let us give them a standing ovation for originality."

Wren laughs, and Kayla frowns, but it doesn't take her long to start laughing, too. And unlike five months ago when I first started here, I walk under the brick arch that reads East Summit High. But this time I'm not alone. This time, I walk under it with two people who are my friends. I have friends. I have *friends*. Do you hear that, past me? You have friends. Ones who care about you, who laugh with you. You get them, someday.

So don't cry.

You have friends.

Sophia was wrong. I'm not pretending to be someone else around them. I'm myself right now, in all my awful glory. This is who I am—I'm not afraid of showing them that. I can show them my true, loud, obnoxious self, even if it's too hard to tell them about my past, and they still like me for it.

I bite my lip and walk faster so they can't see the unsightly water oozing from my ducts.

"Hey! Isis! Slow down!" Wren calls.

"What's the rush? It's just Benson's class! All he's gonna talk about are plant vaginas!" Kayla shouts. I laugh and walk faster. A familiar shaved head passes me, and I back up and explode.

"Knife Guy! How're you doing, old pal?"

"We've known each other five months," he corrects. I sling an arm around his shoulder.

"Five months in dog years is like, ten years. We're practically family."

"Are you crying?"

I sniff. "What, this? Nah, just a piece of teen angst stuck in my eye. Nirvana would be proud."

Knife Guy grunts. "It's good. That you're back."

"Yeah?"

"Yeah. Jack was a pain without you to take him down a peg. Or nine."

He grumpily stares at nothing. I ruffle his almost-forming Mohawk.

"Stop touching me. People might think I'm normal."

"God forbid that." I laugh.

"And Jack will kill me."

"Jack?" I buzz my lips. "Jack doesn't give a jackshit about me. No, wait, I got that backward. *I* don't give a jackshit about Jack the Shit."

Knife Guy ducks out of my arm. When I give him a quizzical "why spurn my beautiful friendship arm" look, he nods behind me.

"I'm smart enough not to get between you two."

I turn around, and there he is. Jack's less than six feet

away, scowling like he's sucked an entire lemon farm. His ruffled tawny hair and ice-blue eyes look different in the light of day versus the pale sickly light of the hospital.

"Ah! If it isn't Jack. Jack the Ripper of female self-esteems everywhere. Jack Sparrow who flies around and shits on heads. Jackoff into everyone's punch bowl and ruin their day."

"The head injury's certainly made you more creative. And fortunately, less coherent," he drones, and then looks at Knife Guy. "And who is this charming young man? An admirer?"

Jack waves a hand in front of his face.

"Is he blind? Or just stupid?"

Something in me draws taut and snaps in a split second. I can't remember much of Jack, but I sure as hell remember Knife Guy and the way he was nice to me. Small, disturbing ways, but ways nonetheless!

"Why do I have the sudden urge to perform violence on your face?" I cock my head. I could be imagining it, but his chest swells slightly. Anger? Of course it's anger.

"That would be your body remembering the time you socked me so hard I saw through time and space," he says.

"Did you like what you saw? Goopy aliens? Supernovas? Mantorok, God of Corpses?"

"I saw an alternate universe without you. It was like paradise."

Knife Guy suddenly chuckles. Jack sneers at him.

"Something funny?"

"You haven't talked to anybody in school in three weeks, and now she's back, and you're—" Knife Guy shakes his head. "Whatever."

I watch him leave. Jack's quiet, his lips drawn. I take

a deep breath and rock on the balls of my feet.

"You really hate me, huh?" I ask. Jack's ice-blue eyes snap up to lock with mine.

"What?"

"Like Knife Guy said. You don't talk when I'm gone, and I come back and you're slinging the insults. So you must really hate me to bother breaking your silence. I get it."

I read the letter you sent Sophia. I know how much you despise me.

Knife Guy has no idea how much it means.

Isis slung her arm around his neck like it meant nothing. She's only ever done that to Wren, and that's because he's less intimidating than a puppy. But Knife Guy is different. He's intimidating, he's angry-looking, he's tall, and he has muscles beneath those Black Sabbath shirts. He's not Wren. He's a man. A month ago, my touch reduced her to panic and tears. It was a memory so painful she blocked it out, and now here she is, touching him like it's easy for her.

My heart beats so hard I can feel it in my fingertips. I'm hot all over, a heat wave sweeping through me like wildfire. I should control it. I should turn on my heel and walk away. I buried my hope. I thought it was dead. But then she revived it that night in the hospital, like a skilled necromancer. Like I hadn't buried it at all. And now I can't possibly control myself. Not when she's there, not when she's touching—

I'm behind her. Knife Guy glances warily at me, and

she turns. Her purple streaks are a little more faded. She's not as pale as she was in the hospital—a rosy bloom on both cheeks. A little smile plays on her lips, and like the moron I am, I let that smile fuel the heat wave in me hotter and higher.

"Why do I have the sudden urge to perform violence on your face?" She cocks her head to the side, like a little angry bird. That one motion reminds me so much of the night at Avery's. I inhale sharply as the memories flood back—her bare collarbone, her smile as she told me she could feel my pulse, her soft sighs—

Control, Jack. Control yourself. You're the old Jack. The one who thought her an annoying nuisance.

Isis asks if I hate her, and the sirens in my head go off instantly.

"No," I blurt, and then stop myself from saying more. No, Jesus, that's not it at all. But how can I tell her that? How can I tell her how I—

"Look, it's fine." She smiles. "I'm still grateful you saved Mom. That's the only reason I didn't hit you just then. Also, I'm becoming a beautiful mature butterfly. But mostly it's for Mom. We clearly rubbed each other the wrong way back then. You stay away from me; I'll stay away from you. We both go on with our lives. Sound good?"

My stomach drops. No. No, it doesn't sound good at all. It's the last thing I want.

"So you're running away? That's your solution?" I snap. "I'm part of your past, Isis. You ran from Will Cavanaugh, but you can't run again. Nothing will be solved that way, and you won't get any peace."

At the mention of his name, she recoils, curling in on herself before straightening and glowering at me. "What the hell do you think you know about me?"

"You can't just write me out of your life like you did that scumbag. I'm not him. So don't treat me like him."

"You hate me," she says dully. "He hates me. I find it better to cut the people who hate me out of my life."

Everything in me screams to move to hold her. To hug her. To show her I don't hate her. But that's not something the Jack she can barely remember would do.

"You annoy me," I say coldly. "I don't hate you. There's a difference."

She laughs. "Not much of one."

"I respect you. I don't agree with you on most things, but I *respect* you."

She scoffs.

"Believe it or don't believe it, I don't care. It's still the truth. Before Leo attacked you, we respected each other. I hope someday you can remember that much."

"All I can remember is that dumb kiss."

"Which one?" I've longed to know the answer to this since she talked about it in the hospital. Her eyes widen, slowly, until they're the size of amber coins.

"Which *one*? What are you talking—"

The bell rings shrilly just above us. She winces at the noise, and I take the opportunity to duck into a stairwell and leave her behind. Calculus can't even penetrate my haze of disbelief. I nervously jiggle my leg the entire lesson, tapping my pencil on my paper. What the hell did I just do? I can't control myself around her. I thought I could. I promised I would. But the idea of her presence and her actual presence are two very, very different things. I blurt things. I let slip betraying body language.

I'm not in control when she's around.

And it terrifies me. Because what she needs the

most from me—no, from any man—is for him to control himself.

After calculus is over, I glance out the window. Isis walks by just under me, with Kayla. She's happier, a smile on her face in place of the frown I caused earlier. I only ever make her frown. And that's when I see it. There, on her scalp, is a pale white scar. It isn't big, but it isn't small. It's jagged and pink at the edges. Just healing. Just barely healing. The sight of it sends a surge of anger into my throat, my lungs.

She got hurt because I wasn't fast enough.

It is Sophia, all over again.

I grab my books and push out the door. I need air. I need not-air. I need silence. The wall behind the cafeteria is the only place in school people can smoke without being seen. A few other people are here, too, laughing. I lean against the wall and light one. The smoke spirals up and the burn in my throat finally matches the burning guilt in my chest.

"Hey," a voice says next to me. Knife Guy.

"What do you want?" I grunt.

He shrugs. "You don't look so good. Thought I'd ask if you were gonna throw up. You know, just so I know not to stand too close."

"You're standing close now."

"If you can talk, you aren't gonna throw up. When did you start smoking?" he asks. "Thought you were all clean-cut and going to Harvard or some shit."

"When did you?" I fire back.

"When my old man told me I was too wussy to smoke. Out of spite, I guess."

"Where's he now?" I ask.

"Jail."

There's a long quiet. Knife Guy puts out his cigarette.

"You've seen it, right?" He looks at me.

"Seen what?"

"That thing on Isis's arm."

"What thing?"

He chuckles. "For someone so smart and observant, you sure are slow."

I don't have the energy to do much more than curl my lip in his general direction.

"It's been fun." He finally speaks again. "Watching you two. Most fun I've had in a long time in this shithole. So I'll give you some advice; don't smoke around Isis."

"What makes you think—"

"She won't like it. Trust me."

"Did she tell you that she hates it?"

"She didn't have to."

Knife Guy squints, and before I can interrogate him further, he's gone around the wall. I mull it over for minutes, racking my brain to put the pieces together. And then it clicks. Just as the bell rings for next period, it all clicks together.

My insides start to boil.

If I ever come face to face with Will Cavanaugh, it will be his death sentence.

Principal Evans is thrilled to see me. And by that, I mean he's pacing around his office popping aspirin like candy.

"Evans!" I throw my arms out and yell. "Long time no see, buddy!"

"Isis, please, I have a headache—"

"HOW'RE THE WIFE AND KIDS?"

He groans. "You like tormenting me."

"I like everything that isn't boring." I flop in the armchair across from his desk. "So? To what do I owe this illustrious summons?"

He gingerly removes his hands from his ears and reaches into his desk, pulling out an envelope with stately ink words on it and a logo of a building of some kind.

"Is that what I think it is?" I ask.

"Stanford," Evans says calmly. "I imagine you'll get one at home, but they sent a faculty confirmation here, too."

"And you practiced enough self-restraint to not open it! You're amazing, Evans. Really. You've grown up from the little boy who pasted my fat pictures everywhere."

He flinches. "How about you open it?"

"How about I switch your apple juice with piss?"

"Isis—"

"Look, Evans." I inhale. "My mom's got a trial coming up. Dunno if you heard. She's gonna need me. Probably for a long time. And I mean, I can do your catch-up homework thing and graduate or whatever, but the truth is, I'm not the best student. Obviously. Obviously you know that. I'm fine on paper, but I cause trouble and I'm immature and I say stupid stuff. So I didn't really earn this. I mean, I did, but I don't belong in college. Especially not a big huge fancy college or whatever. They'd be better off giving the place to like, someone from Korea? Someone really dedicated and mature. Someone not-me."

I push the letter back at him.

"So, you know. You can open that. Or trash it. I don't care. But I'm not going."

Evans is quiet. When he finally looks up at me, he somehow seems so much older. The wrinkles under his eyes are deeper, and his forehead creases with dozens of years of being tired.

"You're doing the same thing Jack did."

"What?"

"Refusing to go because of the people you love. Refusing to—to become amazing. You have so much *potential*, Isis. And you're throwing it away."

"What do you mean, refuse? Did he?"

"You don't remember? He wanted to stay here, in Ohio, to take care of that girl, Sophia. He had offers from every Ivy League in the country, practically."

"But he's going to Harvard now. People won't shut up about it."

"Yes. But he only changed his mind after— I don't know what changed his mind, actually. But I can't let you do the same thing. Please. I know I said it would be your decision, but please. Open the letter, read it, and think it over. And if you still don't want to go, I'll respect your decision."

I snort. I stare at the envelope for a few moments before snatching it back.

"Fine. Fine. But don't expect a happy ending."

Evans smiles wanly. "I never do."

I get up to leave, and he calls out to me.

"Oh, and Isis? Good luck with the trial. I hope that man who injured you gets the justice he deserves."

I clench my fists and slam the door behind me. What does Evans know about justice? He was the scumbag who, in a desperate attempt to please the Jack warring with me and get him to apply to Harvard, pasted pictures of my old, overweight self everywhere, and then he tried to make up for it when he found out I'm decent at grades by shoving me into the gaping, greedy maw of every snooty college in the world.

I push out the doors and into the quad. Chilly February air bites at my ankles, but the sun is out, and it warms my face. It's a calming contrast. I see Kayla sitting on a low brick wall and staring off into the distance.

"You look like you're thinking," I say. "Should I take a picture to commemorate the moment?"

She rolls her eyes. "Very funny. Hilarious, even."

"I try." I sit next to her. She knits her eyebrows and goes back to staring at nothing. Before I think up a quip to jolt her out of her gloomy mood, she turns to me and suddenly says, "Why does Wren act weird when he sees Jack?"

"Good question. I can't be sure, since half my brain leaked out onto my hall floor a while ago, but I'm pretty sure it's because he did something bad. At least, that's what Wren and my foggy memories say."

"Jack did something bad? Like…like what?"

"I don't know." I stare at the grass. "I honestly don't know and it kills me on a daily basis, but I somehow manage to revive and shuffle around in a mockery of living."

"I remember they were friends," Kayla says. "I came here in, like, fourth grade. Wren and Jack and Avery and that Sophia girl were all friends. Really tight. Like a circle no one could get into. I was jealous of them. I didn't have good friends—just people who liked the snacks in my house and my makeup kit."

It sounds lonely. I don't say that, though.

"So it's Wren you're thinking about? Why are you thinking so hard about him? You told me he's a nerd."

Kayla flushes. "W-Well, yeah. He's the nerd king. But— I don't know! He just gets so…so freaked when he sees Jack. It's weird."

"All I know is something happened in middle school. Avery did something to hurt Sophia, and Jack stopped it. And Wren was there, with a camera, because Avery bullied him into filming it."

Kayla's eyes go wide. "Do you think there's a tape of it? If Wren filmed it— "

"I doubt he'd keep it. He's so guilty, he probably destroyed it. You can ask him about it. But it really stresses him out. And he's kind of always on the edge already. Never relaxes. It might not be the best thing to talk about."

"Yeah," she says softly.

"Why all the sudden concernicus, Copernicus? Do you…do you *like him* or something?"

Kayla's face is engulfed in a red-hot blush, and she stands instantly.

"W-What? No! Don't be stupid! He's not my type!"

I laugh and follow her as she strides through the crisp grass.

"You're a bad liar," I say.

"You're a bad…a bad…eyeliner-put-on-er!" she snaps. I try to smother my laughter and mildly fail.

"Look, I'm curious, too. I've been curious for a while about this. Wren said something to me in the hospital about Lake Galonagah. Avery has a— "

"Family cabin up there," Kayla finishes. "Yeah. I've been to it every summer for the last four years. It's beautiful, and huge, and the lake is like, five steps from the door, and the hammock is silk, and the chandelier used to be Michael Jackson's, I think—"

"MJ's table lamp aside, do you think that's where whatever it was happened?"

Kayla shrugs. "I just know Avery has a cabin up there. And a lot of crazy parties happen there, too. Her parents practically let her have the place to herself."

I munch on my lip. A cabin in the middle of the woods on a lake, the lake Wren mentioned, in which Avery is used to total autonomy. Whatever happened all those years ago might well have happened there. If not, at the very least we could look around and see what the place is like.

"We should visit. Maybe not her actual house. Because that would be trespassing. So instead we could lightly trespass *around* her house," I say. Kayla bites her lip.

"Now that you mention it—" She shakes her head. "Never mind."

"Ah yes, the old trick of leaving me in suspense. You crafty minx, you. Stop playing with my heart and my burning desire for the truth."

"No, it's just a dumb little thing," Kayla insists. "I think—I think I remember something about the place. Something weird. But it's so far back I can't remember clearly."

"Well, that's mildly promising."

"Maybe if we go, it'll jog my memory. If it happened a long time ago, there's probably nothing left. No solid clues or anything." She shrugs. "So don't get your hopes up or try to play Nancy Drew."

"I'm not!" I insist. "I just want to see what it's like up

there! Do you think you can remember the way to her cabin?"

"Did Chanel's spring/summer 1991 collection redefine postmodern feminism in the fashion world?" she asks.

There's a pause.

"Translation?" I say.

Kayla throws her arms up. "It means yes!"

"Awesome. Saturday, ten a.m., my place. I'll drive. You provide the atmosphere. And Gatorade."

"Saturday? I'm going with my mom to get her hair cut. Why not Friday?"

"That's when the trial happens," I grunt. Kayla's eyes widen.

"Oh. Right. I forgot about that."

"I didn't," I singsong.

"Do you...do you want me to come? I could, I don't know. Provide moral support? And Gatorade?"

I chuckle. "Yeah. I'd like that. A lot."

Kayla laces her arm with mine and smiles. There's a nice quiet as we walk, the quiet that settles between two people who've said everything they'd been burning to say, only cool ashes floating to the ground. It's peaceful and comforting, and it helps calm my first-day-back nerves like a soothing balm.

And then Kayla promptly starts lecturing me on the fine points of Chanel's spring/summer 1991 collection and why I should care about extended shoulder pads and Technicolor peacoats.

And somehow, that's even more comforting.

The world changes, and I change.

But some things always stay the same.

Mom isn't home after school, so I take my pants off the second I walk in the door and sigh with relief. Hellspawn glares up at me with his big yellow eyes.

"Don't give me that look. I know where you poop. And sleep. Sometimes both at once."

He slinks upstairs to vomit in my dirty clothes basket or something equally elegant. I chuck my jeans after him, and they land on the railing with a sad *thunk*, and then I plop down on the sofa and stare at the envelope Evans gave me, and the one that came in my mailbox. The Stanford logos peer up at me in red and white. They reek of pretentiousness, and I haven't even opened them yet. I can smell the pretense gunk oozing up from the cracks in the envelopes.

They're taunting me. So I get up and throw them in the fireplace.

The cold fireplace. With no actual fire in it. But in all fairness, if I was made of paper, the mere presence of old coal ash rubbing up against my white butt would make me sweat ink for days.

"Scared yet?" I ask. The envelopes remain plucky. By the time I work up the courage to open one of them, I've spent a half hour staring at it. Just staring and watching a bunch of terrifyingly important life choices flash before my eyes. Mom needs me more than Stanford does. But it's Stanford. Stan-freaking-ford. Stan-is-so-loaded-his-last-name-might-be-Ford-like-the-guy-who-invented-that-one-car-Ford. They've got money out the butt and they've contacted me early. It's a rejection. It has to be. A place like Stanford would never want a regular, boring Midwestern white girl like me. I get good grades—so what? I don't do a million charity after-school things like Wren, I'm not Mensa status like Jack, and I'm not loaded like Avery. There is literally nothing to set me apart from everyone else.

But if they accepted me—just if—then Evans is right. I hate the taste of those words on my tongue, but he's right. Stanford would transform me. I'd go there, and learn so much, and become so much more. Or less. Or maybe I'd flunk. I'd fail, probably. But if I didn't, places like Europe and things I've always wanted to do, like learn Spanish fluently or dive into women's studies or peruse the mysteries of microorganisms—all that would be in reach of my grubby little hands.

I could get away from here. I could start over, fresh and new.

The sight of the bills piled on the table hits me like a ton of lead bricks. Who am I kidding? Even if this is an acceptance letter, there's no way Mom could afford it. I'd be working my ass off 24-7 just to make tuition, and even then I'd owe a trillion in student loans when I got out. I'd probably be miserable. It'd be smarter to just stay home, here, with Mom, and get a job and attend the local community college. It'd save both of us money. It'd be the sensible, grown-up thing to do.

I grab the envelope and make a mad dash for my room. I belly-flop onto my bed and pull Ms. Muffin to my side.

"Okay, you open it."

I manipulate her little paws, my hands shaking, and she opens the envelope and extracts the letter. It flops open on the bedspread. I choke on my own saliva.

There's more than just a letter. There's a form of some kind.

Don't be such a wuss! Ms. Muffin seems to chime. *But don't get hasty! Read the letter first!*

"Dear Ms. Blake. Congratulations! We are pleased to inform you you've been accepted to Stanford University for the fall 2016 semesterOHMYGODOHMYGODOHMYGOD."

Breathe! Ms. Muffin wails. *Don't forget to breathe! It is kind of required!*

My mind is blank—all thoughts of Jack, and what he said about "which kiss," flying out the window. I temporarily forget about Lake Galonagah and Sophia's anger. I just have a minor coronary and collapse in on myself like a dying star. The peach tree outside my window is summarily impressed.

"I got in! I got into Stanford!" I shout at the ceiling. The letter shakes in my hand as I eagerly devour the rest of it. There's something about a housing form, and a financial aid form, and at the very bottom is a mention of a grant. Grant? I never applied for a grant. Did Evans...?

And then my eyes widen at the amount on the attached paper. Thirty thousand dollars, for four years or until I get my bachelor's, on the terms I keep a 4.0 average. It's not a lot to Stanford, but it'll put a huge dent in the tuition costs for me. I could actually keep afloat, if I got some more scholarships and worked. It's doable. My heart squeezes and un-squeezes rapidly. I can do it. I can do something different, something wild and massive and incredible with my life—

"Isis?" Mom's voice filters up from downstairs. "Isis, are you home?"

I jump up and rush down the stairs, slipping on the bottom one but catching myself gracefully and launching into her chest.

"I got in!" I scream. "I got into Stanford!"

Mom's eyes widen. "W-What? Stanford? How—"

I shove the letter in her hands and quiver on the edge of a knife for an entire ten seconds as she reads it. Her face lights up from the inside, like a candle through a frosted pane, glowing in all directions at once. She hugs me, harder than when I woke up in the hospital, harder than when I came home from the hospital, harder than when I arrived at the airport in Ohio from Florida.

"Oh, sweetheart. I'm—I'm so proud. This is *amazing*! When did you apply to Stanford? And without telling me?"

"I just…I just put it in for kicks. I didn't expect anything to actually *happen*," I lie. Worry lines overshadow Mom's joy, but she's trying hard to hide them for me. It's then I notice her coat and the new prescription pills sticking out of her purse. But her smile is broad and unwavering, trying its best even if it's difficult.

"Let's talk about this after dinner, all right? Call your father and tell him!" Mom insists.

Dad's just as thrilled. He offers to help me with some of the costs, the pride in his voice unmistakable.

"Kelly! Kelly!" I hear him call to my stepmom. "Isis got into Stanford!"

"Stanford!" Kelly's saccharine voice pierces through the receiver. "Quick, give me the phone."

I suck in a breath and brace myself for the inevitable showdown.

"Isis!" Kelly exclaims.

"Kelly!" I imitate. "It's so nice to talk to you again. Once every two years isn't enough."

"I agree! Stanford…wow. That's incredible. I hope Charlotte and Marissa can be as smart as you when they get older."

"They can try," I say sweetly. She laughs, but under that laugh is the obvious—we dislike each other. We've just never said it out loud.

"You should really come visit us this summer," Kelly presses. "Your father and I are taking the *kids*"—she puts emphasis on "kids", rubbing it in my face that I'm not included in that category—"to Hawaii. We should all go together before you head off."

"Aw, but I like you so much more when you are a generally enormous distance away from me."

She laughs, short and biting. "Well, I'll give the phone back to your father now. Congratulations again!"

Dad comes back on. "So, what's the plan? Do we fill out the FAFSA? I'm coming to your graduation—we could drive out there. A road trip—Ohio to California—for just you and me! How would you like that?"

I smile at the floor. Yeah. That'd be great. If I were five years old. He's trying to make up for lost time. It's so obvious and so ridiculous. He hasn't spent more than a week at Christmas with me each year since the divorce. It's clear he doesn't give a real shit about me. He's started over, with a new family, but he still thinks he can treat me like I'm a child. I'm not a kid anymore. He missed out on his chance to raise me. At least Mom tried, even if it was at the very end of my time as a kid.

"I dunno, Dad. I'll think about it."

"Okay! Keep up the good grades, and we'll talk more about it later. Love you."

"Love you, too."

The words are hollow. He's my dad, but he's never

been my Dad. And he never will be.

Sometimes, realizing the truth feels hollow, too.

Mom bustles around the kitchen making a celebratory dinner. She's forcing herself to be happy for me, but I know something's wrong, and it's not just the looming trial this time. She's so wrapped up in her BLT making I can't get a serious answer out of her, so I go upstairs and turn on my laptop and stare at pictures of Stanford. I do more research; there are amazing overseas programs. England, France, Italy, Belgium. The campus is something straight out of a magazine—perfect green lawns and whitewashed buildings and the California sunshine turning everything golden. Their math program is incredible, with really famous professors I'd only read about in scientific journals. Not that I read that nerd shit. I just, uh, look at them while I'm on the toilet.

But still.

It's everything I've never known I wanted.

I scroll though my email, to thank them for my scholarship, and pause at one particular message. It's new, sent just four hours ago, from a weird address. At first I think it's spam, but then I read the title:

Isis, I know you're there

Creepy-possible-serial-killer title aside, I click on it. What's the worst that could happen? My firewalls are tight, and if it's a phishing email I just won't click on anything inside it. There's a single line in the body:

Jack Hunter is evil, you know.

It's a joke. It has to be a crappy joke email from someone at school. I've heard these exact words from people there—but in an email like this, it's creepy. It's somehow more threatening, and real. I try to trace the email by putting it in Google, but nothing comes up. It's a jumble of letters and numbers that might as well be a spambot, but it's not. It's someone who knows my name, and someone who thinks Jack Hunter is evil. I'm conflicted about him for sure, but I don't think he's evil. He's cruel and callous. But evil? Really, truly evil? That's going a little far.

And that's when I see it.

There's an image attached to the email.

I open it. It's blurry, but I see trees and the pine needles covering the ground. I see the dark lump that looks like it has limbs (a person?) lying on the ground, and I see the hand carrying a bat in the corner. A bat stained with something dark on the tip.

My mouth goes dry. I know that hand. Memories surge up like a rapid tide. I grabbed that hand, with its slight veins and long fingers. I held it, both of us sitting on a bed, and I confessed something. Something that meant a lot to me. Thumping music. The taste of booze. Dancing. A bed.

I know whose hand is holding that stained baseball bat.

It's Jack's.

Jack is looming over what looks like a dead body.

chapter seven

THE THING INSIDE me has no name.

At the age of seven, after Father died, was when I first felt it. After his funeral, I didn't speak to Mom for a long, long while. I didn't speak to anyone. The beast demanded I be silent. The beast demanded I hurt others. I fought with my classmates in elementary. I bit teachers. And when there was no one around to hurt, I'd hurt myself, stabbing pencils into my hand. Mom took me to psychologists, of course, able and willing to shell out to keep her little boy from losing his mind with grief, even as she was losing her own. I was selectively mute after a traumatic loss, the doctor determined, and Mom was depressed. But with a lot of therapy and the good grace of passing time, we managed to pull through. I began speaking again. I made friends. With the help of Wren, Avery, and Sophia, my life began to feel normal again. I began to quell the anger with their friendship, and Mom's unconditional love.

The beast, however, remained. I could only tamp it down for their sakes. They couldn't kill it. I don't know if anyone will ever be able to kill it. Perhaps I'll die with it.

Perhaps it'll be the death of me.

Regardless, it waited, biding its time. It retreated deep inside me, bottled by my newfound adoration for the people close to me. Sophia, especially. When she was around, I felt the thing in me retreat so far away I could barely sense it anymore. She saved me from myself.

And I failed her.

The beast took my failure as a crack in the lid of its cage, and broke free, despite everything I did beforehand to keep it contained. I failed Sophia, and in doing so, failed myself.

And I failed that man, the one whose body haunts my dreams.

The beast hurt so many people, all in one night. The repercussions echo today, in Avery's every avoidant glance, in Sophia's lingering grief, in my own wounds.

Since that night, I've lost the friends who kept it bottled and caged. Mom tries, but she's only one person, and the beast is voraciously hungry for more, always. It wants to fight, to scream, to inflict pain on someone, anyone. It's a deep scar I'll never be able—and don't deserve—to erase. No one can help me save myself. And I swore to myself I'd never let anyone get hurt by the thing again. The farther people stay away, the safer they are.

And so, the "Ice Prince" was born out of necessity.

It worked. It worked for three years exactly, the beast only barely peeking out when the football team wouldn't stop bullying me. They learned quickly, though.

For a while, a short, fleeting while, the war with Isis pushed the thought of the beast out of my head entirely. It was silent, not so much as rattling the bars of its cage. But then she forgot me, and its whispers have been turning to growls in the last few days.

So I'm here, at a seedy warehouse in a part of town where no one knows me, to try to quiet it. I know how it works, what it wants. And this is the safest way to keep it quiet—a controlled environment, with enough people watching so that it never bites too deep.

The roar of the crowd practically deafens me. The warehouse is dim and smells like rust and old cardboard. The place is packed with people I can't see the faces of. All I can see is the man before me—twenty-two? Twenty-three? He's college-aged and built lean and limber. He swims or does soccer. But on the side he takes boxing lessons. I can tell by his stance—square, firm, on the balls of his feet. Boxers always look like they're about to tip over.

"Are you ready?" a man bellows, a microphone clutched in his sweaty palm as he paces between us. His salmon-striped shirt isn't exactly official referee colors, but a match in an abandoned lumber warehouse isn't exactly an official fight, either. The crowd's shouting surges with the ref's encouragement. The boxer and I meet in the middle, shaking hands cordially. Hollywood might like to paint underground fights like these rife with dirty tactics and shit-talking, but it rarely ever comes to that. And if it does, the crowd only roars louder. Do it too much, and they'd get bored or pissed the bets going around were being cheated by an illegal head-butt.

We part after shaking hands. I tighten the cloth belt of my loose pants. Tae kwon do demands fluidity and practice. Which is why I began to enter these a month ago.

The ref throws his hand up, and the fight begins. Our feet shuffle around the makeshift arena, pushing aside remnants of sawdust and dried bloodstains from past competitors.

My eyes are locked on my opponent. The boxer won't strike first. They never do. Boxers excel at stalling—taking a beating and waiting for the enemy to run out of energy or get tired and lower his guard. I have to hit him hard, when he least expects it, or he'll out-sustain me.

The boxer suddenly lunges in. I swing back but not fast enough to avoid his right hook. It clips my shoulder, sending me in a half spin to the ground. The crowd cheers, leering down at me like bloodhounds on a fox. I'm the new guy. I've won barely two matches out of the five I've entered. None of them have bet on me. They aren't here to see me win. They're here to see me get beat on.

I get to my feet. The boxer's danced back to his original spot, a grin on his face.

Wrong move.

Boxers might be able to take a beating, but emotions make humans weak. Confidence makes us weak. I was so confident he wouldn't strike first, and I was wrong.

My memories nag at me with barbed tentacles.

I was so confident, too, that Isis would always be there—always ready to fight me, always ready to snark at me, always ready to bring me down to size when no one else would.

And yet I lost her.

I step in, a quick and precise movement, and heel-kick the boxer square in the chest. He staggers, clutching his rib cage and blinking in soundless pain. His fury is immediate. He lunges for me with that right hook again. I dodge, but he's there to meet me, all flying arms that pound my ribs, close and brutal, and I can't get away until I catch my breath enough to duck out of his grasp.

He's still turning to face me when I lodge my fist into his back, just above his kidney. He howls, reaching for me, but I'm not there anymore. I'm on his other side, and he pivots just as I take his legs out from under him. He hits concrete with a fleshy *thud*, the sound reverberating among the crowd's hysteria. People throw popcorn; someone sloshes a beer on the edge of the arena. The boxer is gasping for air, stunned. The concrete and gravity did most of the work for me—we are fragile little creatures.

I remember the scar on Isis's forehead and wince.

The referee starts counting down. I watch the crowd. They move with a fevered hysteria the likes of which only violence can bring out. But one person—one out of the dozens—remains perfectly still. He watches me, hair streaked with white and his eyes serious. I can only give him a passing glance as the boxer struggles to his feet and throws a punch that nicks my lip. I taste blood. This man fighting me is not Leo; he doesn't cower. Fear doesn't cloud his eyes. Only cowards get scared when force is used against them instead of for them.

I duck another blow. That's what Leo is. A coward. And tomorrow is his trial.

The boxer gets me with a hard jab to my stomach. I see stars, the pain sharp and leaving me breathless. The referee starts counting down, but his voice feels far away. All the voices of the crowd seem muted, underwater.

I came here to work out all the stress of the impending trial. If Leo isn't put away, Isis and her mother will still be in danger. Leo isn't the type of guy to learn his lesson, no matter how badly I beat him. He's the type of guy to take revenge.

I couldn't stop him from hurting Isis the first time,

just like I couldn't stop the men from causing Sophia harm that night in the woods. My own weakness hurt them. And I'd do anything to get rid of it.

I crawl to my feet, swallowing the blood on my lips. The boxer is too busy taking the crowd's admiration with his arms up to notice me.

Boxing is a sport of punches, of outlasting an opponent. Tae kwon do is a sport of kicks, of forms, of landing one strong, good strike that puts your opponent out for good. He turns just in time to see my kick coming.

The blood from his nose flecks my cheek. He drops to the ground, unmoving. The thing in me sings, my own blood pumping hot and fast through my veins, begging me to sit on his chest and whale on his face until it resembles ground hamburger. He's not the boxer anymore. He's Leo. He's the men in the forest. He's everyone who's ever hurt me, ready and waiting for me to give him my anger.

I stand over him, the referee trying desperately to push me away. I want to see more blood, to feel it on my knuckles, to douse it over the angry fire in my heart.

A part of me is terrified of myself. Of the thing. Of the fact that I'm even thinking of destroying him. Since when have I started losing control over myself?

I pull back, icing my heart with every emotionless, subzero thought I can conjure. The referee helps the man up and holds my hand as the winner. The crowd explodes, but I have no interest in their adoration. I only want quiet, somewhere I can gather myself. I slip through the crowd. The white-streaked man watches me the whole way out. What's his deal? Warily, I push through the warehouse door, into the chilly night. I take a deep breath, letting out all the pent-up anxiousness in my chest. I don't know who that guy was, nor do I care. I'm only here for me.

I am Jack Hunter. And I am not my demons.

In the car I wipe my face and pull on a clean shirt. I feel more grounded, but fighting that hard for that long leaves me ravenous. The highway is nearly dead, the city of Northplains nearly empty. The Red Fern is the only place open at this time of night. It's where I took Kayla on a date Isis paid for, and she watched us here. It holds delicate memories of a time I miss, of a girl I miss.

I walk in and instantly recognize the girl talking to the hostess.

"Isis?"

She looks up, purple hair streaks windswept around her face. Her warm cinnamon eyes light up, then dim ever-so-cautiously, but her words are just as exacting as ever.

"You might wanna consider scaling back on the whole 'eating at fancy places' thing if you're going to Harvard. I've heard the tuition is slightly life-ruining."

"Hello to you, too," I deadpan.

"Who am I kidding?" She sighs. "Your mom's loaded. You'll be fine."

"And what's your excuse?" I ask. She shrugs.

"Mom and I didn't feel like cooking. And since the trial's coming up, I figured I'd treat her to something nice, you know?"

"How is your mom doing, by the way?"

"She's fine."

Isis's lips are curled down, her eyebrows knit. She's trying her best to look unaffected, light, airy, but the truth is easy to see on her face.

"You're a terrible liar," I say finally.

"And you're a terrible butthead," she instantly counters. A laugh bubbles up from my chest.

"It's when you resort to the uncreative 'butthead' insults that I know you're really feeling awful."

"Did a girl's boyfriend find out she hired you and socked you in the face or something? Why is your lip all puffy?"

"A new serum," I say. "To improve my pout."

"You pout all the time. You're like, the expert on pouting. They should be asking you to donate cells to make their serum."

"That's…rather disgusting."

"You know what else is disgusting?" She wrinkles her nose and holds up a plastic bag with food trays in it. "Peanut sauce. But Mom loves it. So."

"You poor overburdened thing."

"Shut the hell up."

We both smile at the same time, and I feel somehow more sheepish for it. How can I be smiling when she's just barely remembered me and her mother's trial is coming up? And then I realize that's how it's always been—she's always been able to make me smile. No matter how cold I thought I was, how in control of my emotions, she always elicited humor. No one was ever able to do that for me, until her.

The sudden urge to thank her for it overwhelms me, but I master myself and keep my mouth silent. It would only confuse her, and I don't think I can explain it well enough to her myself. The feeling is foggy, indistinct, but more powerfully bright than any sunrise. I have no words for it.

She would, I'm sure. Incorrect, entertaining words.

I always counted on the fact that she'd be around to

make me smile. So I didn't fight harder to keep her by my side.

"Anyway"—she rubs her nose, an adorable gesture I instantly talk myself out of thinking is cute—"I have to go. Mom's waiting and texting me because she thinks I've been kidnapped slash sold to the human trafficking circuit. See ya later."

"Isis!"

My call to her retreating back stops her. I hadn't meant for my voice to sound that cracked, that desperate. That vulnerable. In the midst of the trial's anxiety, Sophia's surgery, and facing my own inadequacies, I forgot how rock-solid her presence was. Comforting, in a warm and sarcastic way. I want to stay in it, if only for a little longer. If only because it reminds me of the old days.

"What?" Her eyes grow confused. She takes in my face as I struggle for the right words, words that won't betray how I feel too keenly. Finally, she rummages in her purse and hands me a hand wipe and a Band-Aid.

"Put that on your cheek, okay? It'll keep it from getting infected."

"Isis—"

"I'd hate," she interrupts, "to have every girl in the world pissed at me because I let your pretty face contract gangrene."

She turns away from me, but before I can think, my hand darts out and grabs her wrist. She goes stiff from the spine up, her eyes mahogany whirlpools of confusion.

"What are you doing?" she asks quietly.

Stopping you, my brain says. *Taking you home with me, where we can talk in my room over coffee, where you can sit on my bed, my sheets, the same sheets I toss in every night at the thought of losing you again—*

I let my hand drop, staring at it like it's a monster.

"I-I don't know," I admit shakily.

Isis looks torn for a moment, a faint blush creeping up on her cheeks. God, she looks so good flustered. She looks so beautiful when she's red-faced and out of breath. The fight must've flooded me with testosterone, because I can't control my thoughts as they rampage toward the downright obscene.

No, I remind myself firmly. *She barely remembers me. And I have Sophia. I have a duty to her. What I want is secondary, unimportant, and trivial.*

"Drive safe," I finally manage in a hoarse voice. She nods, still glowing with a badly disguised blush, and leaves through the front doors. I watch her go, lit by the bright saffron streetlights.

"Can I help you, sir?" the hostess of the restaurant asks. I turn to her, raking my hands through my hair.

"No," I say quietly. "I'm beyond helping."

Welcome to hell. Population: me, some idiots, and my mother.

Three days before the trial, Aunt Beth comes to visit. I'm grateful for the support—Mom's flashbacks haven't been bad recently, but she's still been withdrawing into herself, barely eating or sleeping. Aunt Beth's arrival has Mom cleaning the house, making food, and getting dressed in the mornings, and that's all I can ask for.

We pick her up from the airport, her long, flowing tie-dyed dress somehow out of place in the dead of

Ohio's winter.

"Aren't you cold, Beth?" Mom frowns. Aunt Beth just laughs from the backseat.

"Ice runs in my veins, Patricia."

"She's so cold she runs an underground crime ring," I chime in. Aunt Beth jumps on my joke lightning-fast.

"Two underground crime rings, thank you very much."

I smirk back at her and give her a high-five. Mom shakes her head and makes a left turn out of the airport.

"You two are incorrigible."

We stop to pick up a pizza and then head home. I fill in Aunt Beth about everything that's happened at school. I show off my cranium scar, and she suggests I get it tattooed into a snake, or a dragon, or something serpentinely badass. Finally, after I've worn out the conversation, she hugs me hard and murmurs into my hair.

"Thank you for watching after your mom all this time. I know no one tells you this, but it's very mature of you. And very thoughtful. You're a wonderful person."

"Aw, Aunt Beth, you gentle liar!" I squirm. "How mature can I be if I still laugh every time I rip a fart?"

"Let me tell you a Blake family secret." She leans in. "You never grow out of laughing at your own farts."

"Dammit! Why did you have to crush my dreams of becoming a graceful debutante?"

She laughs and hugs me harder. "I missed you. The house is so quiet without you."

"I missed you, too," I agree softly.

"I was worried when you left. You seemed so sad toward the end. But you've grown up so much here," she says. "And you look a little happier."

"I am," I assert. "I know it doesn't look it, but I'm

rapturously joyful at all times."

Aunt Beth gives me a flat *you're lying* smile.

"Okay, okay." I sigh. "You got me. I've carved out a life here, sure. And it's good sometimes. But it's hard, too. I know no one's said this in the history of ever, but growing up is hard."

She chuckles and squeezes my shoulder. "Growing up is really hard."

That night, she and Mom talk in the living room around tea and cookies. I announce I'm going out to the store to grab something for a school project next week, and I slip out. I want to give them as much privacy as they need, Mom especially. Aunt Beth is here for her, to talk her through things only two adult women could talk about. Pain, I guess, and how to deal with pain. They both have scars upon scars upon scars, and sometimes, just showing each other's scars can help ease the dull ache of years of heartbreak.

There are no cafés open at this time of night, so I decide to go to the children's park in midtown and spend some quality time with myself and every rusty swing I can find. Thankfully, there're a lot of them. I pump my legs and go as high as I can and then jump off only to repeat the process, the squeaking so loud the previously sleeping squirrels come out to chitter angrily at me.

"Sorry," I whisper. "But I'm trying to get to the moon."

The squirrels politely point out that NASA has sort of figured out a way to do it, and I counter with the fact that their method is much, much noisier and involves a lot more fire. Finally, I get bored of the swings and head to the slide, the squirrels thankfully retreating into their tree mansions. I sit at the top of the slide, watching the stars glimmer.

When was the last time I came to a playground? I remember—we loved them in middle school. We thought it was the coolest shit to stay out late at the playground, defying our curfews even though the parks were only ever a few blocks from our houses. By "we," I mean Nameless's friends and me. Nameless was there, too. We used to play midnight hide-and-seek, the spring-bound horse rides ogling us eerily with their huge plastic eyes as we shrieked and ran from each other. We were so young. Nameless was so polite, so kind. He'd always find me the best places to hide my bulk, and he'd hide somewhere obvious nearby so he'd get caught and could tell the finder he saw me in the opposite direction.

We drank energy drinks we weren't supposed to, ate candy we weren't supposed to. One of Nameless's friends, Ashley, was even cool. She and I got along as only girls who read a lot can. We talked about *Gone with the Wind*, Harry Potter, any and every book we'd read lately. She was the closest thing to a friend I'd had since kindergarten. Being a dumpling gets you more jeers than conversations, even as a child. But Ashley didn't once jab at my appearance. Even Nameless would join in if his friends started joking about my weight, but Ashley never did.

I spot a shooting star and marvel at how fast it moves—here one second, gone the next. I hope Ashley's all right, wherever she is.

And I hope Nameless is suffering, wherever he is.

Movies and books tell me revenge is always the way to go. They tell me revenge is what a girl should go for after a guy wrongs her. But every time I see it happen in fiction, I can only shake my head. That's not how it goes. You don't want revenge, you just want to get away from that guy. You don't ever want to see him again. You want him to never be happy again, but you certainly don't want to beat him up or lash out. Shame and terror floods you after it happens, paralyzing you. You can't move even an inch toward that person. You walk the other way to avoid him.

It would be a perfect world if every girl wronged could take revenge. Revenge never even crossed my mind—I was too busy convincing myself I was ruined forever, that I deserved it for being so stupid and naive. That it was my fault, not his.

I was too busy lying to myself to even think about revenge.

If I saw him now, would I want revenge? Revenge implies you do the same thing to them that they did to you, but I realize I could never do that to another person. I could never inflict what he did to me on someone else. So I'd have to hurt him differently, but just as much.

I'm not sure there's anything on this planet I could do that would hurt him equally, hurt him so badly he hated every inch of his body, hurt him so badly he'd build a shield around himself so thick even a cannonball couldn't pierce it.

I don't want revenge. I want to go back in time and stop it from ever happening.

But I can't. So I keep going as best I can, in the only way I know how—by joking around, sniping retorts, acting dumb to make people underestimate me.

Back at the house, the windows are dark. Aunt Beth sits on the porch, smoking. I walk up casually.

"Has anyone ever told you you're a bad influence?" I ask. Aunt Beth's eyes twinkle.

"My mother. But our mother was diagnosed as a pathological liar. So, only you, Isis."

"The one and only." I puff my chest and sit beside her on the porch. The smell of her cigarette is odd, and I squint. "You're still on that weed jam?"

"Still on that weed jam." She smirks around another drag. "You know me—it's only occasional."

It's true. Back when I lived with her, she'd smoke the odd joint when her knee pain got too bad—she'd broken it when she was young and it never really healed right. She'd tried booze, but didn't want to become an alcoholic, and then opiates—the prescription kind—but she'd gotten addicted. She quit, and found a happy medium. After trying weed with Nameless, I realized I never wanted to smoke it again, and told her so, and she never worried I'd steal it or something equally teenager-y.

"Patricia's asleep," Aunt Beth says after a beat of quiet. "But we talked. It was good. I think she's ready for the trial, at least more ready than she was before I came."

"Yeah?" I hug my knees. "That's good."

"How many joints have you smoked here in Ohio?"

"Seven hundred."

She whistles in an impressed way. "Incredible."

"I go to parties and drink a whole bottle of scotch every night."

"Well, shit. I'd better tell your mom to put a down payment on a coffin real soon."

"No, it's fine. I'm donating my body. The demand for alcohol-ridden kidneys is huge. They eat them as a delicacy in France."

"Bon appétit." Aunt Beth chuckles. I wrinkle my nose. "I gross myself out sometimes."

"Take my advice; if you don't, something's definitely wrong with you."

"Phew. It's so good knowing I'm wrong-free."

We're silent for a while, and then:

"How about you?" Aunt Beth asks. "How're you feeling?"

"About the trial?"

"About anything."

I recall Jack's face. "Confused. A little sad. But I—I'm learning. I'm learning how to like myself again, slowly. And I never thought I would, you know?"

She nods, and I press on.

"But it's not easy. There's my dad, who doesn't care about Mom or me anymore. There's you, the only person who ever really got me, thousands of miles away. And then there're my friends. We'll all go to different colleges—oh God, *college*. I have to spend another four years cramming my brain full of minutiae while learning how to survive in a dorm with a roommate and shared showers and scholarships and essays and the massive ghost of a future unknown career pressuring me—what am I gonna do? How do you find an apartment or pay rent? How do I even *make* money?"

"Strip like I did when I was nineteen," Aunt Beth offers.

"Obviously, stripping is the way to go," I agree. "Don't tell Mom."

She mimes zipping her mouth shut with a wry smile, then immediately breaks it by talking. "Don't strip."

"Gotcha."

The wind ruffles her skirt, and I offer her my jacket,

but she refuses it.

"I'm going inside soon. Keep it for yourself."

"What if I care about your well-being?"

"Don't." She turns her eyes to me, seriousness etched in her face. "Care about your own well-being."

The way she says it is heavy.

She exhales softly. "I'm serious, Isis. You've got to start caring about yourself. Not me, not your mom, not your friends. *Yourself.* You are precious. There's only one person like you in this whole world, and if you get run-down or hurt because you didn't care about yourself enough, I'll never forgive you."

It's not a threat—it can't be when her eyes are shimmering with faint tears. I retract my hand holding my jacket to her and put it back on, the warmth welcome against the bitter air.

"I'm trying," I say finally.

"No. You aren't yet," she corrects. "Not really. But if you are learning to like yourself again like you said, then it'll come in time. And you have to let it happen when it does."

Only half understanding, I nod.

"Okay."

Aunt Beth's stern face breaks into a smile, and she ruffles my hair.

"Thanks, kiddo."

Aunt Beth leaves two days later, after forty-eight hours of Mom cooking delicious food for her and bingeing on a shitload of terrible Netflix movies we can all laugh at. It's rejuvenating, having a third person in the house. Aunt Beth clears the air like an air purifier, a fan, something that keeps the energy moving. I can tell Mom loves having her around, and when she goes, we're both pretty broken up about it. We don't say that, of course, but on the way home from dropping Beth off at the airport, I squeeze Mom's hand over the stick shift, and she smiles sadly.

"We'll be okay," I say.

"I hope so," she returns.

Justice is basically a costumed farce. You learn that when you're three and your parents tell you sharing is caring when quite clearly sharing is *terrible* and there is no caring at all involved, because no matter how loud you cry, no one seems to have sympathy for you and your doll that must not touch anybody else's hands because everybody else is grimy and dumb.

A courthouse is essentially the same principle: a bunch of stuck-up, weary adults telling one another to share and care. With the added threat of jail time.

I sigh and re-button my hideous white blouse all the way up to my chin. At least Mom let me keep my jeans. I can't morally support her when my butt is hanging out of tight black slacks for the world to see. I try to fix my hair—some big bun Mom made for me—but Kayla slaps my hands away.

"Stop it. You look good. For once."

She sits beside me in the courtroom, a similar white blouse barely restraining her considerable chest. She wears a skirt and pearl earrings that are actual pearls and looks totally the part of first lady. If the first lady were seventeen and Latina.

The court isn't exactly what I pictured; I was expecting *CSI* levels of crowded rooms and scowling judges and apprehensive jurors. But instead I get a room that looks straight out of the eighties—weird geometric-patterned carpets and a flickering fluorescent bulb in one corner and a judge who looks like a smiley grandma with purplish hair and bright red nails. The jury doesn't even look serious. They talk and laugh among themselves. Mom sits two rows in front of us, her prosecutor at her table on the right. Leo, the scumbag, sits at the left table, his lawyer whispering to him. He's got a cast on his arm and a bandaged nose.

"Ass," I whisper to Kayla. "Leo's nose is fine. He's just wearing it for show."

She sneers. "He's so nasty. I hope he gets all that nasty delivered right back at him! Via FedEx! Express shipping!"

I keep my eyes on Mom as people filter in. I slept on the air mattress by her bed last night again because she couldn't stop crying. After the Stanford hullabaloo deflated, all that was left was a sad remnant of reality, of the impending trial. Her shoulders are shaking under her two-piece suit and she's wearing makeup to cover her dark circles, but she keeps her head high.

"Is Jack coming?" Kayla asks. I nod.

"Yeah. Why?"

She shrugs. "Just… It might be hard for you. You know."

"I'll be fine."

Kayla's quiet, before she says, "It was hard for him, too."

"What? Who?"

"Jack. When you were gone, he was so different. I know I said that the day you came back, but—but he really, really changed. I've never seen him look that bored. It was almost like he was dead."

"No one to call you names does that to people."

She shakes her head and sighs. Leo's eyes catch mine once, and I mime cutting my own throat to get the point across. He doesn't look at me again.

"For once, your threats are deserved."

The voice belongs to Jack, who slides into the seat next to me. He's wearing a midnight suit—crisp, with a porcelain-blue tie that matches his eyes. His hair's slicked back with gel, cheekbones defiant and profile haughty and regal as ever.

Kayla gives him a cursory glance. "Hey, Jack."

"Kayla. Good to see you." He nods at her. Their exchange two months ago would've been so different, but now it's almost...*mature*? I shudder. Gross.

The image of his hand in the email picture won't fade from my mind. He might've killed someone! Like, dead! Like, not-breathing or -eating! Not-eating sucks because A) food is fantastic and B) food is fantastic! And here I am talking normally to a guy who made people unable to eat. He could be a regular Ted Bundy for all I know, because I *don't* know. I don't know anything about him, except what my fragmented memories tell me. And it makes me feel like screaming. Or puking. Hopefully not simultaneously.

"Your mother looks better," Jack leans in and murmurs. "She was wasting away while you were gone."

"From the sound of things, so were you."

He tenses minutely, his suit straining at his shoulders. Before he can open his mouth, the guard calls out, "All rise," and everyone in the courtroom stands. The grandma-y judge settles in her chair and tells us to be seated.

"The honorable Judge Violet Diego will be presiding over case 109487, the State of Ohio versus Cassidy," the guard reads from a clipboard. "Mr. John Pearson and Mrs. Hannah Roth will be representing their respective clients. Mr. William Fitzgerald is acting court stenographer. Your Honor."

The guard nods to Judge Diego and then retreats to the corner. Diego clears her throat.

"It is my understanding this trial is to address Mr. Leo Cassidy's alleged breaking and entering and assault and battery of Mrs. Patricia Blake and her daughter, Isis Blake. Prosecutor, if you'd like to make your opening statement now."

Mom's prosecutor, a pretty blond lady, stands and takes the center of the room. She makes a speech about Leo's ruthlessness, about Mom's history with him, and how she left Florida to escape him. She presents the restraining order Mom got against him before she left, my cranial X-rays, and the photos the police took of the ransacked house. Our house. Shattered glass and a blood smear on the wall and—

I flinch. A metal baseball bat. Kayla grabs my hand and squeezes.

The defense attorney argues Leo was in a fugue state and suffering from the effects of PTSD from his time in Iraq as a medic.

I lean in to Jack. "You're a nerd, right? You know big words."

He snorts. "Verily, forsooth."

"What's a fugue state?"

"It's similar to the dissociative amnesia you have for

me," he murmurs.

"Aw, stalking my medical records? You shouldn't have."

"I don't stalk, I understand basic psychiatric indications. Regardless, the argument of a fugue state in his defense is idiotic. It's a rare occurrence, and he showed no symptoms of another outward personality. If the judge buys it, I'll be very surprised."

"Aren't you a witness?"

He nods. "They'll call for me, if they think my testimony can help more than it hurts."

The defense suddenly asks for Mom to take the stand. She looks back at me, once, and I smile as encouragingly as I can and give her a thumbs-up. She grins wanly and walks to the stand. The guard swears her in on the Bible, and the defense attorney starts to grill her—where she was that night, what she was wearing, where I was, what Leo looked like, what he sounded like. Mom's resolve wavers, her hands shaking and her lip bitten, but she doesn't break. She keeps talking even though she looks like glass is ripping up her stomach from the inside out. When the defense is done, her own lawyer comes up, and Mom gives a full account of the story with the lawyer's urging. I gnaw my mouth to stay calm and think about unicorns, but even rainbow-pooping horned horses can't distract me from the way Mom's voice trembles as she describes the attack. I want to clap my hands over my ears, or leave, but she needs me. She's looking at me the entire time she's talking, so I keep eye contact with her. I'm her anchor.

"And then Jack—" Mom inhales. "Isis's friend from school, Jack, came in. I saw him over Leo's shoulder."

"Did Jack have a weapon on him that you could see?" the prosecutor asks.

"Objection, Your Honor, visual confirmation of the weapon at the moment isn't relevant—" the defense starts.

Judge Diego shoots him a sharp look. "Overruled. Continue, Ms. Roth."

"Thank you, Your Honor." Mom's prosecutor nods. "Mrs. Blake, did he have a weapon you could see?"

"Yes. A baseball bat."

The prosecutor grills her about what went on—how many times Jack hit Leo and what happened after.

"And then he went downstairs, to where Isis was, and I went with him, and I started crying again when I saw her body so still. I was afraid. Terrified. You don't know how— Oh God—" Mom cuts off, and the prosecutor looks to Judge Diego.

"That's all, Your Honor."

I get up to help Mom to her chair, but Kayla pulls me back down and I watch the guard do it instead. Mom smiles a watery smile at me once she's seated, and she gives me a thumbs-up. She isn't okay. But she's not afraid. I can see that much.

They call Jack to the stand next. The defense attorney is startled at his lack of expression—it unnerves him. I smother a laugh. Welcome to the club, bucko.

"Did you, or did you not, break into the Blakes' house without permission?" the attorney asks.

"Yes," Jack says in a monotone. "I broke in. Through the open door your client left."

A murmur goes around the courtroom.

Kayla pumps her fist and squeals. "Oh, he's gonna kill this guy so bad."

I twist my mouth shut. She has no idea.

"And what did you witness when you walked in?"

"I saw Isis Blake collapsed on the floor. There was a

bloody smear on the wall and blood on the side of her head."

"Did you see my client anywhere in the room?"

Jack narrows his eyes. "No. But I could hear him thumping around upstairs."

"So you did not witness my client 'assaulting' Isis Blake?"

"No."

The attorney smirks and paces. "And did you, or did you not, grab an aluminum baseball bat from your car and head upstairs to confront my client?"

"I did."

"And was my client armed?"

"No. But that didn't seem to stop him from trying to rape a terrified woman."

I flinch. Mom is completely still, focused on Jack. The court rustles again, and the judge bangs her gavel.

"Order! Order in the court."

When the murmurs die down, the defense attorney straightens.

"How do you know the Blake family, Jack?"

"Isis is an"—there's the briefest pause as Jack thinks—"acquaintance. From school."

"I'd like to present exhibit A." The attorney walks up, holding a tape recorder and placing it on the table. It's an interview with Principal Evans, who says Jack and I aren't friendly, that we're practically mortal enemies at school. The attorney tries to twist it like Jack came to my house that day to do something awful to me, out of anger. But Mom's prosecutor immediately shuts it down.

Jack looks to me. If I strain hard enough, I can barely discern the tiniest sliver of worry in his eyes. The jury is looking at Jack like they're suddenly suspicious. He returns to the seat.

"You…you all right?" I say. "I mean, other than the fact that you have a fat, arrogant tumor on your neck you call a head."

"I'm fine," he says softly. There's a beat.

"I didn't, uh, mean it. The tumor thing. It's my instinct to be mean to you."

A wisp of a crooked smile pulls at his mouth. "I know."

And then they call for Leo. The defense attorney builds up his case—that he fought in Iraq, that he got a head injury there, that the army shrink had diagnosed him with PTSD. And with every little half-baked story, the fury in my guts burns hotter and hotter. It makes my stomach want to evacuate lunch onto his shoes. But I can't do anything about it.

"Is it correct that you received a call from Mrs. Blake earlier that day, asking you to visit her at her home?" the attorney asks. Leo adjusts his cast and, with a mock-serious face, nods.

"Yes."

"That's fucking bullshit!" I shout, standing and jabbing my finger at him. "That's bullshit and you know it!"

"Order!" The judge bangs her gavel. "Miss Blake, be seated!"

"He's lying, Your Honor! He's a lying scumbag who ruined Mom's life—"

"Order!" she shouts. "You either sit down right now, young lady, or I'll have you escorted out."

I'm breathing heavily, and my blood sings hot in my veins. I'm ready to punch, to fight, to kick and bite and scream. But I can't do that here. Mom's counting on me, on this trial, to give her some peace of mind. I push through the row and storm out the door. The marble halls of the courtroom are too pristine. They mock me, clean and shiny when my insides are dirty and filled with caked hate.

"Hey!"

I ignore the voice and stride down the hall.

"Hey!"

"AGHH!" I kick a bench with the flat of my sole. "Pathetic shithead! Lying monkey-anus-faced bastard—"

"Isis—"

"If I ever get within five feet of him, there will be blood. Of the not-fake kind."

"Isis, listen—"

"I'm sure they make pitchforks that can fit inside a human mouth. And down the throat."

"Isis!"

Someone grabs my hand. I whirl around and pull it away. Jack stands there, slightly panting.

"Listen to me: you need to calm down."

"Calm!" I laugh. "I'm *perfectly* calm!"

"What are you doing with your hands?"

"Practicing." I wiggle my fingers.

"For what?"

"For when I get my hands inside his guts."

"He's not going to get away with it. Even a moron freshman in law school can see that. So don't get worked up like this. It's not helping anyone, and it's certainly not helping you."

"Oh, you wanna help me now? That's weird, because last time we talked, you basically told me you're going to make my life hell."

"Do I? Make your life hell?"

His voice pitches down, low and deep and cracked

through. The sudden change startles me.

"No." I inhale. "You just make it a little harder."

"Your mom needs you," he presses.

"I can't—can't go back in there. Not for a while. If I see that Neanderthal's face again, I'll—"

Jack quirks a brow. "A word more than four letters long. I'm impressed."

"You should be. I spent an entire year of middle school studying them. And their hairy crotches. But mostly them."

"Would punching me again help ease your fury?"

I scoff. "Maybe. Probably not. It's him I want to hurt, not you."

Jack looks outside the courthouse window, to the playground across the street.

"There're two things I know that calm you down—violence and sugar. Ice cream." He points to an ice cream cart on the sidewalk. "C'mon. My treat."

"Ohhh no. I know how this works. First it's ice cream, then it's marriage."

"Marriage, huh? Tell me," he says coolly as we both walk toward the cart anyway, "who's the lucky sea slug?"

"Why sea slug? Why not, like, a sea dragon?"

"Because a sea slug doesn't have eyes. Or a nose. Or any discernible intelligence beyond eating and shitting. You'd make the perfect match."

I snort. The sun and clear blue sky are a sign February landed on its head when it got out of bed this morning. It's too cold for ice cream, but we're eating it anyway in an attempt to escape the stuffy courthouse. I pick a strawberry cone and Jack gets mint chocolate chip. There's a bench, but I sit on the yellowed grass under the tree instead. Jack sits with me.

"You don't have to," I say.

"It's comfy here," he counters.

"Some butts are better off miles apart."

"No."

With that clarifying sentence, we enjoy our ice creams in the relative chilly peace shared only between two people who are complete opposites. Jack looks ridiculous in the wintery sunlight. Ridiculous and handsome and puke-worthy.

"Can you go back to Abercrombie?"

"What?" Jack looks at me.

"Just, you know. Crawl back into the magazine you came from. So I can hide it under my bed between two *National Geographic* issues on recycling elephant waste and never read it again."

"You're insane."

"You know how people talk about being beautiful on the inside and stuff," I start.

"Yes. And?"

"I just realized people don't have X-ray vision," I whisper in awe. "They can't *see* your insides."

He rubs his forehead tiredly.

"My zodiac sign is Cancer," I insist.

Jack licks his ice cream, impressed.

"One time, when I was seven, I cried so hard I rehydrated a raisin."

My babbling doesn't scare him off like the other 99 percent of the population with dangly bits between their legs. He just grunts.

"Do you know the alphabet backward?" I ask.

"Yes."

"Fast?"

"ZYXWVUTSRQPONML—"

"Can you make cinnamon sugar doughnuts?"

"I can make cinnamon rolls."

"Can you jump rope?"

"Yes."

"A million times?"

"If you gave me cybernetic knees, there's a slight possibility."

I stare into his face. "You don't have bright green eyes."

"No."

"And you're not left-handed."

"No."

"And you probably can't play an ocarina."

"Unfortunately, no."

I lean back and elegantly smash my ice cream into my mouth hole. "Good."

"Those were awfully specific," he says.

"Requirements of my dream man. Sea slug. Whatever. Are you even supposed to leave the courtroom if you're a witness?"

"I already gave my testimony don't change the subject you have a dream man?" He says it all in one breath and has to gulp air. I laugh.

"Didn't think ice princes ran out of breath."

"Your dream man is impossible."

"Bingo." I point at him.

He narrows his eyes. "So that's what you do when you get hurt? You construct a dream man who can't possibly exist, so no one will ever live up to your standards and you won't have to look their way twice?"

"Yup."

"You don't face the pain? You put up a wall between it and you and pretend it doesn't exist?"

The sun filters through the leaves. A dull ache forms above my stomach.

"Yeah."

"You're torturing yourself."

~~I know.~~ "I'm fine, bro."

He snorts. "You're the furthest thing from fine, and you choose to keep it that way."

"What about you?" I snap. "What about Sophia?"

"What about her?"

"She's *dying*, jackass. She's dying and you're here with me, buying me ice cream and asking me about my dream man! She's dying and you kissed me—more than once, apparently! How fucking selfish are you? Are you just setting me up so you have someone to pity-fuck you when she dies?"

His eyes flash with an arctic chill. "Shut up."

"All we do is argue. Sure, respect or whatever, but respect isn't enough. What's enough is tenderness, and love, and you have that with Sophia." I feel something hot prickling in the corners of my eyes. "So fuck you, actually. Fuck you. Don't try to get close to me. Don't try to fucking fix me. I'm not the princess, I'm the goddamn dragon, and you can't seem to see that. So stop! Stop being nice to me! Stop being not-nice to me! Just stay out of my fucking life!"

She comes like a storm, and she leaves like one, heavy steps and hands clenched and hair whipping behind her in the bare winter breeze, amber eyes molten with fire and resentment.

Something in me grows heavy, and then wilts.

I don't go back into the courtroom. I wait in the park and listen to the chatter from across the street as people leave. Leo gets three years' jail time for "assault and battery" and "breaking and entering." Mrs. Blake waves to me. Isis ignores me and walks to her comically misshapen VW Beetle.

She ignores me. Completely. No sneers, no wicked little smiles, no flipping birds. Nothing. Just complete emptiness.

chapter eight

3 YEARS, 26 WEEKS, 6 DAYS

THERE ARE THREE constants in the world: those who like pineapple pizza are criminals, death comes for all of us, and hospital wards never change.

It feels like ages since I stepped through the sliding door, the rush of sanitized air greeting me with a pungent ferocity only achievable by bleach and misery. The hospital looks the same as always—the same night-shift nurses scurrying to and fro, the same tired security guard pouring himself a third cup of lukewarm coffee. The oncology doctor I can never remember the name of walks briskly by, white coat flapping like seagull wings. Everything's normal, so normal it nearly soothes my writhing angsty-filled teenage soul.

"Isis!" A nurse at the front desk smiles. "It's good to see you again."

"Hi," I say. "It's good to see you again, too. This time without a broken head."

"The kids have missed you," she insists. "Do you want me to take you to them?"

"I'm actually going to visit Sophia first, if that's okay." I hold up a bag of warm Subway sandwiches. "Delivery for two, her hands only."

She waves me down the hall. "All right. Just let me know when you're ready to see the kids."

I shuffle warily toward Sophia's room. Hopefully she's in a good mood. Or a mood for sandwiches. I'd take either.

Thankfully, Naomi is coming out of Sophia's room. She flashes me a weary smile when she sees me.

"And here I was, thinking our resident troublemaker was gone forever."

"Nice to see you, too, Naomi."

She laughs and pulls me into a one-armed hug. When we part, she sniffs the air.

"Is that a meatball sub I smell?"

"Good goddamn, Naomi. Not only are you beautiful and charming, you have a nose like a bloodhound. Your worth on the marriage market is astronomically high, I bet."

My sass has little effect on her, as per usual. She motions to Sophia's room.

"She's just about to go to sleep. It's been a long day for her."

"What happened?"

"Just some physical therapy. Her muscles are—" Naomi frowns. "Not in the best condition."

"Are they getting worse?"

"The tumors press down on a part of her nervous system." She sighs. "It makes it very painful to move. The longer they stay there, the more damage they do."

I'm quiet. Naomi puts a hand on my shoulder.

"It'll be all right. Go in and see her. She'll be thrilled."

"Will she?"

"Of course. You're all she talks about these days. You

and Jack, of course. Thank you for texting with her, by the way. It just makes her day to have someone to talk to."

Sophia and I've been texting, it's true. At first I just sent her cat pictures I found on the internet, like I used to do when I was in the hospital. She'd respond with equally adorable dog pictures, and we'd have a sort of cute-animal war back and forth. But the cat pictures turned to talking about our days. I told her about the trial, and she told me about how much it hurt to just live, to exist, to breathe and wake up every morning. One of us was in more pain than the other. One of us felt guiltier about the pain than the other.

I clutch my guilt sandwiches to my chest and open Sophia's door. She's propped up on pillows, an IV of painkillers attached to her wrist. Her hair and skin are the same pale color, practically blending into the white sheets. She scribbles in a black journal, but closes it and tries to hide it when I walk in. She doesn't smile when she sees me, but I can see her try to look happier. Healthier. Not in pain. It's a brave, taxing front for an audience of one.

"Hope you like wads of meat on bread." I hold up the bag. Sophia snickers, the sound so faint and low it's like a cat's hiss.

"You've found my only weakness."

She's weak all over. But I don't say that. I sit on the chair by her bed and hand her a sandwich. She unwraps it slowly, eyes widening.

"It's been a while," she says.

"Since I've come to visit you? Yeah, definitely. Sorry about that, school and the trial—"

"I meant it's been a while since I've had Subway."

She takes a delicate nibble of bread. “Not everything is about you.”

Humbled, I take a massive bite of sandwich to stop up my blabbering mouth.

“It feels like everything is about me all the time.” I swallow. “Is that bad?”

“No. It just means you’re alive—you, a single person with a single brain and a single life, with two eyes and one point of view. Everybody thinks they’re the main character of their own story. That’s just what being alive means.”

“When you put it like that, we all sound like assholes.”

“We are,” Sophia insists. “But you happen to be an asshole who brought me food not of the hospital variety, so you get a pass. And I’m the asshole who’s stuck here, who made you come out all this way. So.”

“You can’t be an asshole when you’re sick. Your body is hurting. You’ve got every right to be an asshole,” I say. Sophia gives me a pointed, half-amused, half-irritated look.

“That’s not how it works. Nobody has the right to be an asshole to people who care about them. And yet I keep doing it. I’m hooked up to a steady drip of pure morphine and I can still be an asshole. Because I choose to. Because even though the pain in my body is numbed, the pain in my head is still there. It’s always there. It infects every thought, everything that comes out of my mouth. And the harder I try to hide it, the worse it gets. The more it wants to come out and ruin everything.”

We eat our sandwiches in the long quiet. Sophia talks first.

“You know what’s the worst part?” She looks at her hands. “It’s not being stuck here. It’s not the pain. It’s the 'why.' It's me asking why every day of my life. It's me praying to every god we've invented, asking him or her or it '*why*.' Why me? Why give me tumors? What's so special about me? Does it like to watch me suffer? Did I do something awful in a previous life, and this is my punishment? Is this a test, to prove I'm worthy of its love?"

I'm struck silent, frozen and yet somehow also trembling. Sophia stares at the whitewashed ceiling like she's looking beyond it, above it.

"And then I realized: there is no '*why*,'" she says. "Things just happen. That's it. The gods have no plan. If they did, why would they make such a horrible one? If God really exists, the good and just God who rewards pious behavior and punishes the wicked, then why does pain exist at all? If he exists, that must mean I'm wicked. I must deserve this. Either that, or there is no God. There are only things, good and bad things, and they happen all the time, to everyone."

She smiles at me, something about it sad.

"But no one wants to hear that. No one is brave enough to accept the universe is empty of meaning, or divine plan. We *want* to believe, so we make things up to believe in, because it's easier. It's less scary to think there's a God out there, a sentient, omnipotent man watching over us, making everything happen for a reason. We want to believe, even if it isn't true. So we make it true. We give it reason, when there is no reason. It's as simple as that. If anything, we are the gods. We make things real by believing."

Her laughter is faint, and she takes another bite of sandwich. I can't say anything. There's nothing to say. I've never thought about what I believe in. I've never given it much thought because I don't have to. I'm not sick. Death doesn't shadow me like it does Sophia. I'm lucky. Above all, I'm lucky I never had to think about it seriously.

"What do you believe in?" Sophia asks suddenly. "God? Buddha? Aliens? Or nothing at all?"

I'm quiet.

"Come on, there has to be something. Even people who don't give it much thought have some belief in their hearts, buried deep down. Is your mom Christian? Do you—"

"Myself," I say finally. Sophia closes her mouth, letting me continue. "I believe in myself."

"That's very magical-girl-anime of you." She laughs.

"It's not. At least, I don't think it is. It's just me. I don't know anything about God, or gods, or aliens. I don't know what happens in the afterlife or if there is one. I just know it'll be a surprise. And until then, all I can do is be myself. All I can do is take care of myself. All I can do is live, until I can't anymore."

It's Sophia's turn to be quiet. She leans back and hoop-shots her sandwich paper into the trash can from across the room.

"Nice shot," I say. She shrugs.

"It's my grandmother's birthday today. Or was, rather."

"Happy birthday, Sophie's g-ma."

Sophia laughs. "She would've liked you. She liked Jack, so she'd definitely like you."

"Here's a bit of fun trivia: I'm nothing like Jack. I'm nothing like Jack!"

"Here's a bit of fun trivia: just because you say things twice and louder doesn't make it true."

"Touché. But I'd at least like sourced footnotes on

these accusations."

Sophia counts down on her fingers. "You two never reveal how you really feel. You always try to make me feel better before making yourselves feel better. Both of you naively, masochistically insist on sticking around me, even if I'm terrible to you."

She curls the last finger into her first. "And both of you can't come to terms with my dying."

"Soph—"

"But that's all right," she continues. "Since I haven't come to terms with it, either."

She pulls out the black notebook I saw her writing in.

"My grandmother left me enough money to get treatment," she says. "She willed everything to me, to be signed over to me when I turned eighteen. But then they found the tumors, and her lawyer got a special exception for me to use the funds for my treatment. After four years, it's nearly run out. Jack's been picking up the slack, but I worry. I don't know where he gets that much money or how. I know it's not from his mom—he's too proud. He wants to take care of me on his own. I'm terrified he's doing something illegal for me. And that just makes me feel horrible."

I knit my lips shut. I don't know what he's doing. What memories I've regained tell me it's something people normally think is shady. If Jack hasn't told her, it's for a reason. He's protecting her from the truth. If I told her what little I think I know, he'd hate me even more. But why do I care? So what if he hates me? I hate him. I hate his face and his eyes and his voice—

"You'd tell me, right?" Sophia looks at me, her deep blue irises more vast than the ocean. "If you knew, Isis, you'd tell me. Because we're friends. Because I deserve to know the truth, even if Jack thinks he's doing the right thing by not telling me."

I hesitate, and Sophia pounces on it like a lion on a baby gazelle.

"Is it drugs? Please tell me it isn't drugs."

I struggle with words, my thoughts a jumble of torn morality.

"It's not fighting," she presses. "He's always been good at fighting, but please, *please* tell me it isn't that. Please tell me he's not beating people up just for me."

The pain on her face is obvious. How could Jack be so cruel as to keep this from her? It's obviously causing her massive amounts of anxiety and guilt.

"I can't—I can't remember." I make a half truth. "Everything about him is so fuzzy."

"You're lying," she says instantly. "You know exactly what he's doing."

"I don't, Sophia," I insist. "Or maybe I do, but I can't remember."

She pauses, and then, "If you remember, will you promise to tell me? Right away?"

"Of course."

She stares at me, judging my honesty. Finally she nods.

"It's a promise."

She scribbles in her black book while I think everything over. My eyes catch a line—it's a list. *Eat cupcakes from that fancy place in New York.* The list is long, with scribbled-out lines and doodles. She sees me staring.

"It's a bucket list," Sophia says finally. "It's cheesy, I know. People only make bucket lists in movies, but Dr. Mernich said it would help. Not that anything can help anymore. But it does make me feel better, planning stuff to do. I can't travel, not for long, anyway. Even if none of this stuff happens, I can at least dream about it."

She yawns, blinking sleepily.

"You can do more than that," I say. "You can do all those things you want to."

"Oh shut up with the hopeful stuff already." She sighs.

She falls asleep so quickly after that I don't have time to apologize. Feeling ashamed, I make for the exit. I open the door only to come face to face with Jack. I close it behind me quickly. The tension is instant, my neck hair prickling and my heart racing like I've seen a shark while diving underwater. My motormouth saves me.

"Why are you always here when I am? Let me guess—social media stalking??"

"No," he says flatly.

"GPS chip in my tooth?"

"I'd never spend that much money on you."

"I told you to stay away from me."

"I'm not staying away from Sophia," he asserts. "And apparently neither are you. So never being near each other again is statistically improbable."

"Statistically, when someone asks someone else to leave them alone, they don't talk to said person."

"You're the one who spoke to me first."

"Why haven't you told her about what you do?" I demand. "She's torn up over it."

His subzero eyes narrow. "I can't tell her. She'd be disappointed in me. She'd hate me. She'd think I was disgusting."

"You're a lot of infuriating things, Jack Hunter," I say. "But you're not disgusting."

"Really?" He laughs bitterly. "What world do you

live in? Everyone thinks sleeping with other people for money is base. Dirty. Don't pretend not to be one of them."

My breath hitches. "Is that— Is *that* what you do?"

He doesn't answer, looking at the floor instead. I study his face, and the memories come trickling in like water through a clogged sieve. A red and black card with the name Jaden on it, eating frosting as I watched him walk arm in arm with a girl in town… I paid him to take Kayla out at one point. His escorting was for Sophia—I remember finding that out, too. He's paying her hospital bills with the money he makes, and he keeps it a secret from everyone—his mom, Sophia, *everyone.* Everyone except me.

"Part of me wished you wouldn't remember," Jack says softly.

"Why?"

"Because." He sighs. "I told you. People are disgusted by it. You were, too, and now you are again."

I set my jaw. "I used to be. I used to think it was gross and wrong. But then I realized I only thought that way because I hated you. Because anything you did was disgusting to me, back when we first met."

"And now?" he snarls.

"Now I— It's—" It's my turn to be unable to look him in the eye. "Now I realize it's your choice. And as long as you're all right with it, as long as it isn't hurting you or making you hate yourself, it's fine. It's what you want to do for Sophia. It's what you want to do, period. So who am I to say it's wrong, or bad? Only bigots think like that."

"So you're fine with it? You're fine with me sleeping with people for money?"

"Trust me when I say I know sex isn't anything special."

His eyebrows knit, the wrinkle between them intense. "It can be, if it's with someone you love."

My face heats, my stomach burbling uneasily. "Then why do you do it with people you don't love?"

"Because it's not— " He exhales. "It's hard to explain to someone who doesn't have experience."

The burbling in my stomach becomes a roiling. "Right. So I'm too inexperienced to bother with."

"No, that's not what I meant." Jack's voice lowers, still even and patient. "Listen, do you kiss your mother?"

"What? What kind of question is that?"

"Do you?"

"Yeah, duh. On the cheek. Or the top of her head, sometimes."

"I kissed you," he says without missing a beat. "And that was different, wasn't it? It felt different. Right?"

It's hard to hear through his careful control, but I swear his last word sounds unsure, anxious.

"Y-Yeah," I admit. "It felt— "

I brave a glance at his face, and my skin prickles as I realize he's looking at me. Not staring, not glaring, just looking at me; me, everything about me, and it feels like not a single thing in my heart is hidden from his gaze. The word I'm searching for is something I don't know. It's undefined, a blank where a definition should be. It's elusive, just on the tip of my tongue, but I can't say it. Frustration builds in me, exploding all at once.

"What's the point of asking me this?" I demand. His ice-blue eyes dim, but don't waver.

"I'm trying to explain to you there's a difference. There's routine affection, and then there's something...

something more. Something *much more*."

The wildfire on my face burns hotter, a third of it shame, a third of it curiosity, and a third of it some deep, instinctual longing; a longing to know what he means, a longing to have him show me what it means.

I manage to douse myself in seven tons of imaginary frigid water and refocus.

"Even if you're just...giving routine affection, it's only okay as long as you aren't hurting yourself by doing it."

"Physically?"

"Or emotionally," I add.

His eyes grow hard. "Why would you care about me? You told me to stay out of your life. You don't get to pretend to care about me."

I freeze. He's right. Why *do* I care?

"It's not pretending," I grit out.

"You hate me," he says flatly.

"You infuriate me," I say. "You confuse me. Every time I talk to you, my feelings turn into a tornado, my stomach twists up. I don't know how to feel about you, okay? I need space. I need time. I need to think without you fucking up my head."

His angry expression cools to an impassive, deathly void. He moves behind me, opening Sophia's door and closing it evenly in my face. Somehow the tornado inside me gets worse. Through the gaps in the blinds of Sophia's window, I can see Jack sitting on the bed next to her, grasping her hand and smoothing away the hair from her forehead tenderly.

Something clicks into place. That's where he belongs. I can feel it, see it, sense it. Holding her hand is what he should be doing, always, forever. They fit like pieces of a puzzle I didn't know we were putting back together.

There's no place for me.

There's no place for a girl who doesn't think about death. A girl who isn't serious or deep or mature. There's no place for a girl who only believes in herself.

Mira and James are a lot easier to be with. I don't have to be serious or deep—on the contrary, they want nothing less than total lighthearted fun. God knows they're bored as hell spending all their time in this hospital. A place for the sick and old is no place for kids to grow up. They deserve other kids their age, candy, school, and zoos and playgrounds and Disneyworld.

"Isis." James's voice brings me out of my thoughts. "Why do you look so sad?"

I smile. "Oh, it's just teenage hormones. Don't worry about it."

"Teenagers sound extremely gross," Mira says sagely.

"We are the grossest," I assure her. "Have you seen a teenager lately? They're absolutely *covered* in grease and sarcasm."

"Like you." James giggles.

"I'm negative seven grease, at least."

"And plus a million sarcasm," Mira says.

"Who gave you permission to be so sassy?" I pretend to look offended. They both point at me instantly, and I burst into laughter. James, sitting by the window, points out of it to the parking lot.

"Hey! Isn't that Jack?"

Mira and I crowd the window beside him. Jack's walking to his car. James pulls out a Nerf gun from under his pillow and aims at Jack.

"Do it, do it, do it," Mira and I chant. He squeezes the trigger, and the little foam bullet goes flying. There's no way it reached him, but at that same moment Jack stops and looks back up at the hospital. James and Mira and I duck under the windowsill.

“Did it actually hit him?” James hisses.

“No way,” Mira whispers. “He’s just staring and being a weirdo like he always is.”

“Weirdo is a really good name for him,” I agree. We poke our heads over the sill and see that Jack’s walking away again.

“Phew!” James wipes his forehead. “I thought I killed him.”

“You can’t kill people with Nerf guns,” Mira snaps.

“Unfortunately,” I say. “Also, if you killed him, you’d be the world’s youngest assassin.”

“Aw, I wanna be that! That sounds awesome!” James pouts. Mira flicks him on the head.

“Nuh-uh. You wanna go to space when you grow up, remember?”

“So?”

“There aren’t any people in space for assassining!”

I laugh so hard I surprise myself. Mira and James laugh, too, just looking a little more confused. I sit up and wipe my eyes.

“I s-swear.” I gulp air. “You two are going to end up assassining me someday.”

“But I don’t wanna assassin you!” James argues.

“Too bad. The wheels are already in motion.”

“Man, that sucks,” he grumbles. “You’re the only cool teenager I’ve ever met.”

“False,” I say. “You clearly haven’t met the Breakfast Club.”

“Who’s that?” He frowns. Mira’s eyes light up.

“There’s a whole club for breakfast?”

"Yup. It's only for teenagers, though."

Mira considers this, then frowns very seriously at me. "I've changed my mind. Teenagers are okay."

I start laughing again, and James rolls his eyes and fires his Nerf gun at the ceiling.

I, Isis Blake, think Principal Evans is a nice guy.

By Disney villain standards.

By every other standard, he's more or less a horrible jerk. And I know this, but I've spent so much time with him now I barely see it anymore. It just is, like the stupid watercolor of the school's main building on his wall, or the fluorescent light above his desk that flickers sometimes, because, hello, public school funding. Summer is hot and I am hot and the sky is blue and Evans is just a straight-up jerk with a continual midlife crisis he likes to take out on me.

I put my feet up on his desk anyway.

"What's up, man?" I ask. I know exactly what's up. But I'm gonna make him beg for it. Evans runs his hand over his balding head.

"I was concerned about my favorite student."

"Oh, you've gotten so much better at lying!" I clap my hands. "You could just say you wanna know what was in Stanford's envelope. You know, be a little more honest with your feelings. I'm sure it'd save you in the long run from buying that inevitable red convertible or a couple years of therapy."

Evans frowns. "I have been trying to make up for my mistakes. How much longer are you going to treat me like the bad guy?"

"As long as you're alive," I say cheerily. "You just want me to tell you I got in early, so you can brag to your other bald principal friends."

"You did? Congratulations."

"Ah-ah." I wag my finger. "Don't assume, and don't try to get me to say it. I know how you work."

"And how do I work, Isis? Please tell me."

"Underhanded tactics and simpering lead-ons. You'd have done well in 1700s France. Except everybody there got beheaded for that stuff." I pause and stroke my chin thoughtfully, then smile. "Yup! You would've done well."

Evans is quiet. His eyes are set and hard, for once, instead of soft and evasive.

"Let me guess." I lean forward. "You want me to tell you I got in, so that you can feel better, feel redeemed, that you entered me in their applications process, like getting me into a prestigious college will make up for the pictures and the bullshit."

He doesn't move or blink. I lean back.

"News flash, Evans—it's called bullshit because it's shit. Because it's already been pooped out, and nothing can be done about it. It can't be cleaned up. It'll always be there. The stink will linger. It'll always be something you've done. So no, I'm not going to tell you."

Evans smiles. "You already have."

I scoff. "Yeah?"

"You wouldn't be nearly as arrogant if you didn't hold the knowledge that you got in. If you didn't get in, you'd have nothing to lord over me. You wouldn't be dragging it out like this."

I inhale sharply. He's right. He's fucking right. I learned how he works, but he's been learning how I work all along. Clever little rat.

"For what it's worth, I'm glad." He smiles a softer smile. "I am glad you have the opportunity. I can rest easy knowing one of my brightest students has the opportunity to become brighter."

I'm quiet. He gets up and stands at the window, watching the people at recess below.

"Because you are, you know. Bright. When you first came, I looked at your records and dismissed you as a troublemaker. But you've done so well. Your paper statistics were deceptive. And yet I judged you on that solely."

"Don't get all cheesy on me," I say.

Evans shrugs. "I'm not. I know you dislike me, with good reason. And that won't change. But I learned from you, Isis. I'd forgotten how to learn from students. Years of being principal, instead of a teacher, distanced me."

He turns back to me and smiles.

"So, thank you, Isis. And I'm sorry for everything. You may go, if you wish."

I stand and put my backpack on. At the door, I turn.

"I got in."

Evans nods, faint smile still in place. Just nods, doesn't say anything preachy or high-handed, and turns back to the window.

I leave, feeling a little stranger. A little sadder. I suddenly don't want to hate him so much. Suddenly everything feels a little grayer, a little colder, the anger-fire burning low in my chest. People make bad mistakes, but so few of them ever apologize for it face to face. So few ever change themselves or try to make up for it. After what Leo did, I realized I couldn't trust adult men to do anything right. I painted them all as villains incapable of doing the right thing. But Evans did this once. And for that and only that, I admire him.

Hiking up to Avery's lake cabin has me pondering several things, one of which stands out brilliantly: there are approximately nine trillion cells in my body and every single one of them hates hiking. And walking. Just moving for extended periods of time in general, really. All nine trillion of us would rather be in bed. In the shade. With a parfait.

"I can't believe I ran myself skinny." I pant and lean on a tree. Kayla is yards ahead of me, pushing over the hill of the hiking trail leading to Avery's cabin.

"We've all done things we regret!" Kayla calls back.

"Like living."

"Or not keeping up with a healthy exercise regimen!" she singsongs.

I stare at an oak's trunk, and it seems to share my incredulousness. *Regimen?* I mouth. The tree shifts in the sunlight—a planty shrug.

"Have you actually been…*studying*?" I call.

"We're adults now. Adults have to know words."

"And here I thought the only words they knew were 'booze' and 'meaningless sex.'"

Kayla laughs as she waits for me at the top of the hill. "Don't forget 'bills,'" she adds when I catch up.

"H-How could I?" I pant.

"I think that's what I'm most afraid of."

"Bills?"

She nods. "Bills are scary. College doesn't scare me.

It's just like high school, probably, except you live there."

"People drink a lot in college."

"We drink a lot now."

"There's lots of STDs."

"What do you think Marina keeps itching her crotch in gym for?"

"And your dreams of being a rock star get crushed."

"I'm thinking more of a rock-et star." She points up into the sky.

I sputter a laugh. "Yeah?"

"Yeah." She grabs her boobs. "These guys would appreciate the zero G. Also there's like, neato space rocks and stuff. And aliens."

"There's no *Cosmo* in space," I warn.

"Yeah but there's *the* cosmos!"

I smirk. I'm rubbing off on her.

We walk for a bit. Or, Kayla walks, and I wheeze. But even through my burning lungs and running nose, the woods are beautiful—dappled with light and fresh air—and the sound of the lake lapping close by is a lullaby only the birds get to hear every night. Kayla stops on another hill and points to the cottage. It's huge, with French windows and marble terracing, but at least there are no cars in the driveway. We're free to snoop around, and as long as we don't get too close to the house itself, we won't trip any alarms.

"Welcome to Château Avery."

"Thanks, ass-tronaut." I tap her butt. She squeals and chucks a pinecone at my head. It sticks to my hair, and I don't bother taking it out, because she gave it to me. She's given me loads of stuff—cake pops and lattes and smiles—but somehow this pinecone means more to me than any of those things. It's a little scratchy, a little uncomfortable sometimes. But it's still with me, and it looks fabulous. Just like Kayla.

"So where do we start looking?" she asks.

"I have zero idea," I admit. "I don't know what we're looking for or where. This journey into Mordor may be completely for naught. But this is the only lead I've got to go on, Samwise Gamgee."

"Ugh, why do I have to be the clingy hobbit?"

"Wren said it happened in the woods." I change the subject. "Avery asked them to come outside, so it couldn't have been too far from the cottage. It couldn't have been too close to the road, though, otherwise she'd run the risk of being seen. We gotta think like Avery."

Kayla makes a disgusted face. I thump her on the back.

"Sacrifices have to be made. The brain cells will regenerate in ten hours. No one will ever have to know." I whirl around and point south. "That patch of woods looks perfect. Far from the road, but not too far from the cottage."

"Okay, I know you're, like, really smart or whatever, but I knew Avery way before you even got here. I know how she thinks and she would not go that way."

"Pray tell why not?"

"Because there's tons of mud. Ew."

"News flash—mud dries up! There might not have been mud five entire years ago!"

"News flash—there's *always* mud over there." She looks around.

I sigh. "What if there's nothing up here? I mean, honestly, what are we trying to find? Evidence? I don't even know what kind of evidence we're looking for, or even what it's evidence of! For all I know this is a massive waste of time."

"It's worth a try," Kayla insists. "If I were Avery, and I wanted to lure people to do something bad to them, I'd do it in that direction. That's where she and her brother went to let off fireworks when they were kids. You can't see it from the cottage, so their parents never busted them. It was like her secret hideaway."

"I would kiss you right now, but currently it is six months too early to experiment with becoming a fabled college lesbian."

Kayla smirks, and we start toward the patch of forest. The trees get thicker as we go in, the trunks so huge they block out the view of the cottage and the lake. It's a perfect, insulated border around a half mile of dastardly evil-has-been-done-here ground.

"So what are we looking for?" Kayla asks. "Bullet shells? Blood? Human bones? Or—" She shudders and whispers, "Ruined clothes?"

"Probably not any of those. Five years is a long-ass time for nature to do its freaky thing. The best we can hope for is nothing at all, but if we gotta search, look for anything that doesn't seem right. Anything that doesn't look like it belongs in the forest."

She nods, and we split up. My hands shake. I'm breathing shallowly. This is it. This is the place it happened. I'm standing where it took place. Jack became a cold, unfeeling husk on the outside here. Sophia got hurt here. Wren's guilt was born here, and Avery started burning here.

I'm not Sherlock Holmes or Veronica Mars. This excursion is half insane, half wildly hopeful. The past is buried in the hearts of Jack and the others. My memories are back enough for me to recall how hard it was to pry any information about that night out of them. But now I'm here, where it happened. Now's my chance to pry an easier target—time and weather.

I kneel on the forest floor, the layers of pine needles squishy. I dig. I turn over rocks. I look between roots and mushroom clumps and massive, rotting stumps. Kayla huffs and daintily inspects tree trunks and moves pine needles with her foot, but I can't blame her. We're not exactly CSI. She's right. What the hell are we looking for out here? We're just wasting our time.

After a half hour of silent concentration, my hands are smeared in dirt and blood around my nails where I dug too hard. Oops. It doesn't hurt, but it will later. It's then I feel something cold and wet on my ankle, and I summarily expire. Loudly.

"Get it off get it off GETITOFF! KAYLA! *KAYLA!* KAYLAGETITOFF!"

"What are you screaming—"

"GET IT OFF!"

"It's a piece of moss, Isis!"

I stop flailing and look down. The slimy green offender peeks out of my jeans innocently. I pull it off, and Kayla rolls her eyes and goes back to searching.

"Y-Yeah?" I adjust my jeans as I stand. "Well, next time a flesh-eating zombie crawls out to eat you, I will just sit back and watch. From a safe distance. Which slightly impairs my ability to hear you screaming for mercy."

"It was *moss*."

"Well, it felt like a zombie, and who do we have to blame for that, hmm? Mother Nature?" I look up and shout at the trees. "Thanks, M-dawg! Next round can you maybe tone down the moss-that-feels-like-a-zombie-hand thing? Thanks, love ya, big fan otherwise!"

"Aren't we supposed to be sneaky?" she hisses.

"Yeah, but it doesn't matter! There's nothing here. I fucked up, okay? My big plan that was supposed to answer all the questions backfired and here we are, scrabbling around in the dirt like Cro-Magnons who haven't learned about fire! Or gloves!"

Kayla's eyes are glazed, and she's staring off into the distance. I wave a hand frantically in front of her face.

"Hello? Don't go to space yet, dumbo, you've got work to do and degrees to earn and boys to break the hearts of."

She grabs my wrist and looks at me slowly.

"I remember."

"Remember what?"

Kayla looks over my shoulder. "One summer, tenth grade I'm pretty sure, because I had my orange tankini and that was, like, SO cute and in style—"

"Kayla!"

"Right, um. So that summer, Avery, Selena, Jen, and I went way far down on the lake, like, took a walk in this direction, which was weird because it's really rocky this way and we usually went the other way, but that day we decided to go this way, and we got about this far, maybe a little farther, and Avery told us—"

Kayla inhales.

"Avery told us to stop. She got really freaked out. Weirdly freaked. She was almost panicking, and she told us we had to go back, and we all asked her why, but she just kept saying, 'because I said so' and 'it's my cottage, you morons, so we go back when I say.'"

My heart soars. I've only ever seen Avery panic like that, lose her porcelain-doll cool, when Sophia stuff crops up. Maybe this wasn't useless after all.

"And that was this way?" I ask. Kayla nods and points over my shoulder.

"If we keep going, I can look over the edge of the cliff and down to the lake and tell you where she told us to go back."

I follow Kayla. She's faster than ever, but adrenaline pumps my legs just as fast, and I can keep up easily. The sun's still high, and it glints off the massive, ice-kissed Lake Galonagah. Kayla peers over the edge of the forest, where the woods and dirt crumble into rocks and shoreline. She shakes her head each time and keeps going, until finally, *finally*, she stops.

"Right here. This is where she freaked out."

I look around. There's nothing here that stands out—just more woods. But if Avery got scared as they walked this way, that means she was afraid they'd see something they weren't supposed to. Something she'd hidden way out here. Something that could definitely be seen from the lakeshore.

"Let's keep going. Keep your peepers peeled for anything weird."

Kayla nods and follows me. We walk slowly, taking in everything. Kayla sees it first and grabs my elbow.

"Isis."

I look to where she's pointing, and my heart sinks. No, "sinks" isn't the right word for it. It falls out through my butt. It's gone, a heavy leaden thing in its place.

There, against a tree and planted in the ground, is a wooden cross, and at the foot of the cross is a small pile of stones.

"Is that—" Kayla swallows, hard. "Is that a—"

"A grave," I finish. "Yeah."

She stays, frozen in place, but I move toward it with

careful steps. I kneel at the gravesite. The wooden cross is shoddy—somebody just put two thick sticks together with twine—but it's withstood the test of time. The bark's eroded off; bleached white wood is all that's left. You could easily see the white color through the trees and from the lakeside, if you caught the right angle. Whoever made the grave knew their stuff, though. The stones probably kept scavengers from digging up the body and eating it.

The grave is so small.

I already know what's inside. I try not to know, the same way you try not to know about a car crash or a pet dying. You close your eyes and block it out, keep it at arm's length, but reality is stronger than any bodybuilder. It pushes its way in, brute strength smashing the truth into my soul.

Even so, I have to see it with my own two eyes. I have to know. I have to finish what I started, what Avery and Jack and Wren and Sophia started all those years ago. I start moving the rocks.

"Isis! What are you doing? Stop it!"

"Go back to the car and wait for me."

"You can't just— You can't just dig that up—"

I look over my shoulder at her. "The truth is in here, Kayla. And I have to know. So go back to the car and wait for me. Pretend I'm not doing it."

Kayla squeezes her eyes shut, but she doesn't move. I pull the rocks off, one by one, and use a flat one to start digging into the soft square of earth. As I get deeper, I can hear Kayla start to sob. Her cries echo in the forest, and somehow I know they aren't the first human tears these trees have seen. My arms ache, my fingers burn, and the blood from my torn cuticles flows over and mixes with the dirt, but I can't stop. I couldn't stop if I wanted to. It's feet down. Two feet, three feet, and then—

And then the dirt comes apart, and there's a tiny piece of pink blanket sticking out of the ground. I bleed on it. I dig faster but more gently, just around the bundle that's starting to form. I dig until it comes loose, and then I pull it out slowly. Brush off the dirt. Put it on the pine needle ground and open it. It's pinned, but the safety pin is long rusted and snaps easily, and the edges of the blanket fall apart like a crusted, ancient flower to reveal the center.

I feel Kayla's heat to my left, her curiosity obviously overcoming her reluctance. But the second the blanket falls apart, she starts crying harder than ever and pulls away like she's been burned.

"No. No no no," she cries. "No. No no!"

A tiny, barely formed skeleton looks up at me, with eyes too small and too black to see anything. It never got to see anything. That much I'm sure of. It's too small to ever have made it into the outside world. And next to the skeleton is a minuscule bracelet, with letter beads. My shaking fingers pick it up.

Tallulah

I stare at the name for what feels like hours. Days. Tallulah.

Tallie, for short.

As an escort, bars are an integral part of the job. It's a place people go to drink, to ease the slog that is their lives. Clients always feel more comfortable meeting in a crowded place, and for good reason. Sometimes clients won't even try anything physical with me—you'd be surprised how much rich, lonely women will pay to be listened to. That's the part of my job I enjoy the most—conversing. Having a good conversation, a mindless conversation about work and people and life, fills me like a hearty meal. It reminds me people aren't so different from me; they're just as angry at the world, just as bitter, just as sad. Sometimes my clients have problems and pasts that eclipse even mine with their tragedy.

I'm not the only one suffering in this life.

And that is a sick, twisted comfort.

The sounds of the basement deafen me the second I walk in. Bull's Tail isn't a nice bar or even a tolerable one—sawdust and piss and vomit crusting in the corners—but it's exactly what I'm looking for.

It's exactly the place people's hopes go to die.

On a Saturday night, it's as packed as it can be. Men swagger and guffaw into their beer and whiskey, the smell of BO and stale peanuts overpowering. Rock music blares from the creaky jukebox in the corner and the flickering LED TV above the bar shows a game only a fraction of the patrons seem to care about. The bartender is an older woman with once-bright blond hair and beauty to spare, but years of wolf-whistles and ass-grabbing have worn her to a pale mockery of that.

"What are you having?" She flicks a half-second strained smile in my direction.

"Two shots of your best whiskey. And a gin and tonic. On the rocks."

"ID?" she asks. I fish it out. Fake IDs are a necessity in the escort world—many of us working are under the drinking age. Blanche secured one for me as part of our contract.

The bartender studies it, nods, and goes to the bar. I wait. I'm the only one here without a potbelly, and the women are starting to notice. Good. That'll make this much easier.

The bartender comes back with my drinks, and I down them as quickly as I can.

"Whoa there," a man to my left says. "You're awfully young to be drinking that hard."

"You're awfully nosy for someone that old," I counter.

He laughs, but it's not an offended laugh. It's amused. I look over at him and realize it's the man who was watching me in the crowd during the fight with the boxer. A tweed suit covers his considerably hefty frame. He isn't fat—in fact, quite the contrary. He has broad shoulders and muscles gone slightly to pasture. He sits perfectly straight, but with an easy demeanor to it. His right index finger and the tendon attaching to it in his arm are very well defined, classic indications of trigger finger. Military, without a doubt. His hair is white-streaked and sparse and his mustache faint. Dark eyes glitter at me.

"People only drink like that for two reasons—to remember something or to forget something," he says.

"Aren't you just full of tautologies," I scoff. The gin and tonic burns on my tongue. The women are moving, and I'm picking my target carefully. It has to be someone stupid enough to assume the worst of me. And that means any drunk man will do.

"It's a girl, isn't it?" the military man asks. I don't dignify him with a response. "Is she pretty?"

I swirl the leftover ice in my glass and remain silent.

"So she's ugly. Must be absolutely hideous."

"No," I snap. "Not that it matters, but no."

"*'Not that it matters'?*" he presses. I pause. He's goading me into talking, but the alcohol is hitting me fast and I have nothing left to lose.

"She's pretty. I suppose." I wince. "It's not that she's pretty. She's pretty, but that isn't all she is."

"Of course not. Otherwise she wouldn't have you here, drinking and tongue-tied."

I slide my glass back to the bartender and face the man. He's faintly smiling, hands wrapped around a bourbon ice. His silence is somehow more irritating than his words, so I break it.

"Men like to categorize women." I curl my lip. "Into convenient little boxes like 'hot' or 'cute' or 'beautiful.' It's easy for them. But it's never been easy for me."

"So this particular girl," the man leads. "She's none of those?"

"She's all of those," I say, a little too quickly for my own liking. "And more than those, and at the same time she's none of those. She is exactly herself, no more and no less. But saying that now is pointless."

"Did she dump you?"

"She told me to stay out of her life."

"And so here you are, stumbling into a backwater bar to start a fight with someone just to vent all that out."

I narrow my eyes at him. His smile remains.

"I've been alive long enough to know the face of someone looking for a fight. And I know the face of someone who knows what it's like to fight."

The man's dark eyes suddenly become unreadable.

"And most of all, I know the face of someone who, deep down in a part of himself he won't admit to, *enjoys* fighting."

I glare at the bar top, the polished wood reflecting my face. The man stops smiling at me and takes a sip from his bourbon before speaking again.

"You see it sometimes, in the guys. Most of us in the army don't like what we do, believe it or not. We join for the camaraderie, the sense of belonging, of order. Not for the blood. But every once in a while, you see a real piece of work come through. And he likes the blood. Some of them are better at hiding it than others, but it always comes out."

"What are you saying?" I snarl.

"I'm saying, son, that you're a monster," he replies evenly. "And you hate what you are."

My fist connects with his jaw before I can stop it. The ice is gone. The poise and calm, rational demeanor I'd kept myself leashed with vaporizes in an instant, and he's pushing back, shoving me by the shoulders outside, and the bartender is yelling something, and the drunk idiots are hooting and hollering, taking bets, following us as we stumble into the night air. I step in a puddle as I duck under the man's right hook. It's so powerful the air trailing behind it makes an audible *thump* noise. He's huge. He's taller and wider than Leo, and I don't have a bat. He lunges for me, and I throw a trash can between us. He kicks it aside, and it crumples against the wall like a tin can.

And for the first time since I saw Isis on the floor with blood around her head, I feel fear. Real, true, cold fear that reaches into my lungs and pulls them up through my throat.

I put my fists up and step around another right hook, but he slams his knee into my chest and I can't breathe, the world reduced to flashes of white and red and pain.

I can barely hear the crowd whooping over the sound of my own surging heartbeat. Someone tries to break us up, but the man shoves him away and lunges for me, and suddenly my feet aren't touching the ground, his fist in my collar as he lifts me above the cement. Our gazes meet for a split second, his curiously empty of emotion, and he throws me aside. Stars pop in my eyes, and my back hits the brick wall with a sickening *thud*. I try to scrabble to my feet, but my legs are pained jelly.

The man leans in.

"No one can tame the monster for you, son. Not your parents, not a girl. Not a college or an institution. Only you can do that."

I spit at his feet, the saliva bloody.

"What do you know about me?"

"Blanche told me a lot about you."

"Should've figured you were one of her goons."

"Don't mistake me. I'm not one of hers, and I trust her as far as I can throw her. Which isn't far, with the way she drapes herself in that tacky jewelry."

We both dislike Blanche, and that alone saps the heat from our fight. All of a sudden he drops his stance, his will to fight gone. The man offers me his hand up. The bar crowd departs, the excitement over for them. I glare at his palm and ease up onto my feet by myself. Every bone in my body screams for me to stop moving, to inject morphine, to roll in bandages, anything to stop the pain. The man dusts off his suit and smiles at me.

"I heard about what you did for the Blake family. Word travels fast in the criminal justice circuit."

"So?"

"So you beat up a grown scumbag, kid."

"It's nothing special."

"No, it's not. You're right. Beating someone up isn't special. Beating someone up three times your size is. You've got a ferocity in you, a ruthlessness. You've got the bloodlust in you. And you'd just be letting it go to waste on civilian life. More than that, if you don't get it trained right, it's gonna backfire on you someday. You know that. You've always known that."

The bastard is spouting half nonsense and half searing truth. Of course I've known. He reaches into his jacket and hands me a card.

"When you're ready to use it constructively instead of destructively, you come see me."

He's gone before I can snipe at him, and I'm alone in the alley with my aching body and bewildered mind. The card is simpler than any I've ever seen—simpler than the Rose Club cards, even. And that's how I know it's seedy, underworld business.

Gregory Callan
VORTEX Enterprises

I nurse my wounds long enough to get up the energy to make it back to my car, and then I collapse. I welcome the warm relief and quiet. I drank too much. I took too many punches. I went looking for a fight. And now I'm hurt, and buzzed, and my mouth tastes like blood, and all I want to do is go back to that night at Avery's, to that absurd sea-themed room, to the bed with Batgirl in it, to Isis, to an Isis who confessed to me with tiny, stuttering, shy words that she liked me, to a moment when everything was simple. Her and me. Her and me in a room, alone.

My phone rings. I wince as I answer.

"Hello?"

"Jack!" Sophia's sunny voice says. "Dr. Fenwall says

the last payment for the surgery came through! Thank you. Thank you so, so much."

I push out the vestiges of the memories of that night and smile.

"Don't thank me. It's the least I could do."

"You worked so hard. I'm really grateful. Remember when I said you could choose the place next time we went out?"

"Yes."

"Well, Dr. Fenwall said he'd let me have a few days out next week. So."

"I'll see if I can't find something fun for us to do."

"Yeah! But Avery wants to throw me a surprise party. For my birthday."

"That's in March."

"I know! But if I only have a few days out, she can only plan it then."

"I thought we hate Avery?"

"We do! I mean, we don't like her, but she's trying really hard. And it just seems unfair. And plus, if I don't make it—"

"Don't talk like that," I snap.

"If I don't make it," she says more sternly, "I don't want things between us to be bad when I… You know."

"You won't."

"Just, *please*. I really want to go."

I sigh. "All right. I'll ask her about it."

"Okay. Thank you. I know it's hard for you, but thank you."

"It's fine."

"Say hi to your mom for me. Or, I guess I'll say hi. It still feels weird, though, just popping up on Facebook and being like, 'Hey Dahlia! It's me!'"

"Don't worry," I assure her. "She loves you. She always will. You can say hi whenever."

"Okay! I'm going to try to get some sleep."

"Good. Good night."

"Good night, Jack."

When we hang up, Isis's words ring in my head.

She's dying, Jack.

Why haven't you told her what you do?

I put my head on the steering wheel and pretend I'm somewhere else. Somewhere warm. Somewhere like that ridiculous sea-themed little room.

chapter nine

3 YEARS, 27 WEEKS, 2 DAYS

SINCE THE TRIAL, Mom's been getting better.

I don't know if "better" is the right word. She had to be so strong for so long, just for me, and now that I'm back, she's leaning on me again, and I don't mind—it's the norm for us—but I can't help feeling sometimes like I'm a cane instead of a daughter, but then I get guilty about thinking that and make her dinner and bring her tea and tell her it'll be all right, instead. Love is being there for someone. If there's one thing I learned from Aunt Beth, it's that family means being there when no one else is. That's why she took me in when Mom couldn't handle the divorce *and* me.

Mom's going to twice as many shrink appointments after the trial, but they seem to be helping. I see Avery at the office sometimes, and she gives me a passing sneer before flouncing out the door. She's bitchier lately, and that means she's happier, and that means Sophia's probably talking to her again. Avery's basically her yo-yo, and Sophia pulls her back and forth for her amusement. I don't understand it, but I can see it happening the way you see a train approach a car on the tracks in slow motion. Avery is desperate to atone for whatever she did to Sophia, and Sophia pretends it's possible. But at the very last moment, she's going to pull the rug out from under Avery and crush her hopes once and for all. Fucking up is the worst. Not being able to make up for fucking up is absolute hell. And Avery's been living with that this whole time. No wonder she has depression.

I feel sorry for her. I pity her. And pity's not healthy, but after everything Avery's done to me, to Kayla, to Jack and Sophia and Wren, I can't bring myself to feel something better toward her. And it's shitty of me, and it's not very Isis Blake-like. The old Isis would've tried harder to be friends with Avery again, even through all this bullshit. The old Isis would've soldiered in with a smile and taken all the blows, because she knew how hard it was to keep living after being broken.

After seeing Tallie, a portion of the puzzle came together. Avery is terrified of people seeing Tallie's grave. Sophia misses Tallie, demands to see her in the midst of her fits. Wren said it happened at Lake Galonagah. The grave is at Galonagah, too. Tallie was so young. Tallie couldn't have been Sophia's baby sister—her parents were long dead by then.

Logic dictates Tallie was Sophia's baby.

Sophia was in eighth grade at the time. Thirteen or fourteen is right around the time everyone else started having sex at school, for better or worse, and much to the stubborn, oblivious denial of their parents. I looked it up—a baby's skeleton begins developing in the second trimester. Ossification, the process of bones forming, is quick. It lasts from two months pregnant to about five months pregnant. The skeleton I saw was tiny, but whole and intricate. Sophia must've been about four months pregnant when she miscarried.

Miscarried. The word rings hollow in my head. When I was enduring the tortures of Nameless, Sophia was pregnant and then losing her baby. She's experienced so much loss and pain—so much more than me. She deserves happiness. She deserves to live. But the world won't let her.

Something in the back of my mind writhes, whispering: who slept with Sophia to make her pregnant?

I had sex with Jack.

I push her echoing voice from that time on the rooftop out of my head and keep moving. The hospital is quiet. Like the grave. Except people here are trying extremely hard not to be in graves. Very hard. At least four morphine drips and two crappy hospital food trays worth of hard. Being back here always makes me feel claustrophobic—the smell of antiseptic, the people in gowns wandering like ghosts from room to room, the nurses and interns all staring and trying to decide where I belong in their mini-ecosystem of healing. Naomi isn't on duty, which I'm grateful for. I don't want this to be any messier than it has to be. For Sophia's sake.

I poke my head into the kids' ward for just a second when the guard steps away to pee. Mira and James wave frantically, and I wink and put down the plastic bag of presents inside the door. They come rushing over in their little cartoon-character pajamas with big smiles on.

"Mira said you'd never come back!"

"Did not!" Mira sticks her tongue out at James.

I laugh and ruffle their hair. "I can't stay long, but I'll come back in the daytime this week, okay? For now just open the presents. But don't tell Naomi where you got them. Just say it was from…uh, Jesus."

They nod frantically, and Mira hugs me around the neck so hard I think she's trying to merge with me on a cellular level. I manage to pry off her fingers and sneak out just as the guard rounds the corner. The sounds of tearing wrapping paper and squealing reverberate behind me. I made some spawn happy. And that definitely does not make me feel all gooey and happy inside.

Sophia's open doorway looms before me. It's dim, and the usual flower vases line her window. I can see her feet under the blanket.

I stand there for what feels like years. And then I take a deep breath and walk in.

She's not asleep like I'd hoped. She's very much awake, blue eyes staring at me over the cover of a romance novel. This one has a knight on it and a very lost-looking busty lady.

"Yo!" I smile.

"I thought I told you to leave me alone," she deadpans.

"Uh, yeah, I've never been very good at following directions. Or respecting people's wishes. Or anything at all, really. So here I am. Doing…here stuff."

She shoots me a withering look. "You're annoying."

"That, my dear, is nothing new!" I sit on the end of her bed. "In fact, 'tis ancient knowledge. The Egyptians foretold of my coming. Actually they mostly told stories about how Isis the goddess of fertility got it on with her brother. Incest was big back then. So was not living past thirty."

Sophia doesn't crack a smile, eyes set and hard like blue-black flint.

There's no avoiding it. Whatever tenuous friendship we once had has been tainted by our mutual insecurities. It was easy when we didn't know anything about each other, and now it's hard. But that doesn't mean it's not worth it. Sophia's presence was always calm and gentle, but heavy, and I feel the weight of it now more than ever.

"I met Tallie," I say. There's a half second of silence, and then Sophia puts her book down slowly. I can't stand the quiet. "I found her. And I'm sorry. I'm sorry for prying. I'm sorry for meeting her. I'm sure you don't want many people to. I'm sorry. I'm sorry it happened to you in the first place—"

"What happened to me?" Sophia interjects viciously. "Please, tell me exactly what happened to me, since you seem to know so much already."

"Whoa, hold on, that's not what I meant—"

"Then why are you apologizing? Do you think that'll make anything better? Do you think that will help at all? Words don't help. They never have. And they help even less coming from your mouth."

I knit my lips shut.

Sophia glares. "I don't need your pity. That's what you came to give, isn't it? Or are you guilt-tripping me with the knowledge you have now?"

"No— Sophia, I wouldn't—"

"You would. Because you think like Jack. And it's what he would do."

And just like that, all my anger wells up and blocks my throat.

"I. Am. Not. Jack!"

My fist swings and accidentally knocks a vase over. It shatters, opalescent shards puddling on the ground. Sophia's glare breaks into a bitter smile.

"It's about time you got mad at me! I knew you weren't as manic-pixie-dream-girl as you make yourself out to be."

"Enough with the insults! Why are you doing this? Why are you being such a horrible poop-face to me?"

She stops smiling, eyes getting heavy-lidded.

"Because you have it all. You have your health. You have family. You have friends. And even though you have all that, you still want the one thing I have left. You coveted it. You tried to take it from me."

"I didn't—"

"You did. You kept pressing. You met him and tried everything to get his attention, and when you had it and found out about me, you still kept pushing. You kept yourself in his life. You wanted him. You still do. And it makes me sick—"

My hand stings. Sophia's face swings to the side, her eyes filled with utter shock and hurt as she looks back at me, her cheek red.

"I've never liked Jack, and I never will," I say through gritted teeth. "He's yours. He's always been yours. So stop. Stop being such an ass. Let go of all this useless hate. I want to be your friend. *Just let me be your friend*."

She goes still, staring at me, and I watch as her eyes slowly start to fill with tears.

"I can't," she whispers. *"I can't."*

Her hands go to her eyes, and she starts to sob. I don't touch her. I want to, I want to hug her and call her Soapy and hold her hand like she held mine when I cried to her about Mom, and Leo, and what happened. But she hates me. I was wrong. Jack might be the bad prince, and the bad prince hurts, but a dragon hurts worse.

By talking about Tallie, by finding Tallie, I'm breathing fire over a village and burning everyone inside to a crisp. Sophia. And Jack. And Wren and Avery. It's not my delicate nightmare, but I'm inserting myself anyway because I think I can what, help? Make things right? Nothing will make things right. Nothing will reverse what happened that night in the woods, no matter how much I dig or how much I try to get them to talk about it. I'm stupid for even thinking I could make things better.

And then, just like that, Sophia reaches out for my hand and pulls it to her heart.

"I want Tallie back," she cries, angelic face swollen. "Please. Just give her back."

I squeeze her hand and nod.

"I will."

Two weeks after we found the body, we decide to finally talk about it.

At school, Kayla's been avoiding me about the baby at the lake. I've tried to bring it up at lunch break, but she refused to mention it. Until now. It's like she had to recharge, get over her own shock, before she could face the reality of it.

She calls it Lake Baby. She didn't see the name on the bracelet, and I haven't told her. Mostly because she already goes the color of thousand-year-old rice when I bring Lake Baby up. If names were attached, she might just combust on the spot out of grief. I think that's what it is. Grief. Maybe she's just been raised in suburban America all her life, hard things like unwanted pregnancies and skeletons far displaced from her life. I've told her it isn't Avery's baby, though, which is what she was worrying and crying about in the forest. It's Sophia's. But that just confuses her more.

"How do you know Sophia had a—"

"I just do. She asked Wren why he hadn't visited the grave lately. They all must know about the grave. God, no wonder they clam up about it."

"Wait, but what about what happened that night?" Kayla munches a cucumber and every boy within ~~five~~ fifty feet is staring, enraptured. "The one in middle school? Did she— Did she lose the baby then? Or before?"

"Avery said she hired some guys to do something to her, and Wren said Jack drove them off. What if the shock made her lose it? What if one of them pushed her and she fell hard, and she miscarried right there in the woods? That'd disturb them enough into the crazy-weird silence they have going on now."

What if they had to bury more than one body that night? The picture from the email is still vivid, like a blind spot you get from staring at the sun too long. But there's another spot that sticks harder to my mind. Kayla voices it first.

"If Sophia and Jack were going out back then..."

My stomach curls in on itself. Kayla's eyes widen.

"...does that mean—"

"You two look way too serious for eleven thirty a.m." Wren slides to sit by Kayla, a smile on his face. Kayla clears her throat and smooths her hair.

"Um. Yeah! We were just, um, talking about the prom! Senior prom feels like such a letdown after junior prom, I think."

"Well, it's the last time we'll have a school function," he says.

"And the last time we'll ever have to buy hand-me-down dresses from Ross," I say, "and put up with groping boys who can't tell the vagina from the anus while a DJ plays something about partying till the sun goes up from the top forty and people sneak cheap vodka from thigh flasks."

Wren and Kayla stare at me.

"What?" I ask innocently.

"You sound like you've been to a lot of school dances," Wren says.

"I've been to exactly zero school dances." I puff my chest proudly and my nipple hits the ketchup bottle off the table and there is a fabulous red puddle on the floor directly in front of the shoes of Jack Hunter. Kayla and Wren freeze, staring at him as if waiting for him to say something first. I keep my eyes ahead, focused on the radical silver perm of the second-in-line lunch lady.

"I'd advise you learn to control your extremities," Jack sneers. "Or lack thereof."

It's almost traditional. My mind nags at me that this is the normal procedure of things between Jack and me. The memories are there, just hazy, and they all say I should snark something back about the way his hair looks like a duck's butt, but I can't. I can't say anything. He's terrifying. The email picture is fresh in my mind, and the image of Tallie's skeleton hangs just before my eyes, and I can't get rid of either of them. They're his. They are extensions of him, and they terrify me—*me*! The girl who's afraid of nothing except centipedes. And the green Teletubby. And the front-row seat of Space Mountain.

So I just stare and don't say anything. Jack waits, and Kayla and Wren wait on him, and nothing moves. Jack's expression is barely there, but the hint of smug wilts rapidly, and he steps over the ketchup puddle and leaves. Wren gets up with a wad of napkins and wipes the puddle.

"What was that all about?" he asks.

"What do you mean?"

"You didn't say anything. You always say *something*."

"Ignoring him is the best way to get him to back off." I shrug. "I've had enough, I guess. It's just boring now."

Kayla narrows her eyes. "That sounds like bullshit to the max."

"You'd rather I fight him like I used to? Didn't that like, end in tears? And a broken head? Let's not go for a repeat performance just this once, okay?"

Kayla and Wren look at each other but don't press it. And I'm grateful. The last thing I need for them to know is what I know. Because I know a lot. And it hurts my head. And possibly my heart. If I had one.

"Did you see his face?" Kayla asks as we walk together to our next class.

"Whose?"

"Jack's. His lip was busted and scabbing. And that was a mean bruise on his cheekbone."

"Probably got in a fight with the mirror when he saw it was prettier than him."

"Isis, I'm being serious!"

"So am I!"

"Look, I know you have like, amnesia about him and your feelings for him are all mixed up or whatever—"

"Feelings? What is this foreign word you speak of?"

"—but you don't have to be such a fucking jerk about

it. He's a person, too, okay? You can't just cut people off and put them back in whenever you want."

The words sting, mostly because they sound too much like what Jack himself said. Kayla's too pissed to talk to me anymore, so I spend the period doodling exploding things on my worksheet.

Wren and I have yearbook together, so it's the perfect time to show him. I print out the strange email picture and pass it to him over the computers. There's a beat, and then:

"What is this, Isis?" he asks.

"What does it look like?" I singsong.

"Where did you get this?"

"Someone sent it to me. Over email. That's Jack's lovely hand, isn't it? Holding that bloody bat and standing over that guy who looks very much dead."

I can see Wren's hand on his mouse, and it's shaking.

"What interests me wayyyy more," I press, "is the fact that the quality is shit. Shit enough to be in a sewage pipe. Or my makeup collection. And see the way the pixels are a little off? Like they're wavy? It's almost like someone took a screenshot of a video—"

"What's the email address?" Wren interrupts. "That sent this to you?"

"Just random key smash. ikwjhk@yahoo.com. Nobody either of us would know just from the address. You can't even say it. Ickwajihuk? Ikewjahooookk?"

I hear Wren typing, and I sigh.

"Trust me, I've already looked. Google's got nothing. I've dug in fifty-two pages and a lot of backlog. Ickwajhuk doesn't exist anywhere else on the internet."

"Isis, listen to me." Wren looks at me from between our computers, expression serious. "Whoever gave you that picture is dangerous. Block the address and don't correspond with him."

"Why?" I laugh. "What's he gonna do, send me an unsolicited dick pic?"

"That's the video I took from that night," Wren murmurs. "I gave it to the federal investigator who questioned us."

"Wait—what? The Feds questioned you guys?"

Wren inhales. "There were…issues. We were the only ones signed into a cabin near the lake, so we were questioned."

"About what?"

He doesn't say anything. I sigh.

"Okay, so you're saying the Feds sent me the picture?"

"The guy who questioned us turned it over to the bureau's vault. He died five years ago of a heart attack."

"How do you know that?"

"I've been keeping close tabs on everything." Wren adjusts his glasses. "So it couldn't have been him. Whoever sent you this picture—he either works there or hacked into it. If he works there, he isn't good news. And if he could hack something that secure, he is really, *really* bad news."

"This is ridiculous. Nobody hacks the Feds except in movies."

"Trust me, Isis. Wipe your computer. Wipe the entire hard drive. Don't take any chances. And don't ask any more questions."

"So that's it? I'm just supposed to forget I've ever seen this? Sorry, I have a better memory and more self-respect than that."

Wren sets his jaw. I lean in and whisper.

"I saw Tallie, Wren. I met her. I know where she is

and who she is. And I know that's what happened that night. Sophia lost her. You all saw it. You buried her together. And maybe you buried other bodies, too. I don't know. But I won't stop until I do."

Wren clenches his fist and stands from the chair. "Then you leave me no choice."

He says something to Mrs. Greene and strides out the door. I try to follow, but Mrs. Greene harps with her shrieky voice.

"Where do you think you're going, Blake?"

"The South Pole?"

She frowns.

"Nicaragua?"

She frowns harder.

"Okay, fine, the piss palace."

"Emily left with the bathroom pass. You'll have to wait till she gets back."

"But what if I wet my pants? Do teacher salaries really pay enough to replace student underwear? I'm wearing very expensive underwear."

This is a bluff. My underwear is blue and three years old. We both know I am not That Girl.

"Sit. Down. Ms. Blake."

I cross my arms and flop in my chair with considerable grumpy pizzazz.

For the first time in nearly five years, Wren walks up to me. He peeks into study hall, finds my table, and walks over, looking me in the eye as he does it, too.

This is my first indication that something has gone

very wrong. He's cowardly. He's hesitant. And he's carrying years of guilt toward me on his shoulders. He would never approach me this boldly unless something dire was happening.

He slides a paper across the table. It's a printout of a picture, of a very familiar bloody baseball bat, and my hand, and a dark shape in the background I know all too well. I see it each night my brain decides to grant me a nightmare.

"Isis had this," Wren says, voice strong but low. My lungs splinter with ice at her name, but I quell the pain and quirk a brow.

"And?"

"You know what it's from," he hisses. "Someone sent that to her in an email."

"Did she say what the address was?"

"ikwjhk@yahoo.com. All in lower case."

The letters are simple to memorize. I sit back in my chair and struggle to look casual. "Sounds like a trash-byte spammer."

Wren leans in, now closer to me physically than we've been in five years. His green eyes are dark behind his glasses.

"I know you know more about computers than I do," he says.

"Correct."

"And I know—God, the whole school knows—you like Isis."

I have to force the chuckle, and it comes out bitter. "Really? Fascinating. I love hearing fresh gossip."

"It's not gossip, Jack, and it's sure as hell not new. It's the goddamn old truth and you and I both know it."

He's breathing heavily, his face flushed. He's

frustrated and flustered, not angry. Wren never gets truly angry. I give him my best glare.

"Didn't you see her in the cafeteria?" I ask. "I don't exist to her. She clearly has no concern for me. Why should I care who she's emailing?"

"She'll find out the truth about you!"

"It's about time someone other than us did."

"This p-person—" He splutters and jabs his finger at the photo. "This person is dangerous. And he's talking to Isis. What if he hurts her?"

There's a long silence. I scoff and look him up and down.

"I'm sorry, am I supposed to care?"

Wren's face falls like someone's slapped him. He grits his teeth and grabs the paper back.

"I thought you did. I guess I was wrong."

"Yes. Now, if you could turn around and march back the way you came in, I'd be very grateful."

"I care about her!" Wren shouts suddenly. Study hall goes quiet. The librarian looks up, but Wren doesn't seem to notice. His hair comes undone from its gel, and his glasses skew minutely. "I care about Isis! She's done more for me than anyone, and if she gets hurt again, I swear to you—"

"You'll what?" I laugh. "Slap me with a ruler? Sic your student council lackeys on me? Oh wait, I know—you'll call in some favors and have my pudding privileges revoked with the cafeteria."

And then he snaps. Wren, the coward behind the camera and my mild-mannered ex-friend of ten years, *snaps*.

Before I can move, he's grabbed my shirt and shoved me against a bookshelf. The librarian frantically dials security. Girls shriek and boys start to clamber around us in an encouraging, scattered circle.

"Come on." I smirk. "Punch me. Do it."

Wren's green eyes blaze, his muscles taut for someone who isn't in any sports clubs. I eye his fist, and just as I see it pull back, he drops me and snarls.

"No. That's exactly what you want. Someone's already ground you into pulp by the looks of it, and now you want me to do more damage because you're a self-absorbed, masochistic asshole."

"You don't know what you're talking about." I laugh.

Wren nods, fast and hard. "Yeah. I don't. I just know that before her, you were dead inside and out, walking around like a zombie. Anybody could see that. And then she came, and you lit up like a fucking candle. And we could all see that, too. Even Sophia."

"Shut your mouth," I growl.

"Is that why Isis ignores you now?" Wren laughs. "Because she realized Sophia means so much to you, and you were out here fooling around with her?"

"I never— No one ever—"

"You did!" Wren hisses. "You did, Jack! Isis's been through more shit than any girl should go through and *you got her hopes up*! And then she met Sophia and you fucking *crushed* them!"

"You have no—"

"How could she compete, you moron?" Wren's voice gets softer, but not any less deadly. "Just use that huge fucking brain of yours for two seconds; you've given up everything for Sophia. You send her letters. You've been with her since middle school. You had Tallie, and she knows about that, too—"

My mind goes white, a horrible keening noise

starting in the back of my skull.

"She *what*?"

"She knows. She saw it. She went out and found it herself because she's Isis and that's what she does."

Something in me plummets.

"What do we do?" I whisper, my own voice surprising me by how hoarse it is. Wren's eyes grow brighter.

"You tell her the truth. Before this emailer does, and gets her involved deeper."

"You forget she doesn't acknowledge my presence anymore."

"I'll take care of that," Wren says. "Just promise me you'll tell her when I give you the opening."

"You've become quite the little dictator," I sneer.

"I've had it"—he clenches his fist—"with running away. Every time I do, someone's gotten hurt. But not this time. I won't run this time. We have to own up to what we did. We can't keep living like this."

He turns and leaves before I can verbally cut him down to size.

The rest of the day passes in a panicked blur. I watch Isis from the parking lot, feeling every bit the stalker but bent on studying her face in a new light. She knows what I did that night. That's why she's ignoring me. She's too smart not to put two and two together.

And she knows about Tallie.

My biggest secrets are in her hands now. Just as I've known hers for months. I've had her number for months. But I've never texted or called. Until now. My thumbs fly over the keyboard.

We're even.

I see her stop and pull her phone out, Kayla chatting aimlessly at her. She looks up and scans the parking lot, and our eyes meet for the briefest moment. For one second, the warm amber engulfs me, and I let it.

And then I release it and turn away.

Tonight is the last night.

This woman is the last woman.

She's older—the trophy wife of a lawyer, confined to a house and left to treadmill and Martha Stewart her way into being ignored by her husband, who has enough hookers and blow to far outlast a wife. They have no children. She is miserable and in shape and anxious, and the hotel room is nicer than normal, and when she's satisfied and exhausted, she starts crying.

"Thank you."

I pull on my jeans and nod cordially.

"How— How old are you? I know I asked that in the lobby, but really, you can't be twenty-three."

I flash a smile. "Over eighteen. You're safe."

She covers her eyes with her arm. "Oh Jesus. I practically cradle-robbed."

I think of all the women who came before her, who were deceived by the fact that I'd looked twenty-one since I was fifteen. She has no idea. I grew up fast, and she has no idea.

"This is my last night," I say as I button my shirt. "Of this job."

"Oh? That's good. Someone as nice as you doesn't need to stay in this field. It ruins good people."

And yet you still use our services. I curl my lip where she can't see it. There are plenty of good people at the

Rose Club. She's ignorant, just another person who considers sex work base and below her. Hypocrite. She showers and dresses, and I pull out my laptop and sit on the bed, taking advantage of the free, harder-to-trace wifi.

"The room is yours for the night," she says when she comes out, now in a pressed pink suit and perfectly styled red hair.

"Thanks," I grunt. The woman—I forget her name—leans over my shoulder.

"Ooh, what are you doing? It looks fascinating—"

"I'm running seventy-two targeting executables for a free-roam IP trace."

She gives me a blank look. I sigh.

"I'm trying to find someone."

"Oh! Girlfriend? Ex-girlfriend?"

Tiresome. Women like her always jump straight to romance. I roll my eyes.

"An anonymous email sender."

She laughs nervously. "Right, well, I'll leave you to it. Thank you again."

"It was a pleasure doing business with you." I nod. It was no pleasure at all. The last time I felt honest pleasure—not sickly release—from sex was the last time Sophia and I slept together. And that was nearly a year and a half ago. Before the pain flares got so bad she couldn't walk sometimes.

Before her soul got darker.

I wait until the door clicks shut behind the woman to pull up the trace results. I parse them down twice—once using the email address name and once using Isis's email address. Which I also happen to have. She didn't exactly hide it when she put up posters around the school asking for people to contact her with dirty information bits about me.

She knows about Tallie.

I shake Wren's words out of my head and work quickly. I'm by no means gifted at computer hacking—if you could even call it that—but I know my way around a program or two. Ruby and C++ are far easier languages than any drivel humans speak. People much smarter have made sinfully simple IP trace programs for people like me to use and abuse.

After two hours of parsing, I'm left with 137,108 possible IP addresses the email could have originated from. I could go through them all one by one, but there has to be some connecting factor. And that factor is no doubt Isis. Why her? I check Maryland and Washington, DC. There are two IPs there, but none of them from the federal bureau where the investigators have the tape. The tape Wren gave to them behind my back.

I'm not mad about it. I was at first. But then I learned the tape was badly damaged, and video-imaging technology back then wasn't the best. The police discovered Joseph Hernandez's body days after the incident, but ruled it an accident. The other three men Avery hired were conveniently paid off by Avery's parents, who knew something terrible had happened because of their daughter but never quite knew what, preferring to make the problem go away instead of linger on it. Those three men never spoke a word of what happened.

That reminds me—Belina, the woman whose husband is gone because of me, because of that night in middle school, will be needing her check sometime soon. I'd give it to Wren, but this was the last lump sum I'd have for a while. Of course, I'd invested a small amount in a hedge fund so she wouldn't be completely cut off when I went to college, but she'd quickly run out in a year or two. Hopefully, by my second year, I'll have an internship that pays well. No, I have to have one. It's the only option.

By then, Sophia's surgery will be over.

And she will either be dead or alive.

I press my fingers to my temples and try to focus. The majority of the IP address near-matches are located in Florida. I narrow my eyes. Florida is where Isis used to live. That can't be a coincidence.

But there's one IP address that bucks the norm, way out in Dubai. The rest are in America. Whoever this person is, he clearly knows how to access information that isn't his. He's good. Rerouting his IP through proxy servers to Dubai would throw anyone looking for an American off the trail. Unless he kept his IP in Florida, purposefully, knowing something like Dubai would stick out like a sore thumb. Basically, every one of these dots is suspect.

I sigh and pick up the phone to order room service and a change of bedsheets. It's going to be a long night.

Between coffee and eggrolls at 1:00 a.m., I get a text. From someone in my phone I've labeled "Never." I ignore the palpitation in my lungs at the sight of that name on my phone.

What would you do if everyone hated you?

I pause and consider my answer carefully. Everyone has hated me at some point. Women, because I turn them down. Men, because I turn the women they love down.

I would ignore them.

I try not to stare at my phone, waiting. I have work to do. But I slog through it reluctantly until her answer comes, ten minutes later.

That's what I'm doing. But I don't like it much.

Then stop doing it. Do what you like, not what you don't.

But what I like hurts people. I get in the way. I mess things up.

Sometimes people need to be messed up. It reminds them life is short.

There's a long silence. Just as I start regretting what I said, my phone lights up again.

She would have been a very pretty baby.

My eyes sting. The cold numbness of the woman I'd slept with earlier and the single-minded focus on finding the mystery emailer melts. Just like that, with a single sentence.

Thank you.

chapter ten

3 YEARS, 29 WEEKS, 6 DAYS

THE DARK, DRY TREES loom like massive sticks of cinnamon. Lake Galonagah at midnight looks like a sheet of glazed black sugar. The moon resembles a perfectly white round of Brie cheese.

I am lost as hell. Also, hungry. But that's nothing new. I am hungry approximately 363 days of the year. The one day I am not hungry is Hitler's birthday. And also the day after Thanksgiving. Thankfully these two days are not on top of each other, otherwise we would've named it "ThankGodHitlerkickedthebucketbackinthefo rties-giving" and that assuredly does not carry the same ring capitalist America likes so much for their holidays.

In my vast and strenuous consideration of the importance of holiday cheer, I manage to get myself even more lost. Contrary to popular belief, flashlights don't contribute all that much to awesomeness other than being a cool thing you can use to put on a makeshift rave. I rave alone for two whole seconds and since it is horrible and quiet I give up immediately and sit down. On a skunk's home. The great brute is understandably displeased and pokes his butt out just in time for my ankle to get completely soaked by hellacious spray.

"Oh holy—" I gag and cover my nose with my hoodie sleeve. "You knave! Hear ye, hear ye, this stripey beast of yonder wood is an ASSHOLE! Oh Christ, this is never going to come out, is it?"

The skunk admires his work for a split second before taking off. I shake my fist at him impotently. I can't mess around with the local bitchy wildlife. I have to find Tallie again. The forest in the day is way different from the forest in the dead of night, and when I hear a crow caw hoarsely, I start to regret my decision to wander onto the apparent set of a horror movie. But I stick to the cliff side, careful to always know where the edge is, and follow it around.

Finally, the white cross peeks out of the trees, and I dash to it. The dirt's still soft where I dug it up and put it back, and I dig it up for the second time. Grave-robbing isn't my ideal job, but I'm getting pretty freakin' good at it. Not that anyone needs to know that. Ever.

"Hey, Tallie," I say in a low voice. "I'm back."

The little pink bundle is dirty. I brush the mud away and pick pine needles off it. Tallie looks up at me with her tiny, fragile eye sockets. They'd be blue, since Sophia has blue eyes and so does Jack. I bet they'd be stunning, like lapis lazuli or the ocean on a summer day. And she would've been beautiful—with Sophia's hair and Jack's height and face. I smile and open the bundle and grasp the bracelet with her name on it.

"Is it okay if I take this with me?"

Tallie lies there, and I nod and take it, the silver flashing in the moonlight. I close the bundle back up and rebury it for what I hope will be the last time.

"I'll come visit," I say. "Your mom can't, but I can."

"Hey! This way!"

Someone's voice cuts through the night, and the forest rustles with newcomers. Footsteps, heavy and deep, reverberate through the ground. Lots of them. Lots of potential serial killers ready to chop off my head with a fire ax. Or it's Avery's parents. Either way, I'm fucked. I duck behind a rotting log and hold my breath. I can barely hear their words; they're a good distance away but close enough.

"Find anything?"

"No, sir. Are you certain this is the place?"

"Of course. My source at the police department is reliable. Keep searching. We need that leverage."

Leverage? My ~~foolhardy~~ marvelous curiosity gets the better of me, and I peek over the log. A man in an impeccable tweed suit stands with two other men in dark, matching suits. The man in tweed is so tall and broad-shouldered. His hair is a shocking white, and he has an old-white-guy-in-charge aura about him that makes me instantly dislike him. Not Avery's dad—I've seen him at open house. And he's rich, but not rich like this guy—Rolex watch, Italian leather shoes, and anybody who runs around with two guys in suits taking orders from them is rich enough to have a lot of enemies.

"Sir, if you don't mind my asking—is Jack Hunter really worth all this trouble? He's just a high school student," one of the suits says.

Tweed Guy sighs. "Yes. He's in high school. But he's four months away from college. It's just a matter of time before the Harvard scouts sniff out his brilliance, and I intend to recruit it before them. I won't let Aramon take this one from me. He's too smart, too ruthless. He's perfect. Now, get back to searching. The body has to be here somewhere. Look for a badly dug grave, small enough for a baby."

Body. They're talking about Tallie. I can't let them find her. I have to get to her first—

I move my leg because it's cramping, and it's the last thing I ever do. Theoretically. In the alternate reality where they have guns. But they don't. All they have are ears. Which is still slightly problematic.

"What the hell was that?" One of the suits looks up.

"Deer?" the other offers.

"No deer here," Tweed Guy says. "Moriyama, check over there."

A suit starts moving toward me, his back hunched and his fists clenched. Saying I don't wanna get caught by these guys is like saying being on fire is a mild discomfort. My heart throbs in my ears. I scrabble for a rock and chuck it to the left of me. The suit freezes and then starts gravitating toward the noise, and I move in the opposite direction around the log, slowly.

And then something fuzzy scampers over my leg, and, unable to contain my fabulous voice, I yelp. Or sing an opera. I can't be sure, because all of a sudden there's chaos, and I'm running, and someone's running after me, and the tweed guy is shouting, and a hand grasps my hair and I stop dead in my tracks and duck, and he goes soaring over my head down the hill, a chunk of hair in his hand.

"Thanks for ruining the do, doo-doo!" I scream. My gloating's short-lived, as the other suit catches up with me and puts his arms around my torso, pinning my arms to my side.

"Fuck you! Unhand me at once!"

"Don't think so, princess." He struggles to contain my

flailing. I switch up my voice to make it sweet.

"Please let go of me. Your future children will thank you."

"What?"

I take his moment of confusion and dig my heel into his crotch. He lets out a strangled moan and collapses, and I tear away and slide down the hill. My car isn't far down the trail. Air burns like cold flame as it goes down. My legs want to collapse and never work again. It's not fear. Okay, it's a little bit of fear. But like, 15 percent—60 percent is elation at what a fantastic ninja I'd make, and the last 25 percent is my mind screaming at me to let Jack know about these fuckers. Platonically. We'd texted earlier and I said some dumb shit about Tallie, but he didn't seem mad. Hopefully my luck sticks long enough. Hopefully my stupid newfound butthead fear of him keeps its voice down.

Finally the trail gives way to the parking lot, and I scrabble into my lime-green Beetle. Don't let me down, baby. It coughs and sputters as it starts, and I glance wildly back at the trail entrance. "C'mon, c'mon, now is not the time to fart out on me! Pick another time! Like, you know, when I'm not running for my life from mysterious gangsters with thousand-dollar suits and tiny nuts!"

The engine roars to life, and I do the greatest U-turn in Ohio. Which is saying a lot, because everyone here drives like they just got their license and are celebrating with six beers.

I pull over only when there are ten miles between Lake Galonagah and me, and fourteen McDonald's to choose from. They'll never find me. Unless they saw my car in the parking lot and are looking for it now, which is likely. I consider a midnight paint job. Maybe I could just, I dunno, bathe it in the blood of my enemies really quick and turn it red? Avery doesn't have enough blood, though, and I feel kind of sorry for her, and the only other people I really hate are the people chasing me, and they are not an option because they are *chasing* me, and—

"Did you want ketchup with that?"

I look up, the cashier handing me my order of fries. Just fries. An entire bag of fries.

"Ketchup is the great illusion. Only when you put barbecue sauce on your fries will you know truth and freedom," I chastise.

He looks appropriately enlightened. I head to the nearest, least-greasy table and inhale my kill. When my writhing stomach is appeased slightly, I text Jack.

I need to talk to you. In person. Right now.

His response is nigh instantaneous.

What happened? Is something wrong?

I don't wanna talk about it over text. Where are you?

Come to the Hilton on First and Broadview. I'll meet you in the lobby.

I grab my bag of fries and head out. I shouldn't be scared. I shouldn't be feeling nervous. I told him off, but I'm the dragon, and he's just a prince, and I breathe fire and I meddled and hurt the people he loves, and him, but I'm still the dragon, and I can fly away if I need to. I'll be fine. I am always fine. I survived Nameless. I survived Leo. I can survive this. I'm fine. I'm *fine*.

I find a parking space four blocks away. The Hilton

is small here compared to the one in Columbus, but it's fancy—fresh orchids and a fountain in the marble-floor lobby. The concierge smiles at me. Jack is waiting, sitting in a leather chair with too-perfect posture and a lazy flannel shirt and jeans. He's on edge. The second I walk through the doors, he bolts up and walks over.

"What happened?" he demands. "Are you all right?"

"I won a million d-dollars," I say. I can't look at his face for some reason. Shame. Shame and guilt, probably.

"You're shaking like a leaf. Come on. It's warmer in the room."

"No— I—" I pull away. "I just, I just want to tell you something, and then I'll leave. I don't want to— I don't want to—"

"Be in the same room as me?" His voice is low.

"Just...don't be nice to me. I'd appreciate it if you'd just momentarily forget I've been pretending you don't exist for the last few weeks long enough for me to tell you this. Just like, develop amnesia. Wait, shit. Don't. I've been there. It's terrible. Also, there's a lot of Jell-O involved."

"Isis—"

"There're some people digging around in your past. Other than me, I mean. I saw them at the lake."

Jack's eyes narrow.

"I'm sorry, I went to see Tallie again, because Sophia—she asked me to, and—"

He starts walking away, to the elevator.

"Hey! Wait! I'm not done talking to you!"

"Get in."

"Uh, no? Have you not seen any Japanese horror movies? Getting in elevators after dark is asking for the voodoos."

"You either get in this elevator and come back with

me to the room, or you leave."

I puff my cheeks out and agonize for four whole seconds.

"Fine! But I'm leaving right after!"

"I'll kick you out promptly," he promises. Somehow, it makes me feel better, but in a weird twingy-gut way. The doors close and he hits the button for floor eleven. There are approximately thirty seconds of us standing together in a closed space. He smells like mint and sweat in the best way. I mash myself into the farthest corner and think about how much he and Sophia like each other, and it works, keeps my head above the swirling memories lurking just beneath the surface of that smell.

The elevator opens and he leads me to room 1106. It's not a big room, but it's beautiful, and the queen bed is perfectly made. I expected it to be messy and full of sex, whatever that looks like. Not that I'd know, and I really have to stop thinking about sex while I'm facing down my nemesis, who I incidentally do not like in any way, I am just concerned about various creepy suited men in my neighborhood because I am a Good Samaritan, that's all—

"Stop thinking out loud." Jack takes off his shoes.

"I am overwhelmed," I say. "By certain recent events."

"You were thinking out loud. About sex. Has it been a recent event for you? Congratulations. Who's the lucky man?"

"Sea slug," I correct, and sit on a chair. Warily.

"I was trying to be nice."

"Don't. You suck at it."

Jack's lips quirk in the shadow of a smirk, but it's gone quickly.

"Did you cut yourself?"

I follow his finger pointing to my jeans. A massive tear along the thighs shows an angry red cut, the blood staining the fabric around it.

"Aw, man! These were my favorite jeans! I saw my first concert in these!"

"I'd be a little more concerned about the gaping wound in your flesh," he snarls.

"Well, that's your deal. Personally, I'm okay with blood. Happens every month. Also you should stop rolling your eyes that much because I read somewhere that really hurts your eyesight and you wouldn't exactly be as aloof and enigmatic if you're running into walls all the time now, would you?"

"Get in the shower."

"You get in the shower!"

"You smell like skunk. And you're bleeding. You need a shower."

"There was quite a large skunk. But really this will only take two seconds and then I'll be out of your duck-butt hair, so listen up—"

He crosses his arms over his chest.

"Unfortunately, my powers of immense concentration are compromised by the stench of wildlife and the sight of blood. Take. A. Shower. There are towels, and a robe, and I'll have room service wash and dry your things."

"You're being nice, dude. It's sickening. The color does not match your eyes. Zero out of ten would not buy that nicey-nice makeup again."

"I'm being practical. I have work to do that's important, anyway. I'll have finished by the time you come out, and I'll be able to devote my full attention to your apparent chaotic experience involving my past.

Now go."

"Oh, I hate you so much."

"Good. I prefer it to the silence."

He turns to the laptop on the bed and types away, lost in it. The guilt solidifies, clamping down on my chest. I move mechanically into the bathroom and wince as I peel off my muddy jeans and jacket. I'll have bruises for millennia. Thanks, Small-Nuts. The knock on the door makes me jump into the ceiling.

"Give me your clothes," Jack says.

"Thanks, thanks a lot. Now I have a lightbulb for a head."

"What are you babbling about? Just give me your clothes."

"Go away! I'll drop them on the floor! I can't risk your cooties infecting me!"

"Fine. Just hurry up."

"You hurry up," I grumble wittily. The truth is my heart is pounding. Everything in me is pounding, bashing against my skeleton and skin to escape and slink away like a fleshy, independent meatbag. I'm naked. I'm naked and a boy is within ten feet of me and I am panicking, but I don't let it leak through anywhere, not in my voice, not in my choice of words, because panic is normal, panic is what I'll always do when I'm naked and a boy is around, and I'm shaking suddenly as I open the door when I'm sure he's gone, and I drop the clothes on the floor and lock it behind me.

My underwear is stupid. It's pink with a panda on it. He'll think I'm a kid. He'll think I'm immature.

Stupid little girl. You're ugly. Do you think anyone on this planet would want to go out with a fat, ugly girl like you?

I shake my head. Why the hell should I care what he thinks about me? He's Jack Hunter, the greatest douche who's ever douched. Or not douched, because he's a guy. Ugh, I really do gross myself out sometimes.

I decide to wash myself clean in the waters of Jesus and emerge as a less gross, more mature girl. The hot water is a luxurious relief and helps with the shaking in my hands, and the fancy shampoo and soap smell like milky almonds. The adrenaline of my escape winds down, and when I exit and tie the robe around myself, I feel like a new person. A person who's not-me. And that'd be nice right now. Any other girl wouldn't shake. Any other girl wouldn't be panicking that I have to walk out there in only a robe. Any other girl would be calm and collected and know exactly how to act and what to say in this "hotel with a boy" situation. There's another knock on the door.

"What is it?" I snap.

"I've got clothes for you. They aren't yours, but they're better than a robe. And there's a box of Band-Aids."

I deflate a little. He even thought of Band-Aids?

"Just drop them outside."

I peek out and pull the clothes in quickly. It's a soft skirt, long and shimmery and black, and a white dress shirt. The shirt is obviously Jack's; it smells like him. And there's a pink lip imprint on the collar. I roll my eyes. No wonder he has a lady's skirt on him, and he's holed up in the Hilton. I put a Band-Aid on my cut and walk out of the bathroom.

"Just got done working, huh?" I ask. He looks up from the laptop briefly, pauses as his eyes find the shirt and skirt, and nods.

"Yes. For the last time."

"You mean, your last appointment? Ever?"

He nods.

"That's great!" I clap my hands. "Jesus, that's— That's really great. Congratulations on not being a sex slave anymore!"

He curls his lip. "Oh, be quiet."

"How's it feel? To be free and all?"

"It's riotous fun," he deadpans.

"Ah! You're distracting me!" I point at him. "Listen, some guys were looking around the woods where Tallie is. I overheard them talking, and they were looking for a body. A baby's body."

Jack closes the laptop. "What did they look like?"

"Two guys in black suits, lackeys obviously, and one huge guy in a tweed suit. He had like, white hair and a really jerk-y presence, like he owned the place. Superrich watch. Superrich in general."

"Did he say who he was? Any hint at all?"

"No. Just that you were going off to Harvard and he wanted to recruit you for his company before all the other scouts. And he called you brilliant and ruthless and some other such nonsense, but I forget most of everything after that because I always tend to zone out when people start complimenting you. They were looking for Tallie's body."

Jack's eyes narrow. "What happened after you overheard them?"

"Well, they overheard *me.* Specifically, my feet on the noisy ground. So I ran. Threw one guy down a hill and kicked the other in the balls. Not a bad night, if I may say so myself."

"And you just…got in your car and came here right after?"

I hold up the bag of fries. "Refueled a bit."

He pinches the bridge of his nose. "Dammit."

"Something wrong? I mean, other than the corporate dudes after your neck? Protect your neck, by the way. That's a Wu-Tang song. Also it's a mildly good neck. I've stared at it many times while considering choking it."

He chuckles. I cross my arms over my chest.

"What's so funny?"

He shakes his head, a bit of his stupid hair glancing across his stupid eyes. His bruises are faint but still there, like inky imprints of a harder time.

"It's nice. Having the old you back."

"Oh."

"I missed it," he continues. His eyes are softer, but all at once they become hard. "Never mind. Forget I said that."

There's a silence, and suddenly I'm blindsided by a headache. It throbs, sending lances of white-hot electricity up and down my spine. It's the same pain I felt in Mernich's office. Shit, shit shit. Not now, brain, not now—

I've worn his shirt before. The smell is the same. He gave it to me to wear for bed, because my Halloween costume was too tight, and I was drunk, and the room had pictures of the sea in it and smelled like lavender, and I was happy; for a few seconds he was leaning over me and kissing me and I was happy. We sat on a bench once, our backs pressing against each other as the stars watched and a party raged on around us, and yet we were an island of quiet, of peace. I felt at peace with him. Reality and my memories blur together. I'm in the hotel room but I'm in the seashore room all at once. The shirt is soft. The smell of him is the same. Except the

Jack now is sitting at his computer, staring at me with concerned eyes, and the Jack of the past is leaning over me, his lips on every part of my neck, my collarbone, my mouth and the corner of my mouth, and—

"Isis, are you all right?" Hotel Jack asks. "Forget what I said. I'm trying to let the past go. Sometimes it's difficult, and I say ridiculous things. You're not a part of my life anymore, just like you wanted. I've blocked you off. I promise."

I like you.

Something painful and monstrous opens up in my chest, like a massive, shadowy Venus flytrap. The two me's reach for his hand at the same time.

"I remember," I whisper. His fingers are long and delicate, but I can feel the strength in them. "I remember the Halloween party. I said I liked you. You— You kissed me. We—"

Sophia's words reverberate in my head.

That's why he kissed you. That's why he even bothered getting to know you. Because you're exactly like me. Hopeless like me.

I drop his hand like it's burned me.

"I'm sorry. Shit. I'm sorry."

"For what?" Jack murmurs.

"I'm assuming things! My memories are back, but I know the full story now, too, so I'm sorry for even bringing it up!"

"Your memories are back?" His voice is strangled, but he clears it. "That's— That's good. You don't have to be sorry for—"

"I just mean that wasn't— Obviously that night wasn't a real, uh, kiss thing. I mean, we were both pretty drunk! You didn't really mean it; you were just being weirdly nice like you sometimes are once in a blue-ass moon, and I was super drunk, so when I said I liked you I just meant as a nemesis, you know? As a friend I could fight with verbally and stuff! Yeah. I really did like you. As a nemesis. Man, fighting you was fun!"

I laugh, but it sounds hollow even to my own ears.

"And, you know. I remind you of Sophia. We are kind of similar, deep down, so it makes sense you'd get confused and kiss me! Totally cool. Totally understandable. Man, I'm just sorry I drunkenly forced myself on you like that, and then did a total one-eighty and got scared like a little bitch. Like, wow, nobody deserves that ever, you feel me? I'm really sorry you had to go through that."

I've wanted to hold her for months. It's a need I've tamped down, a carefully controlled fire kept locked in the center of an iceberg. And she's unknowingly tested me, over and over; she's prodded and poked and sometimes taken a chain saw to the ice, but she's never gotten through because I am Jack Hunter, and I am in control of myself at all times.

Except that one time, in the seashore room. The time she thinks was false. The time she is heaping piles of guilt on herself for. Guilt that's coming from her past and from Will Cavanaugh. If I don't stop this now, she'll hurt herself with it. The cycle of Will's damage will only dig its thorns deeper into her. If she can't do it, it has to be stopped now, by someone. By me.

"I don't want to scare you," I say finally. She looks up,

warm cinnamon eyes surprised.

"What?"

"And I don't want to make you uncomfortable—"

"Um—"

"—but you are nothing like Sophia. You are Isis Blake—stubborn and ridiculous and kind and strong. You are exactly you. And that's why I kissed you that night, because I wanted to kiss Isis Blake. And I did. It was uncalled for. You had every right to stop and every right to pull away. You were afraid, and I exacerbated that fear by trying to kiss you, and it's my fault. Not yours."

Her face goes blank with shock, and she's silent for once in her life.

"Yes, we were drunk," I continue. "You were, more specifically, and I was a little. So I'm the one who should've known better, and I apologize. I went too far, too fast. I was happy." I chuckle darkly. "For once in my life, I was happy. It's no excuse, but I hope it helps you understand my actions that night."

Her shell-shocked expression doesn't change.

"I'm sorry." I smile. "It won't happen again."

She doesn't say anything. I have to break the tension. I get up and stretch, cracking my neck and wrists.

"You should go. It's getting late, and I'm sure you're tired. You need to get some rest. Thank you for telling me about the men. I'll look into them—"

Something crashes into me from behind, and it takes me a second to realize it's her, wrapping her arms around my stomach and pulling my spine to rest against her chest. She buries her face in my back.

"I want it," she whispers. "I...I want it to h-happen again."

The web of anxiety in me snaps, thread by thread, and every muscle in my body relaxes. It is relief, pure and bright, coursing through me. I'm not the only one who wants it. *I am not the only one*, and my skin warms and my breathing comes easier as that knowledge sinks in with each passing second of silence. What she said that night in the seashore room wasn't just a drunk babble. She likes me. And I soak in that realization for as long as I can, before she rubs her face against my shirt like an animal, something wild and used to marking others with its scent.

"I want to show you something," she says.

"All right." I keep my voice carefully even and low.

She puts her arms out on either side of me and pulls up the shirt on her right arm. She's always, *always* kept that arm covered. She's never worn short-sleeved T-shirts, and even when I saw her in that blouse, she kept the sleeve carefully covering it and her arm faced downward. It's almost a reflex with her, to keep the arm out of sight.

My breath catches.

There, on the delicate underside of her wrist, are the marks. Round, puckered white scars. Dozens of them. They molt her skin, the pockmarks overlapping like a dappled pond. Cigarette burns.

"How—" I stop myself, even though I know the answer already. "I'm sorry. It's not my place to ask."

Her arms tremble as she speaks. "Nameless."

I close my eyes. Hearing the confirmation from her is more infuriating, more heartbreaking than any conclusion I reached on my own.

"It's ugly, I know." She laughs shakily. "Sorry, I didn't mean to gross you out."

I turn and lace my arms around her, careful not to put too much pressure or squeeze tight to the point she'd feel trapped. Her mouth against my chest makes me shiver, but I suppress it at the last second. I can see her scar on the top of her still-wet head. She smells like almonds and forest pine.

"There is nothing about it that's ugly," I say. "Can I?"

She hesitates, then nods. I reach around and bring up her wrist, gently running my fingers over the marks. The raised ridges are rough, but in other parts, silky. I trace around each circle with my thumb.

"It looks like a galaxy," I say. "Full of stars and supernovas and conductive cryogeysers and a lot of wonderful science things I could go on to list that would probably bore the hell out of you."

She laughs, the sound vibrating in my ribs.

"I have another one." She gestures to her head. "It's not as ugly, but it's a lot bigger. Just call me Scarface. Head. Cranium. ScarCranium is definitely a Swedish death-metal band."

I lean in and kiss the top of her head, the scar smooth under my lips.

"We'll have to listen to them someday," I say. She makes a sound halfway between a squeak and a sigh. "Something wrong?"

"N-No. Just…having someone—kiss—um— Having someone…doing that—um—"

"You don't like it?"

"No! I-I do. It's really—um, just really, it's nice. It feels nice. Um." She buries her face in my shirt like she's trying to disappear, but I can see the red flush creeping up her forehead.

I feel like I'm melting. My insides are warm, and I'm all weirdly relaxed. And I don't ever want it to stop.

I feel safe.

For the first time in a long time, I feel really, really safe. Like nothing can get to me. Like, for once, Nameless can't reach in his fingers and get to me through my memories.

"I was scared," I murmur. "When I was running from those guys. And I'm scared they saw my car."

"You can stay here, if you want," Jack offers. "I can take the couch."

"That'd be rad."

"All right. I've got work to finish, but feel free to take the bed." He grabs his laptop and sits on the couch. I'm almost sorry for the loss of his warmth, but then I remember he's a nerd. I spot the empty plate of what looks like soy sauce, and my stomach makes a noise like a dying cow.

Jack raises an eyebrow, smirking. "Hungry?"

"Shut up." I flush. "I've got my fries."

"Those are embalming you from the inside out," he says and picks up the phone. "Let's get something that doesn't survive radioactive deterioration, shall we?"

I dive under the blankets and try not to think about the fact that Jack had sex with some old lady in them. He got the sheets changed, obviously, but it's still a used bed. Then again, it's a hotel! A lot of people have probably had sex in this bed! And it's so fluffy I might as well be lying on my own flabby belly.

"Hello, yes, this is for room 1106. I'd like the salmon

Parmesan, with the spinach salad, and an order of the crème brûlée. Yes. Yes, thank you."

When he hangs up, I raise an eyebrow.

"Yeah? Suddenly rolling in cash?"

"My final client is paying for the room. We could order a dozen lobsters and she'd have to pay it."

"Ah, the perks of sex work." I flop into the pillows. He doesn't answer, absorbed in his laptop. "Hey, who was that tweed guy, anyway?"

Jack shrugs. "Going by your description, I think I've met him."

"Oh yeah? At a gathering for the rich and snooty?"

"At a bar. Where he beat the shit out of me."

"That's where you got the beaten-hamburger look?"

Jack nods. "He's good. Trained, probably. Karate, if I had to guess by his forms and strikes."

"And you're just trained in bat, right? Not the billionaire playboy vigilante kind, but the baseball kind."

"I took tae kwon do until high school. He's much better than me."

"Someone sent me a picture," I say. "Of your hand on a baseball bat, and a body—"

"I know. Wren told me about it. More accurately, he screamed it at me. In the library."

"Wren? Screaming? C'mon, lying isn't funny. Except when it is."

"He was very worked up. Agitated. He's a lot of things, and we have a complicated history, but he's surprisingly loyal to the people he considers friends. Not that it mattered when he turned tail and ran that night, but still. It's the thought now that counts. Reform and second chances and all that drivel."

"You killed someone," I say. There's no fear behind

it now. I've shown him my scars, and he didn't flinch. So if he says yes, I won't flinch, either. His icy eyes flicker up. There's a long, languid silence in which I'm sure he can hear my thunderous, anticipating heartbeat from ten feet away.

"I don't know if I did," he says finally.

"What do you mean?"

"It was dark. The police—the police told us he walked off the cliff because he didn't see it. But he couldn't see it because I gave him a black eye."

"He still had one good eye—"

"That's no excuse," Jack says sharply. "I may as well have killed him myself."

He's telling what he thinks is the truth—the guilt in his eyes is obvious. If it were a lie, they'd be clear.

"That's not true."

Jack glares at me. "As far as you know, it is. You're not concerned? I killed someone. I'm a murderer, Isis."

"You were defending Sophia. Just like you defended my mom and me from Leo. That's what you do. You protect people."

He opens his mouth, then closes it and stares at the floor.

"Look," I start. "I've done some things I'm not proud of. I know what it feels like to want to kill someone. I really do. I was going to try to kill Leo, when my mom first told me about what happened with her and him. I had it all planned out—I'd drug him with chloroform, and if that didn't kill him, I'd slice his dick off with a butcher knife, and then his fingers, and then his throat. I dreamed about it sometimes. I wanted it more than anything. I wanted to make him pay for what he did to her."

Jack looks up at me. I shrug.

"So yeah. I know what it's like."

There's something like gratitude that flickers behind his eyes.

"So the guy in the tweed has an inside man on the police force," I say. "How would the police know about Tallie?"

"They don't," Jack says. "But they saw Sophia. The EMTs or the doctors probably told him she…she lost Tallie. And the cops saw the blood in the forest when they were investigating the crime scene. It'd be simple for them to put two and two together, and for Tweed Incorporated to find that out. But the cops never actually found Tallie. Avery saw to that. She buried her somewhere no one else would find, if they didn't know the area like the back of their hand the way she did."

"So why is Tweed looking for Tallie, then?"

"I don't know his motives," Jack says. "Information on me, maybe? The more he knows about me, the more ammo he has to try to convince me to join him."

"Because you're the perfect candidate for his weird corporation?"

"Because I am perfect, period." He smirks. I throw the extra pillow and it graciously arcs over his laptop and hits him smack in the face.

"Thanks, physics!" I thumbs-up no one. Jack belligerently coughs out a feather.

"What are we going to do?" I ask. "We can't let them find Tallie. I don't want them to, and I'm sure Sophia doesn't want them to."

Jack's eyes get sharp, then soft all at once. "I'll figure something out."

He turns to his keyboard and types rapidly.

"Wow, you're super dedicated to that computery thing over there. Wow. I can't stop saying wow."

"Stop saying wow."

"What are you wowing? I mean, doing?"

"Tracing the email address that sent you that picture."

"Oh. Then what? What happens after you find him?"

"Then I blow him up," Jack growls.

I raise an eyebrow.

"Crash his hard drive," he corrects.

"Slightly more legal," I agree. "Alas, not as fun."

The food comes, and the maid wheels it in and leaves after Jack gives her a tip, and I inhale every little thing on the tray in less than five minutes.

"Jesus, woman, you're going to choke."

"Worth it!" I chirp, and slurp crème brûlée. I start coughing massively.

"Choke quietly." He turns back to the laptop and mutters to himself. "There. Finally. This guy is ridiculously good. But if I run the byte scan, I can— "

He goes still, like a deer hearing a gun cock.

"I'm…dying…" I remind him from the general vicinity of the floor.

"The IP traces back to Good Falls, Florida. Your hometown," he says. "Someone from your hometown sent you this. It has to be someone you know. Who do you know from back then who's good at computers?"

My heart stutters, and I stop pretending to die and start actually dying.

"Isis? What's wrong?"

I stare up at the hotel ceiling, debating how many steps it'd take for me to get to the toilet. I don't wanna throw up on Jack again, no matter how marvelous the last time was. Jack's face looms over my vision.

"Isis? You're pale—"

"Him," I say softly. "He won the state computer programming competition for the middle school division every year."

"Who?"

I thought he'd left me alone. I never thought the email could be him. An almost-year of silence convinced me I was free.

I grit my teeth and put my hands over my eyes, like it'll block out the darkness. It can't be, but it is. I had nightmares about this exact thing, about him finding me. I'd spent so much time away from him, I was lulled into a false sense of security, security built up by my new friends, and with Jack's help. But I was stupid. Naive. I haven't gotten smarter at all. Deep down, past all my newfound strength and courage, I knew the safety wouldn't last long. It never does. Nameless is a scar in my life that will never go away. The darkness he's planted in me hovers in every corner of my soul, waiting for an opening, a weakness to force its way in. And no matter how hard my armor, no matter how loyal my friends and how gentle Jack is, there's always a weakness in me. Maybe their kindness has made a weakness in me.

The darkness always finds a way in, just like it has now.

"Nameless."

chapter eleven

3 YEARS, 30 WEEKS, 0 DAYS

JACK TRIES TO CONVINCE me he'll do everything he can to block Nameless from contacting me again via email. But I know it won't work. Jack's okay at the whole computer tracking thing, but Nameless is much, much better. He always has been. He used to spend entire weekends working away at strands of hugely difficult codes. Sometimes he'd shrug off our dates at his house to practice. He was good because he practiced, and all that practice ended in him becoming talented. The computer science teacher at our school wouldn't shut up about him.

If Nameless can get access to a video in a federal vault, then he can get to me. If he knows about the video, he knows about Jack, probably through Wren. Not that Wren would ever tell him purposely. Maybe he let it slip. Or maybe Nameless just tracked me all the way here and somehow found out about Jack through the school's computers. People talked about our war on the beat-up old Macs in the computer lab, I'm sure. Or maybe—

My stomach sinks, and the wonderful crème brûlée taste goes sour in my mouth.

Maybe Nameless had my email hacked all along, and he read my emails to Kayla about Jack.

"Wipe your old hard drive, just in case," Jack says. "Get a new email address and change the passwords on everything."

"He'll just break in again."

"He won't," Jack says sternly. "He *won't.* I won't let that happen."

"He's been watching me this whole time." I laugh. "I was so stupid. I thought I got away from him for good."

"You will. You can. You just can't give up. Work with me, okay? We'll fix this together."

"It's no good." I roll over. "He's gonna torment me for my entire life. He's always gonna be here, just like this stupid—this stupid fucking scar—"

I wrap it in the sheet so I don't have to look at it. Jack walks over and unwraps it, pulling it to his lips.

"Listen to me, Isis. He won't be with you forever. Someday, you'll force him to leave, and he will, and you'll be happier for it. The memories won't go away, but they'll become less clear as you make more."

I flinch. His eyes don't leave mine.

"I want to help you make more, if that's all right with you."

"What about…Sophia?"

"She'll always be a part of my life, and I'll always support her. But I know now who I want. The truth is here, right now, staring me in the face and sitting on a hotel bed, wearing my shirt and looking ridiculously cute."

My face heats like a brushfire. Jack stands.

"Let's get some sleep. We can worry uselessly tomorrow. Have you told your mom where you are?"

"Shit," I hiss. "I gotta call her. It might be one of those nights."

"*Those* nights?"

"She relapses sometimes. The memories come back to haunt her and she freaks out and can't sleep unless I'm there."

"Jesus, Isis, how long has this been going on?"

"Ever since we moved here to get away from Leo," I say. "It's not a big deal."

"It's a huge deal," he insists. "Your mom can't sleep without you sometimes? That's a huge burden on you."

"It's not!" I protest. "Look, I just do what I can to help her, okay? She's my mom. I love her. She needs me."

"You need *yourself*. You can't be there for her forever."

His words ring true, reminiscent of what Aunt Beth said to me. But then I remember Mom's tears at the trial.

"I can try," I snipe.

"Isis, this isn't healthy. She needs to get help—"

"She's getting help. But it's not enough."

Jack closes his mouth, a frown forming on his lips. In the sudden quiet, I dial Mom. She sounds good. She ordered Chinese takeout for us, but when I tell her I'm spending the night at a friend's, the forced happy in her voice throws me off.

"Oh! That's great. Which friend?"

"Kayla," I lie. "I can give you her phone number."

"Sure, that'd be great. Should I call her parents and say hello?"

"Her parents are…out of town."

Mom clucks her tongue. "Are you two drinking?"

"It's just one bottle of wine," I agree. "I'm sorry—"

"No, no, honey." Mom laughs. "It's okay. You don't

have to lie to make me feel better. You deserve to relax. God knows you deserve to have fun with your friends after everything I've put you through. Just promise me you won't drive anywhere or get in a car driven by someone drunk, and that you'll be home by noon tomorrow."

"I promise." My heart lifts. "I swear to you, I'll be safe."

"I know you will, sweetie. You're the best daughter a mom could ask for."

"You, too. Not that you're a daughter. Even though you are. I'm sure Grandma thought you were the best daughter ever, bless her wrinkly, dementia-addled soul."

Mom chuckles. "Sleep well, you."

We hang up. Jack is watching me with an appraising gaze.

"What?" I ask defensively. "Why are you looking at me like that?"

"What are you going to do for college?" he asks. "Don't tell me you plan to stay here."

"You were planning to stay here for Sophia," I retort. "But all of a sudden you're going to Harvard?"

"Sophia asked me to go," he says tiredly. "I'm coming back to visit her every month. Besides, a Harvard degree will get me a much better job—one with enough money to cover her costs for a long time."

"You talk about my relationship with my mom not being healthy, but you and Sophia are no different."

His handsome face twists, but after a moment it lightens.

"I despise your logic," he says. "But sometimes it's right. I'm a hypocrite."

"And a fathead," I say. "But I forgive you."

His exhale is laced with a laugh. "Let's get some rest."

He turns out the light and takes a spare blanket from the closet, draping it over the couch and lying on it. I snuggle under the blankets and try not to feel guilty. I can't fall asleep at all. It's a repeat of what happened at Avery's house, but this time, I'm not drunk, and I'm not as scared. It's just the darkness gnawing away at me. Nameless feels like he's everywhere. And I'd give anything, do anything, to chase him away and feel safe again.

"It's cold," I say. I hear Jack roll over.

"Do you want another blanket?"

"No, um." I swallow. This is the hardest thing I've ever done, second only to my first-grade spelling bee in which I spelled "fabulous" wrong, and third to when I had my first period ever and bled through my pants and onto the metal foldout chair during band class and had to attach the chair to my bottom as I walked sideways to the bathroom so no one would see the damage. I gained a whole new respect for crabs and their walking style. Shit's straight difficult.

"Can you—" I try to raise my voice, but it cracks. "Can you—please— I'm usually not this bad at talking." I laugh. "This is so stupid. I'm sorry. Never mind."

I roll over and pull the blankets over my head so he won't hear me whispering curses at myself. But then I feel a weight on the other side of the bed, and my lungs rapidly decide they want to burst.

Jack's voice is close. "This?"

I pull the blankets off my head and nod, too furiously. Too eagerly. Jack chuckles, low and soft. With my eyes adjusted to the dimness, I see him roll and face away from me, pulling the blanket over him. His legs are just a few feet to the left, his back even closer. I'm shaking, but I pray to whatever god is listening that he can't feel that through the bed. I don't want him to get the wrong idea—that I'm afraid—and then leave. I *am* afraid—a deep-down, rock-solid fear burned into me by Nameless—but I'm not scared. I'm not shallowly breathing or panicky or jumping at every little thing. And that makes all the difference. It's not chaotic fear; it's orderly, and I know the causes for it. I can control it.

I reach out, slowly, and put my hand on his back. I feel his muscles tense under my fingers. When he doesn't say anything, or move, I lean in and press my weight against him. He's warm, warmer than a blanket. There's a long pause as our breathing moves in and out of each other's rhythm. And then finally, he speaks.

"You're the most confusing girl I've ever met."

"Yeah." I smile. "Not sorry."

"Good."

The sun barges in and sits its butt on my eyes and the world is ending and I'm blind and everything is over. And then I roll over and see Jack's face on the pillow and then everything is really over. Permanently. Because my universe explodes.

I make small screeching noises under my breath as I try to remember how I got here, in the hotel room. It all floods back at once and I'm more than a little mad at myself for giving in and staying here without a fight. Jack cracks open one sleepy blue eye. He runs his fingers through my hair idly as he groans.

"Who gave you permission to be conscious before six, and how can I end them?"

"Why are you touching me?" I whisper. "Is it really that fun? Because most people say it feels squishy and gross."

He laughs and puts his hands over his eyes, stretching like a freshly woken cat who likes to arch its back.

"What do you want for breakfast? I can run out and get something, or we can call in. Checkout isn't until one."

"There was a café I saw on my way in last night. Looked really swanky and smelled permanently like bacon. You should go there. While I sneak out the window."

"I think we should go together."

"Hear me out on this one: What if we don't stay near each other for extended periods of time?"

He rolls over and leans on his elbows, playing with a strand of my purple hair.

"That's an incredibly contradictory statement considering what you did last night."

"I touched your back! Stop making it sound sexual!" I gasp. "Did I just say sexual? Out loud? Without stuttering? Praise Jesus. Wait, does Jesus like people having sex? I keep forgetting who likes what."

"I like you," Jack murmurs. I elegantly fall off the bed. There's a silence, and then I peek my head over the mattress and raise my hand.

"Uh, hello? Me here. I would preferably not like to be given a heart attack before I reach legal drinking age."

"Did that really surprise you that badly?" Jack smirks. He pauses. "I like you."

"Ah!" I put my arms up to shield myself.

"I like you."

"Stop!"

"Oh, this will be fun."

"I will kill you slowly," I retort, but he's already up and pulling on his pants. I set my entire facial region on fire involuntarily when I realize he slept in boxers. Next to me. And in the split second before he pulled his pants on there was a distinct bulge, and I am dying, this is what dying is, you burn up and then the ashes blow away and someone gets them in their eye and they walk around with a red eye all day and their coworkers think it's pinkeye when really it's just your dead carbon—

"Isis. Shhh."

"You shhhh!" I hiss. "I'm having a seventeenth-life crisis here upon seeing a man's junk for the first time."

He pulls on his jacket and grabs his wallet off the nightstand.

"I'll wait for you downstairs."

He shuts the door, and I'm alone. Alone but with him waiting for me downstairs. In a fancy hotel. For breakfast at a café. I pinch my feet and yelp when I don't wake up. There aren't any hidden cameras I can see, but then again if I could see them they wouldn't be very good hidden cameras now would they? I don't think this is a setup, at least. It's an impossible little dream probably, cooked up by my waking subconscious, but for now I'll let it slide. For now I'll go along with it. I slept in the same bed as Jack Hunter, my nemesis, my rival, and now apparently something a little more than my friend.

And I felt safe.

Over breakfast at the café, Jack and I talk logistics. He'll keep an eye on Nameless's IP, and I'll do a thorough cleansing of my computer. When we're standing in the parking lot with bellies full of bacon and toast, we linger. I shuffle my feet. I have no idea what to do. How is a girl supposed to say good-bye to a boy she slept with but didn't really sleep with? Is there a handbook for this shit? Should I write one real quick and mail it to my past self? Does publishing even work that fast?

Before I can agonize any longer, Jack reaches his hand out and pats my head.

"You'll be okay driving home?"

"Duh." I feel miffed that he'd pat me like a child, but also weird and glowy on the inside in places I don't even wanna think about. "I'm like a NASCAR driver. Minus the millions of dollars."

"Shame, really. Imagine how many more people you could annoy if you were a millionaire."

"At least ten whole people. And their grandmas."

"Ah yes, the time-honored Blake tradition of annoying grandmas."

"All it takes is like, a dirty pan and a cat without a furry pink sweater on it."

"Say hi to your mother for me."

"You, too. Um. If she still remembers me. Actually, don't, it's fine, I didn't exactly make the best impression when I went over there—"

"She remembers," Jack insists. "She thinks you're sweet."

"Hah. Must've met my doppelgänger. The one who doesn't exist anywhere ever."

Jack smiles. It's not a bright smile, like the one I'd seen him give Sophia in the hospital once. But it's warm and without ice, and that's all I can ask for, really.

"You have my number," he says.

"Yup. I'll text if there're issues. Tissues. Not tissues, tissues are disgusting and so are issues."

He starts to walk away. I want to say a thousand dumb things at once—*thank you*, and *I'm sorry you chose a shithead like me*, and *you deserve better*, and *drive safe*, and *be safe*, and *sleep well* and *eat well*, but all the words and feelings come up in a jumbled mess and dissipate into the air as I open my mouth to say nothing at all and close it again.

"YOU WHAT?"

I hold the phone away from my ear to preserve my future hearing for eighty years to come.

"Slept. In the uh, same bed," I whisper.

"YOU HAD SEX WITH JACK HUNTER?"

"Jesus, Kayla, no, stop shouting, it's indecent."

"I'LL TELL YOU WHAT'S INDECENT—SLEEPING WITH JACK HUNTER!"

"We didn't sleep together, dork! Do I look stupid enough to ever touch that bag of germs?"

Kayla finally takes a breath. "That's true. You can't even say 'dick' without vomiting in your mouth a little. And sometimes on desks. And small children."

"That was one time, and that kid totally walked *into* the flight path of *my* vomit. It's not my fault if he had no grasp of liquid physics."

"But you totally slept in the same bed and, like, hello, isn't that at least second base? Second and a half base?"

"Uh, like a second moon base?"

"Ugh, no! Never mind, I'm not gonna explain really

outdated sex terms to you."

"For the last time! There was no sect…ional things going on, okay? I would never do that with your ex. Ever."

"I would. With your ex. If you had one. If he was smoking hot. If you gave me your sure-as-hell approval, obviously. Which I totally give you, by the way, because, duh—it's Jack Hunter! Someone in this school has to bed him before he gets to Hollywood or model-land or whatever and contracts a bunch of icky diseases!"

"You are insane."

"Omigod! Did I tell you?"

"That you're insane? Already figured it out, thanks."

"No, dummy! Wren asked me to prom!"

I feel my mouth drop open. "The one with glasses?"

"Uh, duh, what other Wren do you know?"

"Was he…was he drooling or shuffling or moaning about brains?"

"Ew, no! He was in his right mind and I'm like, ninety-nine percent sure he wasn't a zombie, okay? Is it so weird that someone would want to take me to prom?"

"No, it's just— Wren isn't exactly bold?"

"I know!" she squeals. "Which is like, the biggest compliment, if he got all gung ho to ask me and stuff, right?"

"Yeah. Are you gonna say yes?"

"I already did!"

"What happened to him being a nerd king?"

"He's a slightly…cooler nerd king now? I mean, I just— We've had woodshop together and it's been really fun, we made this birdhouse and it came out really cute, and I cut my finger on the band saw a little, and he got really concerned and took me to the nurse's and—"

"You like him."

Kayla chokes on nothing. "I-I do not! Like him! I just happen to want to go to senior prom! And he's cute enough! And he's nice!"

"He doesn't drive."

"That's fine! I do! And anyway I'm totally gonna ask Daddy for a limo, and you and Jack are definitely invited."

"Uh, thanks? But me and Jack aren't a thing."

"You slept in the same bed."

"Yes?"

"You're a thing," she asserts. "I'll see you on Monday!"

I sigh and hang up. Having friends is great. Having friends determine your romantic status is not so great. Yeah, Jack and I slept in the same bed. And he touched my hair. And smiled a lot. And he was warm, and—

I run into the bathroom and grace my head with a cold shower. Mom's surprised to see my wet hair when I drive up to her shrink's.

"Did…did something happen?"

"Jesus blessed me with his holy water."

"Oh?"

"Took a shower. How was your session?"

She laughs. "It was…it was all right. We talked about you, mostly, and Stanford."

"Oh yeah?" My voice pitches up. "Cool."

"It would be so wonderful for you, honey. And with your dad willing to help with the costs—you could really do it. You'd meet so many new people and learn so many amazing things."

"Yeah. And they've got these awesome foreign exchange programs." I pull onto the highway. "I've been looking at this one in Belgium; it's like, four months, so one semester, but you live with a host family right in the city and there's all this cultural exchange stuff in your program, like going out to the countryside and visiting France for a week, and it sounds so—"

I stop when I see Mom raise her hand to her face out of the corner of my eye.

"Mom? Are you okay?"

"I'm sorry." She sniffs, laughing. "I'm fine. Really, I'm okay."

"Are you crying?"

"I'm fine, sweetie! I-I'm—"

Her crying gets louder. She's shaking, her shoulders quivering and her hands quaking as she desperately tries to hide her face from me.

"Mom!" I pull over onto the shoulder and put the car in park, lacing my arm around her. "Mom, are you okay? What's wrong? Tell me, please."

"N-No," she whimpers. "I'm being selfish. I'm sorry. Please, just drive us home."

"No! Not until you tell me what's making you cry like this!"

She sobs into my shoulder, every echo of her pain tearing a hole in my heart. I shouldn't have gotten so excited about Stanford. It probably hurts her just to hear me talk about going away so far.

"I don't want you to go," she cries. "Please, stay here. I need you here."

I wince and shut my eyes. I pull her closer to me, her trench coat enveloping both of us.

"Hey, it's okay," I say softly. "Mom, it's okay. Don't worry. I'm not going anywhere. I promise."

"No! I want you to go." She looks up, eyes panicked

and red. "But I don't want you to go. I know you have to. You have to grow and learn and fly on your own. But I don't know what I'll do without you. I'm sorry. Please, go. Please do whatever you want. Just…just promise me you'll come back and visit sometimes, all right?"

"Mom, I'm not going—"

"You are!" Her expression suddenly turns furious. "You are, don't listen to me! Don't hold yourself back for me. I want you to go to Stanford."

"But I don't want to."

"Yes you do, Isis. I know you do. And you're giving it up for me, and I can't have that. You need people as smart as you, sweetie. You need challenges, and you'll get that at Stanford. God, my little girl, going to Stanford. I'm so proud. So, so proud."

She composes herself, and I start driving again, and she smiles and talks about mundane stuff like grocery shopping and what the neighbors said about her yard and how work was, but I know she isn't done with the sorrow, because when we get home, she locks herself in her room and turns on her music. And she only does that when she doesn't want me to hear her crying.

My chest burns as I look over the Stanford brochures again. They're a wonderful, impossible dream.

I can't leave her. There's no way I can leave Mom here with a good conscience. I'd be too far to help if anything happened again—and she'd be too lonely. She wouldn't get better if I was gone; she'd only get worse. I have to be close. Very close. I have to stay with her until she's strong enough to stand on her own two feet again, and going to Stanford won't make that happen.

My path is clear.

My path has always been clear.

I put the brochures in my desk drawer and cover them with my old sketchbooks from elementary school. Things I don't touch. Things I won't touch, ever again.

My email beeps, shakes me out of my misery, and then piles more on. The email's from the same address that sent me the picture. Nameless.

Hi, Isis!

How've you been? You got my pic, right? That Jack guy seems really cool. Have you guys fucked yet?

Aw, who am I kidding? You don't gotta tell me. I'll see you again someday. :)

I fight the urge to puke and lose, fantastically.

The darkness wells up in the bathroom. It bleeds out of my eyes and my mouth that cries with no sound. I lock the door and huddle on the floor, hugging my knees.

He'll see me soon.

I'm not safe. I've never been safe.

I'll never be safe. I'll never be free. Jack's wrong. He can't do anything. He can't help. Nameless lives inside me and always will. The darkness will always be here.

There is a nest inside me, and all it takes is a few words from the boy who raped me to bring the monsters roaring out of it.

chapter twelve

NAOMI ISN'T PLEASED with the fact that I'm leaving town. She's never been pleased when I leave, ever, because Sophia gets sad, and that probably makes her job harder. She escorts me to Sophia's room grumpily.

"Something the matter, Naomi?" I inquire.

Naomi grunts eloquently. "Don't try to schmooze me, Jack."

"I'm just wondering why your face is more lovely than usual. New eye cream?"

"Are you really going to Harvard?" she snaps. "Do you know how far away that is?"

"In another state, I believe."

"What about Sophia, hmm? What is she going to do when you're gone?"

Naomi's words dig a needle straight through my heart. She seems to see that, and sighs and rubs her forehead.

"I'm sorry. I— She's been here so long, I care about her so much, and with the surgery coming up I'm just so worried. Dr. Fenwall says her likelihood of pulling through—"

"She'll be fine," I say. "She's tough, even though she doesn't look it. She'll live. She'll be able to live her own life when it's over."

Naomi nods. She pushes open the door to Sophia's room and gasps. It's empty. I walk over to the windowsill, where every single one of the vases I'd bought her are smashed. The floor's littered with pottery, sharp and gleaming and just begging for someone to step in it and shed blood.

"Where is she?" Naomi moans. "I told her you were coming and to stay in her room so I could bring you here. Oh no, oh, no no no—"

"We'll split up. Check her usual spots," I say. "I'll take the top floors, you check the bottom. And ask Dr. Fenwall if he's seen her."

Naomi nods, and we run out the door. I take the steps two at a time and weave around wheelchairs and interns. She's not in the cafeteria, and the servers say they haven't seen her all day. The recreation room is nearly empty, and when I ask a kindly old woman if she's seen her, she shakes her head. Nurses who work with Naomi say they haven't seen her, either. The bathrooms are fruitless. Finally, I get to the kids' ward, where Mira and James are playing video games. They look up, and Mira smiles.

"Hey, Jack! Sophia was just here."

"Where did she go?"

"Upstairs. To the roof, I think. Even though we're not supposed to be up there."

Four flights of stairs leave me breathless and sick to my stomach. Why the roof? She only goes there when she's irrevocably sad or depressed. And with all the smashed vases? She loves those vases. She'd never—

I climb faster and burst through the emergency door and into the weak sunlight.

Sophia's standing at the edge. Not on it, like I'd found her so many times, like I was afraid she'd be. She peers over it, watching the world spread out below. Her hands are clasped behind her back, her silvery hair ruffling in the strong wind.

She looks over her shoulder and smiles at me.

"Hey."

"Sophia—" I run toward her, turning her to face me and inspecting her for wounds. "Are you okay?"

"I'm fine. Just wanted some air. You don't look so good, though."

I exhale all the worry out. "I was— I came to visit, and your room, all the vases were broken. Did you do that?"

She nods. "On accident. I was dancing to music and got a little crazy. I didn't want to deal with it, so I just left it there for the janitor to clean and came up here. Mean of me, I know."

"No, no, it's fine— You just worried Naomi and me."

She cocks her head and hugs me. "Oh, I'm sorry! I didn't mean to, really."

I put my arms around her and inhale the smell of her hair, making sure she's still here. She's real. She has a scent and a feel and she's realer than anything in my life. She always has been.

Half of me wants to tell her about Isis, about Gregory Callan looking for Tallie. The other half knows she'd take it badly either way, and with such an important surgery coming up, her mental stability has to be rock solid. I'll tell her after, when she's healthy and whole again. If I worry her now, the stress could tip her over an edge she can't come back from.

"I love you," I say.

She giggles and pets my hair. "I know. I love you, too. Thank you for being so strong for me all this time. Thank you for trying so hard, for so long. It'll all be over soon."

"You'll be able to do whatever you want. Go wherever you want. You'll be free."

She laughs and hugs me tighter.

"I already am."

Today is easier.

It's not any brighter—the darkness still lingers on the edges of my vision, but I punch it in the gut and drive to the hospital anyway. I pause in the doorway of the ER.

The first time I came in here, I was a different person. Also, unconscious and bleeding. But also extremely different. Louder. And more obnoxious. And less evil. It's clearly not a fair trade. But no trades are ever really fair. Life gives and takes constantly and deeply. I've learned that much.

"Isis!"

I look over to see Dr. Mernich coming toward me, her flyaway hair even frizzier today.

"M-dawg! What's going down in crazy town?"

She laughs. "Nothing much, really. All the interesting pranks conducted around here suddenly and mysteriously stopped once you left."

"Ah, well. What can I say? Poltergeists are fickle. Also, supernatural and imaginary. But mostly fickle."

"Are you here to visit Sophia?"

"Yeah."

"You look much better," she says, looking me up and down. "You sound better."

"Do I? Because I feel like shit now more than ever."

"But now you're feeling it. Not running away from it. That's a good start. Little steps, remember?"

I nod. "Yeah. I think I'm getting there. I mean, a fancy mind-wipe machine like in *Eternal Sunshine of the Spotless Mind* would be helpful and extremely welcome, but hey, you scientist guys are slow and always out of funds. I forgive you."

Mernich smiles, but it fades quickly. "Isis? Just between you and me—how is Sophia doing, you think?"

"I dunno. One minute she likes me, the next she hates me, the next she's crying on me. But she seems like she's stronger, somehow. She's focused on the things that really matter to her. And sometimes she tries to be nice."

"Except when she doesn't," Mernich offers.

"Yeah. That."

Mernich turns my words over and then finally claps me on the shoulder.

"Well, thank you for coming to visit her so often. She really does like you, you know. Deep down. She sees you as a friend and wants you to be happy like she can't always be."

"Really?"

"She has a very hard time showing it." Mernich sighs. "Being terminally ill is the most stressful state a human brain can be in. Your emotions run wild constantly, and it doesn't help that the tumors are also altering her personality."

"Yeah. But that's understandable. None of us can be happy all the time," I say.

"Yes. But you certainly try more than anyone else, don't you?"

Her words hit hard. She smiles one last time, then turns and walks down the hall, calling out to another doctor.

I peek into the kids' ward, but Mira and James are out to lunch in the cafeteria. Sophia's door is open, and I walk in to see her and Jack, hugging. I back up immediately, but Sophia hears me first and pulls away.

"Isis! Hey!" She runs over and hugs me. It's a sudden 180 from her behavior the other day, but I'm so happy she's being nice to me again I let it slide. I look at Jack over her shoulder. He's expressionless, the slightest frown on his face.

"Hi, sorry, wow. I just barged in here without even knocking first," I say.

"It's okay! I'm just glad you're here. You, and Jack, and me, all together for once. It's great. Isn't it?" she asks, turning to Jack. He nods, stiffly, and then locks eyes with me. It's quick, but it lingers, and reminds me of everything that happened that night in the hotel—how kind he was, how warm. I feel my face burning up and Sophia staring at me.

"I should go," Jack says suddenly.

"What? Why? Work again?" Sophia tilts her head.

"No. I just don't want to get in the way of any girl talk."

"Periods," I say to Sophia immediately. "Huge, bloody periods."

"Tampons!" she shouts.

Jack pushes past us and out the door. "I'm going to get something to eat. I'll be back."

When he's gone, Sophia turns to me.

"So? What's up?"

I'm confused by her sudden cheeriness. For a split second, it was like we were back to how we used to be, before I regained my memory. People say knowledge is power, but in my case, it's a curse. A curse to lose a friend I'd made during a really hard time. Maybe she's not in pain today, I muse. Maybe she's feeling better. Maybe she's *getting* better! The surge of hope is instant and half blind, a tiny voice whispering she'll never get better, no matter how much she deserves to, no matter how unfair life is.

I rummage in my pocket and hold out the silver bracelet with TALLULAH on it. It jingles faintly in the air, the sudden silence between us deafening. Her blue eyes widen, and she reaches out reverently and takes it. She strokes the name engraved on it with her thumb.

"Tallie," she whispers.

"I couldn't bring back…um. The rest of her. I mean, that's her grave, so that's where she should stay, you know? That's where she rests. But I thought you'd like the bracelet."

Sophia's quiet for a long time. She traces the bracelet chain over and over. Just as I start to feel awkward for staying, she raises her voice.

"Jack got it for me. After it happened. It's nice to have it back."

I try to smile, but it comes out crooked.

"He didn't know," she says. "I never told him about her. But that night in the woods spilled the secret in front of everyone. That night—"

Her fist clenches the bracelet, a darkness creeping into her eyes that wasn't there before.

"He was the only good thing in my life," she continues. "I would've done anything to keep him with me. You understand. You wanted Nameless to stay, too, right?"

I nod slowly. I told her about him, in the softest, most vulnerable moments of my recuperation. Not everything. But enough. Enough to have her link us together in the same way—her and Jack, me and Nameless.

"This bracelet's been with Tallie for years now," she continues. "In the ground with her. I couldn't see her or visit her. And it tore me up every day. But now it's with me."

"Now *she's* with you," I offer. Sophia looks up, eyes wet, and flings her arms around my neck.

"Thank you. Thank you so much. I'm sorry for everything I've said. Everything I've done. Let me make it up to you, okay? I really wanna make it up to you."

"You don't have to, actually, I know things have been really hard? And like, your life is hard? So I don't want to make it extra hard?"

"You won't be! Avery's planning the entire party, so I won't be doing anything stressful. All you have to do is wear something 'rad,' or whatever, and come!"

"Uh, historically I haven't had the greatest experience at Avery's parties."

"Neither have I," she reminds me. "But it's my birthday party, and she's promised to behave herself. And I'll be there, so I'll keep an eye on her. I'd just like it if you came. Wren's coming, and so is Jack. And a bunch of other people I was supposed to go to school with, so like, most of your class."

"Big party?"

"Huge! And there's a cake, and a DJ, and please, *please* come!"

Her face is shining in the same way it used to shine when I'd make her laugh, back at the beginning. Back when I first came here.

"Yeah. Yeah, all right. I'll come."

Sophia smiles, relief carving her features.

"Great. It's on the twenty-eighth, up at her house. It's supposed to start at seven, but you should arrive fashionably late, because the booze is also arriving fashionably late."

"You know me too well."

Sophia shakes her head and laughs.

"I thought I did. But, no. No, Isis. I don't know you at all. You're the only one. You're the only one who brought me what I wanted. Not flowers. Not food. Not medicine or pity. You brought me my baby, after everything I did to you and said to you."

She hugs me again.

"You don't pretend to be a good person like everyone else. You *are* one."

"But I'm the dragon. I'm evil. Jack and I—"

Sophia pulls away and smiles faintly.

"You and Jack are my greatest friends. My only friends. Thank you for sticking around this sick little idiot."

There's a moment of quiet, in which all we can hear is the shuffling of nurses and patients outside and the faint beeping of distant monitors.

"I like Jack," I blurt. The words hang there, pushed out by my guilt. Sophia doesn't miss a beat.

"I like him, too."

"I think…I think I want to be with him."

"I want to be with him, too." Her smile widens. "But I can't be. Not for much longer, anyway."

"But the surgery will—"

"I don't know what the surgery will do. No one does. The future is funny like that. No matter how much we plan and scheme, the tiniest hole in the ship can sink us. So I've learned to stop planning. To just...let things happen."

My mouth won't say words, tightening into a thin line instead. All of my feelings for Jack, for her, war with each other. Imaginary blood spills. Someone probably loses an arm or five.

"Whatever happens," Sophia continues, "I want him to be happy. I think that's what Dr. Mernich means by coming to terms with my own death. It's not about accepting death. It's about accepting the lives you're leaving behind. Accepting their feelings, their wants and needs. At first I hated the idea of that—I wanted everyone to suffer like I was suffering. Avery, Wren. Even Jack. Even you. But now I realize..."

She looks down at the bracelet and smiles.

"Now I realize the only thing I can do is make it easy on all of you."

"Sophia—"

"Let's go upstairs." Sophia grabs my hand suddenly. "To the roof. One last time."

The wind is gentle today. There are no pigeons, but a few crows perch on the radio antennae above the door. The winter light is pale and washes the world out—all gray roads and white buildings. Sophia sits on the edge of the roof, and I sit with her. We watch the people go in and out of the hospital, bustling about their daily lives. She points to two kids playing on the rusted swing in the recreation area.

"James and Mira look good. Well, better than when

they first came."

James takes a flying leap off one of the swings and Mira chastises him loudly. Sophia laughs.

"James might get out, someday. If he fights it off. But Mira is pretty much like me. When they first came, I was jealous of them. They have parents who visit, parents who love them. I was alone."

She leans back, stretching her thin arms out.

"I got close to them to try to siphon some of the parental love. It worked, for a while. But then the jealousy got to be too much, and I snapped at them one day. And they haven't looked at me without being afraid since."

"It wasn't your fault—"

"It was my fault," she says dully. "Mernich helped me see that. I was manipulating my surroundings because I didn't have any control over my life."

"Why all the past tense?"

She shoots me a crooked grin. "I'm just talking about past therapy sessions. Don't get all worried-mom on me."

I hold my hands up. "All right, officer. You got me."

"To jail you go," she orders. "Solitary confinement. No comic books."

"Alas! How will I discover who Captain America sleeps with next?"

"The internet will scream about it, I'm sure."

For a while neither of us says anything. The sun starts setting, turning the grays of the world into pink gold.

"Be gentle with him," Sophia says finally. The way she says "him" means Jack, I can tell that much. "He's been through a lot because of me. The fact that he doesn't hate me after all this, after everything I've put him through, only makes me love him more. And it only makes me feel more awful."

"He's a good guy," I say. "And so are you."

"I wish." She laughs. "But no. I wasn't a good guy. Not in this life. Maybe in the next. If there is a next life at all. For all my disbelief, I still like to think there is one. Secretly. Does that make me a hypocrite?"

"It makes you human."

I don't want to ruin this moment by asking about what Jack did that night, but the shadow of Nameless looms over me, darker in the silence.

"Nameless sent me a picture," I say. "Of Jack with a baseball bat. It's bloody. And I can't help but think— "

"He didn't do it," Sophia says instantly.

"What?"

"He didn't kill that man. He didn't kill anyone. He chased them off, all of them. One of them just happened to run the wrong way in the dark and fell to his death."

My lungs feel like they're frozen. Sophia shakes her head.

"Why is Nameless sending you things?"

I shrug. "I don't know."

"It sounds like he wants to torment you."

"Probably. Knowing him, definitely."

Sophia inhales. "That night, there was an investigation. We called the police. Well, I didn't. Wren did. I was busy having a seizure. I was so scared I tripped on a root and slammed my head on a tree. It was a chain reaction—Tallie came out. I couldn't stop it."

Her eyes are distant, glassy. Her words sound robotic, as if she's said this to someone else before.

"They panicked. Wren, Avery, Jack. They were just kids. We were all just kids. I'd kept it a secret from them.

Jack called an ambulance. Wren ran. Avery buried Tallie so my grandmother wouldn't disown me. She was hardcore Catholic. They'd all been to my house and knew that. Jack tried to protect me, until the last. Wren did, too, toward the end. So he doesn't deserve my hate."

Sophia kicks her feet against the edge of the roof.

"The paramedics came for me; the police came for the man's body. I was unconscious the whole time. At the hospital they did a CAT scan and found my tumors, and found out about Tallie. The doctors didn't tell Grandma about her, because of patient confidentiality and all that. When I woke up, Jack told me what happened, what my life would be from then on."

She looks to me.

"He blames himself for that man's death, even if the police ruled it an accident. Avery's parents paid for major PR work. The papers reported the guys as drunk fishers out on the lake for the weekend, even when the police knew the real reason. The news said Joseph Hernandez just...disappeared. Ran off. Nothing about Avery hiring them. Nothing about how they worked for her parents' company. After that, the rest of the men moved out of state. Everything was cleaned up by Avery's parents. It was terrifying, watching the efficiency money could buy."

"So, Belina," I start. "Wren took me to see a woman Jack is sending checks to. She was—"

"Joseph's wife," Sophia agrees. "And Jack tries to fix everything with money, because it's the only thing he can do. Because the other wounds are too deep to fix."

"How do you know about Belina?"

"Wren told me," she says. "He's still afraid of me. But texting works wonders for talking to people who can't look you in the eye. He hasn't told me how Jack gets the money. Or from whom."

I'm suddenly very interested in my shoes. The whole night I'd been wondering about is out in the open now. I know what happened. And it's every bit as terrifying as I thought it would be. Things like this don't happen to normal people. But they happened, anyway. And I can't change that.

"Things just happen," I echo Sophia's words back at her. "Good or bad."

"And we live with the consequences," Sophia agrees. "Or not. Some people decide to die with the consequences, instead."

"Some people are pretty dumb."

We watch the sun go down and the moon rise. Each day passes as it always does, in slow, twenty-four-hour increments, but for Sophia, I realize, it must feel like the blink of an eye.

Eventually it gets too cold for us to stay up on the roof, and so we go inside and get hot cocoa from the cafeteria. We talk about the party, what to wear and what music to play. Sophia insists she doesn't want any presents, save for my presence.

When I finally get home, Mom is filling out bills at the kitchen table. I hug her from behind, and she turns and laughs.

"What's the occasion?"

"I realized," I murmur into her shoulder. "I realized people are fragile. Everything could change in a second. And I don't—I don't want to waste time not hugging you or telling you you're the best mom I could ask for."

"Oh, honey." Mom turns and hugs me back. "Are you all right? What brought this on? Is this about Stanford?"

"No. A friend," I say. "She's shown me a lot of stuff. About life. And not-life. It's so short. Life is so short and weird and things keep happening all the time, and I don't know what to do anymore. I can't do anything except be me."

Mom's hug tightens.

"That's all you need to do. No matter what you do, I'm here for you, sweetie. Always. You'll always have me on your side."

"I know." I bury my face in her chest and say the words that hold the most truth, the most gratitude. "Thank you."

I stare at the last email Nameless sent me for what feels like forever. He wants me to suffer. That's why he keeps doing this. He won't let me go. He can't. Not after what he inflicted on me. He wants to feed off the pain as much as he can, while he still can. Just like Leo. But I won't let him. Life is too short.

Responding would just give him pleasure. I click on the emails and delete them and, for good measure, my email account. I start a new one, the fresh, blank inbox a comfort. I can still start over.

Next year I'll have to start over, because college demands it. The next step of life demands it.

But I can always, *always* start over, because I'm here, outside a hospital. Because I'm alive and healthy. Because I won't let my past chain me down like it has Jack, and Sophia, and Wren, and Avery.

Because I'm not Mom. I'm not Jack. I'm not Sophia. I am not my past.

I'm Isis Blake, and I'm my own future.

chapter thirteen

3 YEARS, 31 WEEKS, 1 DAY

AVERY'S HOUSE IS FAMILIAR in all the wrong ways. I park in the same place I always do—easy to back out and easy to drive away fast if I gotta. The music is thumping across the lawn, down into the street, and permeating the gated community. It bounces off the trees and the dozens of cars parked haphazardly in her yard. People are already drunkenly stumbling out the front door, lying on the lawn, wrestling with each other, and chasing each other with toilet paper and the hose.

I smooth my shirt one last time. It's the Florence and the Machine one I wore here the first time, and I didn't even realize I was wearing it until I got in the car. My jeans are frayed on the thighs—not because I bought them at some high boutique that purposefully frayed them, but because I'd eaten pavement so many times on my bike. The cool air on my thighs through the fray reminds me how broken the jeans are, and why they're broken, and how I broke them myself. I did it. I broke them, but I can still wear them, and they work just fine at what they're supposed to do—cover my fabulous butt.

Things are broken, but they still work.

I get out and pull my jacket closer to me. It's bitter cold. Did spring not get the memo? Does spring ever get memos? What are they written on, leaves? Petals? The carcass of a newborn deer?

"Getting maudlin this early in the night, are we?"

I look up. Jack's standing there, in a preposterously gross leather jacket and dark jeans. Wren's standing by him, looking a little shaken up in his usual plaid shirt.

"It's sort of my job," I say. "Provide the searing atmosphere, throw a few shallow but well-meaning compliments, mutter to myself, maybe break a bottle or two."

"Please don't break a bottle." Wren wrings his hands. "We've had three people cut themselves already."

"Whoa, what's that on your chest, Prez?" I blurt. A little golden star pin that has the number one on it is tacked to his shirt. His glasses slide off as he looks at it, and he pushes them up.

"Um. Just something Sophia gave me. From when… from when—"

"Is that the math rally pin?" Jack interrupts. "Wow. I didn't know she still had it."

"Neither did I." Wren lets out a half laugh. "I mean, I thought she got rid of it a long time ago."

"Math rally pin?" I ask.

Jack nods. "Back in the day, Wren and Sophia competed in this math rally. They were really into it, invested like only competitive smart kids can get. They studied for weeks, months. Sophia wanted to win so badly. But Wren did. They tied, technically, but the judges gave it to Wren for some extra calculation he did."

"Sophia was furious at me," Wren says. "She wouldn't talk to me for a whole month. So I gave her the pin, and she started crying and said to not be so nice to her."

Jack laughs, low, and Wren shakes his head, a wistful smile on his face. It's a history I'm not a part of, but it gives me a warm feeling just to see them remember that time when they were all friends, and close, and cared for one another, without the darkness between them.

"Look, I'm gonna go get a mood fluid. Thirst burst. Flavor saver," I say.

Wren and Jack raise their eyebrows in sync, and I laugh.

"A drink. I'll be back."

I recognize a lot of people—not just Avery's group is here. She's invited the not-populars; Wren's student government friends, the band kids, the hipsters, even Knife Guy. And I know he didn't just sneak in this time like he usually does, because I see Avery nod at him as she passes, instead of curling her lip.

"Pretending to be civil? Color me surprised," I say. Avery looks me over. Her hair is straight and glossy again, her skin perfect and makeup on-point. She looks much, much better than usual.

"Sophia wanted me to be nice. And I figured, hell, I can do it once in my life. It might kill me, but I'll do it for the sake of getting to say I did. I was nice." She ponders this and sighs. "Should've put that on my college résumé. They love nice people."

I chuckle. "Most people like nice people. Good thing I'm not most people."

"You've never liked me," she sneers. "And I've never liked you."

"True. But we're willing to put up with each other. That counts for something, right?"

She stares at me, green eyes flaring. And it's then I

notice she's been crying. She's applied makeup over it, but I can barely see red puffiness under her eyes, and her nose is swollen.

"Have you seen Sophia?" I ask.

"I was just talking with her upstairs. She's been bugging me to tell you to come find her when you get here, so, go talk to her. Quick. Before she explodes."

"That happy, is she?"

For once, Avery smiles. It isn't a sneer, or a sour grimace, or a catty, petty grin. It is exactly a smile, no more and no less. It is a younger Avery that shines through in that smile—a lighter Avery. A more innocent Avery. She nods.

"Yeah. She's happy. She's really, really happy."

I pat her on the shoulder and then walk upstairs to the third level. It's quieter up here but less like a soundproof room and more like the top level of a jungle infested with monkeys in heat. Correction: monkeys in heat with access to EDM. The noise dulls, and I wander around aimlessly, but with a very specific aim. I spot a wisp of platinum-blond hair at the end of the hall, where French doors open to a mini balcony. Sophia's leaning on the banister of it, watching the stars, a drink in one hand. She's in a beautiful, lacy white dress with a short skirt and no sleeves, and she looks stunning, like a dove about to take flight.

She hears me coming and turns.

"Hey! It's about time you came. No drink?"

"You were a little higher on my priorities list. Which is weird because no one comes before booze. Except Tom Hiddleston. But even he has to take a number and wait in line a little."

She smiles, and I lean on the balcony with her.

Someone streaks by below, completely naked and yelling about the "king of alien invaders."

"It's a good party. People are having fun, losing their pants—"

"Possibly their minds," Sophia interrupts.

"—and most definitely their minds. I take it back. It's a *perfect* party."

She giggles, then drinks out of her cup. It's something blue and frothy, and she sticks out her stained tongue and waggles it at me.

"Gross!" I push her playfully. "You really are sick!"

"I'm contagious!" she insists. "That was my plan all along: hold a massive birthday party, infect you all, and start the zombie apocalypse."

"'Bout damn time. I've been waiting for that thing for years."

There's a comfortable silence. I look over and notice then her wrist is decorated with Tallie's bracelet. It's just barely big enough, and her wrist is just that thin and tiny. The silver glints in the moonlight. It's breathtaking.

"I wanted to thank you," Sophia says. "Properly."

"For what? Making your life hell?"

"For trying."

The wind plays with her hair, and she tucks it behind her ear and smiles at me.

"Not many people try. Once they see the real me, the one who's suspicious and bitter and angry and hopeless, they leave or give up. But you stayed. So I wanted to thank you for that."

"Wasn't a big deal. I just…I was just sort of pigheaded around you. I didn't really do anything."

"You tried to help," she insists, grabbing my hand. Tallie's bracelet is cool on my skin, and her palm is surprisingly cool as well. "You tried to help, and for that I can never thank you enough."

We stand there like that, our hands joined, me looking at her and her looking at the sky.

"Do you know about Van Gogh?" she asks suddenly.

"Cut off his own ear and painted LSD sunflowers, right?"

She laughs. "Yeah. His paintings…everyone says they're beautiful, but they've always made me a little sad, and scared. They're frightening—all those bright colors and all that chaos. But I suppose that is beautiful, in its own way."

I nod, quelling the snark in me to try to enjoy this moment of peace.

"He painted *Starry Night* while he was in a mental asylum," she says.

"Oh yeah?"

"Yeah. Right before he died, he painted a lot of wheat fields. I like those paintings the best—they're calm, peaceful."

"I wanna see 'em someday."

"You will," she asserts. "They're really nice. It's sad, though; he killed himself. With a gun. Well, he tried to. He missed and crawled back to the inn he was staying at, and died in his bed after hours and hours of pain."

"Jesus." I suck in air through my teeth. She shakes her head and smiles.

"But his last words were 'The sadness will last forever.' And I think he was right, but I also think he was very, very wrong. It doesn't last forever. Because we don't last forever."

The darkness I'd put bars over to appear cheerful at this party bubbles up from my heart. Sophia must see it, because she squeezes my hand gently.

"Hey, it's okay. Go and get me some more of the blue stuff, will you? I'm not nearly tipsy enough to dance yet, and that's gotta be remedied."

"Hah, I know that feeling. I'll be right back."

I take her glass and squeeze her hand as I leave. Downstairs, the party is batshit insane and only getting batshittier insaner. I wave to Jack, and he follows me into the kitchen.

"So? Is she all right?" he asks.

"Yeah, she just wanted a refill on the booze. You should go see her. Drag her down here, dance with her, something."

He flinches, but it's well-hidden.

"I still haven't told her."

"I know." I nod. "And I haven't told you some things, either. So. Everybody's not telling everybody else stuff. It's fine. Secrets are kind of the crappy bread-and-butter around here."

"I haven't told you something very important. And I want you to know it," he starts, icy eyes burrowing into me.

"Don't," I start. "Don't, seriously, Jackoff. Not now."

"If I don't tell you this, Isis, it's going to drive me crazy." He leans in. "I need you to know. I want you to know—"

"Isis! Come dance with me!" Kayla appears at my side, obviously tipsy and pulling me by the hand toward the dance floor. Jack's hand on my other wrist is instant, yet gentle.

"Please, Isis. It'll just take a second."

The earnestness in his voice catches me off guard. Kayla doesn't stop pulling, and I trip over another guy's foot. Kayla's pulling keeps me from falling, and I stagger forward. In a split second of shifting bodies I'm enclosed on the dance floor, the music jackhammering straight into my skull. Kayla's way drunker than I thought she was, because she wraps me in a hug, half swaying with the music.

"It's almost over," she shouts.

"What is?"

"School. Graduation. What if I—you're— You're the bestest friend I've ever had, Isis! What if we get to college and stop talking? What if we stop being… friends?"

Her voice is loud and quaking with emotion all at once. I wrap my arms around her and lean in.

"We won't," I say. "I know it's hard to say that for sure, because the future is the future and we don't know the future."

"What?" Kayla knits her eyebrows.

"It'll be okay, is all," I assert. "You can't worry about the future. All we've got is right now."

"You sound like a Hallmark card!"

"And you sound drunk!"

She laughs and releases our hug. I tiptoe and see Jack's face over the crowd, my heart beating faster with every moment our eyes linger. He wanted to say something, something important to him. Deep down, I know what it is. I know what it has to be—the same thing I felt in the hotel room, in Avery's sea room on Halloween. It's the one thing I'm afraid of, the one thing I crave. I want to run to him and run from him all at once, as fast as I can.

I'm scared in the best way.

A little shove from Kayla brings me back to the

dance floor. She's smiling.

"Go on. He's waiting. Sorry I dragged you off. I had no idea it was deep-talk time with you two."

"It's not," I say shakily.

"It is." She nods. "It's okay. You can't worry about the future. All we got is right now, yeah?"

I push her playfully. "I hate it when you stab me with my own cheesy words, you foul betrayer."

Her laughter is just barely louder than the music as she turns from me and starts spinning, dancing, her arms high in the air.

It shouldn't feel like a movie, but it does. As I walk toward Jack, slinking through the dancers and the crowd around the dancers, everything seems to slow. His eyes are patient, the sort of patience I never thought I'd see from him. He's waiting, a hundred mishmashed emotions on his face. The ice mask I'd seen on him so many times is gone, and all that's left is a smile half hidden by anticipation, his sky-blue eyes practically glowing in the dimness. There are no butterflies in my stomach, just a gentle humming.

I'm scared, but not afraid. Not anymore.

And then I'm in front of him, and he's so close, and we both wait for someone else to talk first.

"Isis—"

"I didn't know—"

We interrupt each other at the same time, and laugh at the same time.

"Sorry," I say. "You first."

"What if I want you to go first?" he asks.

"Why? Historically, I haven't had anything important to say."

I feel a warmth on my fingers, and look down to see

him holding my hand.

"Wrong," he says. "Everything you've said has been important."

"Even the poop jokes?"

"Especially the poop jokes." He chuckles. "I'm too serious, you know."

"Really?" I feign innocence. "I had no idea!"

His hand squeezes around mine, smile twisting sardonically.

"I'm too serious, and this year I've learned…" He pauses, looking me over. "I've learned it can kill you. From the inside out. I was no better than dead for so long. And it's cliché and masochistic, but when you punched me that first time—"

He laughs, shaking his head.

"It was like waking up from a coma, like coming up for air from an ocean dive. I was angry. For the first time in a long time, I felt something. My life wasn't still and silent anymore. It moved. *You* made it move. *You* made noise when no one else could."

My chest feels heavy and tight all of a sudden. His face looks so sad.

"I was sure, after everything that happened, that nothing would ever make me feel like that again. But you came along—in all your irritating, righteous glory—and proved me wrong."

He holds my hand to his lips, gently.

"There's something you need to know—"

A scream rips through the party, piercing his words down the middle. That's typical, but what's not typical is it doesn't stop. Someone is screaming, and they're screaming over and over, and it's like metal scraping over slate. It is panic and terror, pure and unfiltered, and it's coming from outside. Jack drops my hand and looks up, and I follow his gaze.

"What the hell is that?" I hiss.

Jack and I push through the crowd that's running in the direction of the scream. The night air is crisp and people's breaths float up as a suspended ring of clouds around a certain patch of grass on the left side of the house. People are swearing, some are sobbing, some are frantically dialing on their phones. Jack keeps pushing through the people, Wren pushing with him, but I'm frozen to the ground as I look up and see the balcony just above.

Everything goes quiet, but people's mouths are still moving. Jack's screams are barely audible above the ringing in my head. I move achingly slow, like I'm in a sea of sludge. People won't move. I lean on them until they do, until the last person in the circle parts and shows me Jack leaning over Sophia's lovely white dress, Tallie's bracelet around her contorted wrist, her head twisted at a perfect ninety-degree angle and her deep blue eyes staring at me, wide and open, like a mannequin, like a doll, like a bird that never learned how to take flight.

The sadness will last forever. And I think he was right, but I also think he was very, very wrong. It doesn't last forever. Because we don't last forever.

bonus content

Read on for a never-before-seen scene from Wren's POV!

wren

IT ISN'T RAINING at Sophia's funeral, but it should be.

This is the first funeral I've been to. It should be my second. I should've been there for Tallie's funeral, when Avery buried her in the woods. It was so dark that night that Jack never saw Tallie. He only saw the blood covering Sophia, and panicked. He rode away with her in the ambulance.

Avery and I noticed, though. But I ran, terrified by it all. Sometimes, if I close my eyes, I can still hear Avery shouting "Coward!" after me.

I look at Avery's face now. She's standing away from the rest of the crowd gathered around the coffin on the grass. She's practically hiding in the shadows of a tree, to the very end ashamed of what she'd done to Sophia.

As she should be. As I should be.

There are so many *should*s—things we didn't do and can't do, anymore. Regrets hang heavy over all of us at Sophia's funeral.

Isis stands solemn, next to Naomi—Sophia's nurse—and Jack's mother. It's a small funeral; all of Sophia's family is dead, and her friends few. The priest drones Bible verse after Bible verse. Isis meets my eyes, her own wet and miserable. Her every emotion is written on her face.

I turn my eyes to Jack and see the exact opposite.

His expression is blank, completely devoid of any feeling at all. It's like looking at an empty canvas or a blank sheet of paper. There should be something, anything, even the slightest splash of color, but there isn't. He's always been cold, but this is...*unnatural*. If I look at him too long, I feel a shiver coming on. A human being shouldn't look like that, unless he's totally and completely lifeless. His mother clutches his elbow, sobbing, and yet he doesn't move an inch, watching the casket with a steady gaze.

Avery is crying, too, but silently. She's afraid she'll draw Jack's attention, I'm sure. Ever since that night, she's always been afraid of him. After what she did, I'm sure Jack wanted to make her life a living hell, but something stopped him. If I had to guess, it was Sophia, calming him down as she always did so expertly.

And now she's gone.

Jack's lost a part of himself—anyone can see that. Isis's brown eyes skitter over to him every so often, lingering on the hard lines of his face, his slack hands at his sides. She looks like she wants to go over and comfort him, but she doesn't know how. She looks like she's unsure if she's even allowed to touch him in his grief.

It's obvious Isis likes him. And for a while, it was obvious Jack liked her. But now? Whatever the two of them were beginning to feel for each other is over. It has to be. Sophia's death leveled us all, all the friendships we'd been building, all the relationships. I confronted Jack earlier this month, something like respect blossoming between us again, but I know that's gone now. I've even been pushing Kayla away, embracing fully the gray cloak of sadness around me. Do I even deserve to be happy with someone, after what I did to Sophia? Do any of us?

The priest finishes his prayers, and the pallbearers lower the coffin and begin to shovel dirt on it. Naomi collapses at the pit's side, wailing and reaching for her. She'd taken care of Sophia for so long—she was the closest thing Sophia had to a mother. Naomi knew better than any of us that Sophia was going to die, but not like this. Not by her own hand, out of despair, or tiredness.

That's the worst part—that we'll never know why she did it. There was no note, not a single clue left behind as to why. When Isis and I first saw each other in the graveyard parking lot, she walked over and shook her head.

"I'm sorry, Wren. It's my fault."

"What are you talking about?" I asked.

"I should've seen the signs." She clutched her head. "I was the one who hung out with her the most—she told me. She told me she was going to do it in a thousand different ways, but I was too stupid to see them. Too naive. I should've known. *I should've known* and I'm sorry. God I'm sorry—"

She started to cry. I offered her a hug, and she took it, clutching at me like I was a lifesaver thrown overboard to a drowning person.

I tried to say "it'll be okay," but the words got caught in my throat. There's a chance things will never be okay again. They'll never be the same, no matter how much I want them to be.

I watch Sophia as they lower her into the ground and feel a wave of sick heat wash over me. She's gone, forever. It hits me just then—I'm never going to see her again. I'm never going to get the chance to apologize to her. I spent years working up the courage and failed. I failed her. I betrayed her friendship; all those years spent as kids together, growing up together, all forgotten just because I was afraid of Avery.

Isis starts crying as the last dirt goes on the coffin. Unlike Naomi, she cries completely silently, tears streaming down her face.

Jack doesn't shed a tear.

After the funeral, my mom picks me up from the graveyard. She leaves me alone, thankfully, not asking a single question. Emotionally exhausted, I collapse into bed.

My phone won't leave me alone; a text message blares on the screen. It's from Kayla.

Hey you, it reads. **How are you doing?**

Tired, I text back. **It was awful.**

Kayla's grandmother had fallen down some stairs, and her mother rushed her out to the East Coast to see her, just in case. She'd tried to get out of it to come to Sophia's funeral and support Isis and me, but her mother had an iron fist—family first, friends second.

I'm sorry, she says. **I'll be home in two days, and then we can talk about it.**

Yeah. I'm looking forward to that.

Stay strong! ☺☺☺☺

Somehow, the cartoonish smiley faces make me feel a little better. Kayla in general makes me feel better—something I've always known but never told anyone. Since that night at Avery's party when Avery locked the two of us inside the room, Kayla and I have gotten closer. It started with me trying to calm her down that night, and then grew to walking to class together, bonding over our shared experiences of how horrible Avery was to us. Soon, she was asking me to help her with her math homework, and offered me rides home in exchange.

She's gorgeous, and much smarter than anyone gives her credit for. She doesn't have the razor wit of Isis or Jack, and she's a little naive, but that only makes me like her more.

But I haven't told her.

I've asked her out to prom, and somehow, beyond belief, she said yes. But now? Now I don't know how to go to prom. I don't know how to wake up tomorrow. What should I say? What should I do? Do I show my sadness, or hide it away where no one can see? I have to pretend I'm okay, for my family and Kayla. I can't make them worry more than they already are.

"I'm sorry, Sophia," I murmur into my pillow, the tears finally coming to me, far too late. Only in the quiet privacy does my numbness wear off. The sorrow grabs at me, deep and aching.

The sun sets, thick clouds lashing rain against my window, as if the world is crying with me.

In the midst of the storm, Kayla texts once more.

I just talked to Isis. I'm worried. Will things be okay? Will you guys ever be okay again?

It takes me a moment to sit up and wipe my eyes enough to see her words. My own hiccups sound so pathetic. But at least I can still cry. At least I'm alive to keep crying. Sophia doesn't have that luxury anymore.

Whatever she was feeling, killing herself wasn't the answer. Even if it was what she wanted, it wasn't what she needed. She needed time. She needed more life, not death. That's all I know for sure anymore.

I don't know, I text back finally, my fingers shaking. **But I'm going to try.**

The next morning, I hike up to Avery's cabin by Lake Galonagah. Tallie's cross is right where we left it that night. I haven't seen it since I was thirteen.

Someone stands in front of the grave, someone wearing a stylish jacket and jeans, her red hair dancing like flames as the wind teases it. It's her first time up here since that night, too.

I pull air into my lungs and use it like courage. Like iron.

I walk up to the girl, and the grave, for the first time in five years.

"Hello, Tallie," I say to the cross. Avery is quiet, staring at the little patch of dirt that holds our greatest regret, and then she echoes me softly.

"Hello, Tallie."

Collect all the books in the Lovely Vicious series

Love Me Never

Discover where Jack and Isis's relationship first heated up in *Love Me Never*, available now.

Remember Me Forever

Don't miss the stunning conclusion to Jack and Isis's story in *Remember Me Forever*, coming soon.

acknowledgments

Thank you to every reader; to you, the one reading this. I know it's hard, but things will get better if you hold on. I promise.

When I was in high school, my sister's boyfriend was diagnosed with an inoperable brain tumor. They gave him five months to live, and it was the roughest five months I can remember in my life—for my family, for my sister, and especially for him. We saw him go through so much pain. It was nothing like the movies and books told us—tragic but somehow enlightening/heartwarming in its tragedy. It was just sad. Sad and difficult.

This book is, in some ways, for him.

There is no romance in death, or suicide. If you're in that low place, please, please call your friends and family. If you can't bear to talk to them, please call the National Suicide Prevention Hotline (1-800-273-8255). A majority of them have been through the same thing and can help you when it feels like no one else can. You are valued; you are loved.

Thank you to Stacy Abrams, Lydia Sharp, and the entire Entangled/Macmillan team for being flawless human beings willing to put up with my every typo and melodramatic nonsense.

A special thank-you to Andrew, a wonderful writer who constantly inspires me to work harder and be better.

Thank you to the entire NK Beach Party gaming circle in general—you guys have kept me sane in the midst of revisions/my hectic life. I promise to suck less this season. ☺

And lastly, thank you to Jack and Isis, Wren and Kayla, Avery and Sophia, for growing up so fast, and so well.

It'll be all right.

Grab the Entangled Teen releases readers are talking about!

Chasing Truth
by Julie Cross

At Holden Prep, the rich and powerful rule the school—and they'll do just about anything to keep their dirty little secrets hidden.

When former con artist Eleanor Ames's homecoming date commits suicide, she's positive there's something more going on. The more questions she asks, though, the more she crosses paths with Miles Beckett. He's sexy, mysterious, *arrogant*...and he's asking all the same questions.

Eleanor might not trust him—she doesn't even *like* him—but they can't keep their hands off of each other. Fighting the infuriating attraction is almost as hard as ignoring the fact that Miles isn't telling her the truth...and that there's a good chance he thinks *she's* the killer.

The Replacement Crush
by Lisa Brown Roberts

After book blogger Vivian Galdi's longtime crush pretends their secret summer kissing sessions never happened, Vivian creates a list of safe crushes, determined to protect her heart.

But nerd-hot Dallas, the sweet new guy in town, sends the missions—and Vivian's zing meter—into chaos. While designing software for the bookstore where she works, Dallas wages a countermission.

Operation Replacement Crush is in full effect. And Dallas is determined to take her heart off the shelf.

Olivia Decoded

by Vivi Barnes

This isn't my Jack, who once looked at me like I was his world. The guy who's occupied the better part of my mind for eight months.

This is Z, criminal hacker with a twisted agenda and an arsenal full of anger.

I've spent the past year trying to get my life on track. New school. New friends. New attitude. But old flames die hard, and one look at Jack—the hacker who enlisted me into his life and his hacking ring, stole my heart, and then left me—and every memory, every moment, every feeling comes rushing back. But Jack's not the only one who's resurfaced in my life. And if I can't break through Z's defenses and reach the old Jack, someone will get hurt...or worse.

The Society

by Jodie Andrefski

Not everyone has what it takes to be part of The Society, Trinity Academy's secret, gold-plated clique. Once upon a time, Sam Evans would have been one of them. Now her dad's in prison and her former ex-bestie Jessica is queen of the school. And after years of Jessica treating her like a second-class citizen, Sam's out for blood. But vengeance never turns out the way it's supposed to...and when her scheming blows up all around her, Sam has to decide if revenge is worth it, no matter what the cost.

Life After Juliet
by Shannon Lee Alexander

Becca Hanson was never able to make sense of the real world. When her best friend Charlotte died, she gave up on it altogether. Fortunately, Becca can count on her books to escape—to other times, other places, other people...

Until she meets Max Herrera. He's experienced loss, too, and his gorgeous, dark eyes see Becca the way no one else in school can.

As it turns out, kissing is a lot better in real life than on a page. But love and life are a lot more complicated in the real world...and happy endings aren't always guaranteed.

The companion novel to *Love and Other Unknown Variables* is an exploration of loss and regret, of kissing and love, and most importantly, a celebration of hope and discovering a life worth living again.

The Sound of Us
by Julie Hammerle

When Kiki gets into a prestigious boot camp for aspiring opera students, she's determined to leave behind her nerdy, social-media-and-TV-obsessed persona. Except camp has rigid conduct rules—which means her surprising jam session with a super-cute and equally geeky drummer can't happen again, even though he thinks her nerd side is awesome. If Kiki wants to win a coveted scholarship to study music in college, she can't focus on friends or being cool, and she *definitely* can't fall in love.

Wake the Hollow
by Gaby Triana

Forget the ghosts, Mica. It's real, live people you should fear.

Tragedy has brought Micaela Burgos back to her hometown of Sleepy Hollow. It's been six years since she chose to live with her father in Miami instead of her eccentric mother. And now her mother is dead.

This town will suck you in and not let go.

Sleepy Hollow may be famous for its fabled headless horseman, but the town is real. So are its prejudices and hatred, targeting Mica's family as outsiders. But ghostly voices carry on the wind, whispering that her mother's death was based on hate...not an accident at all. With the help of two very different guys—who pull at her heart in very different ways—Micaela must awaken the hidden secret of Sleepy Hollow...before she meets her mother's fate.

Find the answers.

Unless, of course, the answers find you first.

Remember Yesterday
By Pintip Dunn

Sixteen-year-old Jessa Stone is the most valuable citizen in Eden City. Her psychic abilities could lead to significant scientific discoveries, if only she'd let TechRA study her. But ten years ago, the scientists kidnapped and experimented on her, leading to severe ramifications for her sister, Callie. She'd much rather break into their labs and sabotage their research—starting with Tanner Callahan, budding scientist and the boy she loathes most at school.

The past isn't what she assumed, though—and neither is Tanner. He's not the arrogant jerk she thought he was. And his research opens the door to the possibility that Jessa can rectify a fatal mistake made ten years earlier. She'll do anything to change the past and save her sister—even if it means teaming up with the enemy she swore to defeat.

True Born
By L.E. Sterling

After the great Plague descended, the population was decimated... and humans' genetics damaged beyond repair. But there's something about Lucy Fox and her identical twin sister, Margot, that isn't quite right. No one wants to reveal *what* they are. When Margot disappears suddenly, Lucy is forced to turn to the True Borns to find her. But instead of answers, there is only the discovery of a deeply buried conspiracy. And somehow, the Fox sisters could unravel it all…

Thief of Lies
by Brenda Drake

Gia Kearns would rather fight with boys than kiss them. That is, until Arik, a leather clad hottie in the Boston Athenaeum, suddenly disappears. When Gia unwittingly speaks the key that sucks her and her friends into a photograph and transports them into a Paris library, Gia must choose between her heart and her head, between Arik's world and her own, before both are destroyed.